THE LIES OUR CHILDREN TELL

LISA TIMONEY

Boldwood

First published in Great Britain in 2026 by Boldwood Books Ltd.

Copyright © Lisa Timoney, 2026

Cover Design by JD Smith Design Ltd

Cover Images: Shutterstock

A CIP catalogue record for this book is available from the British Library.

Paperback ISBN 978-1-80557-053-0

Large Print ISBN 978-1-80557-054-7

Hardback ISBN 978-1-80557-052-3

Trade Paperback ISBN 978-1-80656-157-5

Ebook ISBN 978-1-80557-055-4

Kindle ISBN 978-1-80557-056-1

Audio CD ISBN 978-1-80557-047-9

MP3 CD ISBN 978-1-80557-048-6

Digital audio download ISBN 978-1-80557-051-6

This book is printed on certified sustainable paper. Boldwood Books is dedicated to putting sustainability at the heart of our business. For more information please visit https://www.boldwoodbooks.com/about-us/sustainability/

Boldwood Books Ltd, 23 Bowerdean Street, London, SW6 3TN

www.boldwoodbooks.com

To all the anxious mothers of teens, I see you.

PROLOGUE
NICKY

Nicky should have known something was seriously wrong before they got on the plane. The fact that Betsy didn't argue when her older sister took the window seat was another clue. Ordinarily, eleven-year-old Betsy would dig her sharp elbows into Lola's ribs and make whiny complaints about how it wasn't fair, that Lola knew she liked to watch the clouds. Usually, she'd throw out some spiel about how, just because Lola was five years older, it didn't mean she was in charge.

Instead, Betsy watched in silence as Lola shuffled into the window seat and sat, pulling the hem of her jersey shorts down to cover more of her bare legs, tanned from a week in the Zante sunshine. Betsy then sat in the middle seat without comment, stealing quick glances at her sister as she tugged the belt around her waist, lifted the metal fastener and clicked it into place. This unusual compliance washed over Nicky. She was too busy stretching to reach into the overhead locker, shoving aside cases to make room for their backpacks. She groaned when she remembered the sugar-free lollipops she'd stowed in the side pocket of hers, to stop her daughters' ears from popping on the ascent. She dragged the heavy bag back out, almost hitting herself in the face with it, and dropped it on the seat.

A man with a sunburnt nose slid past her in the aisle. She tried to tuck herself in towards her seat, but still felt the man's groin brush against her bottom as he passed. He muttered, 'Cheers,' the smell of his beer-breath wafting towards her. Unexpected tears pricked the corners of her eyes. She imagined Julian watching from where he'd always sat on flights to family holidays – across the aisle from Nicky and the girls, so he could relax with his fitness magazines and drink his whiskey in peace. He'd have said she gave the man the eye, encouraged him to push against her for the cheap thrill. That's what he'd said she did; teased but didn't deliver.

She shoved the thought away. Julian wasn't here and that was a good thing. Why did she have to keep reminding herself of that? It was as if the years of him telling her how good she had it had made it true, despite all the evidence to the contrary. The video that had changed everything replayed in her mind's eye. She pressed pause. She would like to press stop – better still, to delete it altogether – but it seemed to be branded on to her brain with hot knives.

'All ready?' she said, with forced cheeriness as she fell, exhausted and dry-mouthed from her hangover, into the aisle seat. Betsy nodded, but Lola stared out of the window, the side of her angular face silhouetted against the blinding Greek sunshine outside. Nicky marvelled at the way shadows deepened under her sixteen-year-old daughter's cheekbones and along her jaw. Both had been soft with puppy fat only months before. How quickly she was turning from a girl to a woman. Too quickly for Nicky's liking. 'Lola?'

Lola turned, her green eyes watery. She lifted the corners of her lips in a brief smile. 'Yeah.' She glanced past Nicky to the row of seats set slightly back on the other side of the aisle, to where Nicky's best friend since university, Sabine, was sitting in the centre seat, her son, seventeen-year-old Elias, next to her, staring out of the window with a face equally as miserable as Lola's.

'You sure?'

Lola turned back to the window.

'What's up with her?' Nicky whispered to Betsy, a familiar uneasy feeling in her abdomen churning the coffee and greasy croissant she'd eaten at Zante's tiny airport.

Betsy turned to Lola. 'Tell Mum,' she said.

'Shut up,' Lola hissed. She glanced past her mother again to Sabine and Elias.

Nicky followed her gaze to Sabine, her skin tanned a rich brown, dark head craning to see the last of the island where her family had holidayed for decades as the plane's engines thrummed into life. Sabine said something to Elias, but he didn't turn to his mother, just stared into the white glare, his soft curls bouncing as the plane taxied along the runway.

Turning narrowed eyes back to her own small family, Nicky leaned towards her eldest child and whispered over the engine's high-pitched wail, 'What's happened?'

Nicky's stomach clenched as Lola swiped tears from her cheeks, wiping her palms on her shorts, the water darkening the grey jersey. 'Nothing,' she said, shifting her whole body towards the window. 'Betsy's just being dramatic.'

'I am not.' Betsy crossed her arms and huffed at the accusation so often levelled at her.

'You don't cry over nothing,' Nicky said, feeling the constant dread she had spent the last week trying to expunge returning. Betsy might be prone to tears, but Nicky had always admired her eldest daughter's self-possession. She got that from Julian. Never had a man been so sure of himself. His confidence had been so attractive, at first. He knew his own mind, and he wanted her above every other woman in the world. She'd never felt so desired, and that feeling had been intoxicating. She'd been drunk on love and had only sobered up when it was too late. Even then, his insistence that she was the one to blame for everything that was wrong in their marriage had made her question herself more than him. It had been a long road to this point where she was single and at no risk of returning to her husband, and the journey had left her tender heart shattered and her brain frazzled with self-doubt.

Nicky had done everything she could to stop the girls from seeing or hearing the worst of it, and there had rarely been violence... usually no more than a shove, or a wrist held too tightly, anyway. But she knew the atmosphere in their home often crackled with a kind of tension it was impossible to hide and that her girls had suffered. Lola had become vigilant, asking her if she was okay more than any child should, and Betsy played the jester, trying to distract everyone from the electricity that was so often in the air. Nicky would never forgive herself for putting them through that.

She reached across and put her hand on Lola's warm leg. She noticed a dark red bruise on her thigh. That hadn't been there yesterday, she was sure of it. She looked closer and saw a graze on her daughter's shin. Nicky touched the skin below the bruise. 'What happened here?'

Lola glanced at the bruise, and her lips tightened. She paused. 'I fell.'

It was the pause that made Nicky's insides pitch. 'When?'

Lola covered the bruise with her hand. 'Last night.'

Nicky thought back to the previous evening. The kids had gone to bed before her and Sabine. There had been no fall. 'You can tell me anything, you know that.'

'It's nothing,' said Lola, her voice barely audible over the roar of the engine. 'Seriously.'

Nicky leaned in further. 'I'm starting to worry now, Lola.'

'Tell her why you're upset,' said Betsy, her voice unnaturally gentle.

'I wish I'd never said anything to you,' Lola said, crossing her legs and covering the bruise. 'Please, can you both just leave me alone? I'm fine.'

Nicky knew she wouldn't get any more from Lola. She would try again later, or failing that, push Betsy to share what she knew when she got her on her own. She cursed herself for drinking more than she should have on the last night of their holiday. She'd taken her eye off the ball, and something had happened between her daughter and Elias. Something bad enough to leave her bruised and make her stoic child cry.

Ice creeping through her veins, she glanced back at Elias, her best friend's only child, foreboding stitching her stomach into a twisted knot.

1

A WEEK EARLIER

Nicky

Two hours into the flight to Zante, the novelty had worn off. The girls had been giggly at the airport, but the excitement of boarding and take-off faded quickly and they were all feeling the effects of getting up at 4 a.m. A tiredness headache pulsed behind Nicky's eyes. She was the one who'd pushed for an early flight, reminding Sabine that they only had seven nights away. This was the start of her new life with her girls, the one Julian had told her she would fail at. Well, she wouldn't, not with her best friend by her side to support her. Though she hated herself for thinking like that. Why did she always need someone else to prop her up? She should be more self-reliant, like Sabine herself was.

Her thoughts had to fight to become clear through the fog in her head. She hadn't slept well; she rarely did these days because it was impossible to switch off her brain. Then she'd been up before her daughters, checking and rechecking the cases, worried she'd forgotten something crucial. She didn't know why she was suddenly convinced she couldn't pack effectively. It wasn't as if Julian had ever helped on previous trips. And she couldn't share her anxiety with Sabine. She'd roll her eyes and say something like, 'We're going to Zante, not the Gobi Desert. The shops have tampons as well as novelty T-shirts with dicks on, for God's sake.' She would have a point too. Nicky resolved to stop stressing. To try, at least.

Betsy squiggled in her seat. The stains on the white T-shirt Nicky had optimistically suggested she wore could tell the story of their trip so far: red from the strawberry smoothie at the airport as they waited for their gate to be called, and brown from the Minstrels Nicky foolishly allowed her to buy in addition to her meal deal in WHSmith. Once again, Nicky's belief that at least the chocolate was in a hard shell, therefore less likely to make a mess, was hopelessly optimistic. Betsy systematically chomped on them, somehow managing to coat her fingers in a half-chewed mess of sludgy brown, which she then wiped across her chest.

'I said you had to eat your sandwich before those,' Nicky said, leaning across Lola and trying to take the almost empty packet from her youngest daughter.

Lola smiled and raised her eyes skywards as if the two of them were in a playground spat. 'Behave yourselves, children,' she said mockingly as her mother and sister tousled. Lola was so sensible. Nicky sometimes wished she was in charge instead of her.

'I'll eat my sandwich,' said Betsy, clinging on to what remained of the chocolates in her tight fist, 'in a minute.'

'Your sister's eating hers.' Nicky knew that was a mistake as soon as it came out of her mouth. What right-minded parent openly compared their children? It was hard, though, since Lola always toed the line. Growing up in a tense household with a mother who was always on edge seemed to have made her eldest daughter into a perfectionist, so it was Nicky's fault Lola had grown up before her time. That's what Nicky told herself. It was easier than seeing Julian's traits in her child.

Betsy was a different creature. She seemed oblivious to what was going on around her most of the time, thank God. She pushed herself back in her seat and stared out of the window, shoving three more chocolates into her mouth. Nicky patted her knee by way of apology. She needed to relax. This holiday would be fun. Sabine always brought out the best in Nicky; she made her feel carefree in a way no one else did. She needed that now more than ever.

Nicky sat back in her seat and stole a glance at Lola. She was eating her ham and cheese sandwich in neat little bites, catching the crumbs in the packet. She'd chosen a small tub of pineapple instead of crisps in her meal deal, which made Nicky first pleased and then worried. She was glad her daughter wanted to eat nutritiously, but did that mean she was overly conscious about her weight? Everyone knew you had to be on the lookout for eating disorders with girls her age. She thought back to Lola's sixteenth birthday last week, feeling relieved when she remembered her stuffing a wedge of birthday cake into her mouth. Good. That was one less thing she needed to worry about... unless Lola had binged on cake, then gone into the toilet to make herself sick. The thought hijacked Nicky's brain and sent prickles of anxiety over her skin.

She shook her head. She was being ridiculous. Lola was perfectly healthy; it was she who was a wreck. She'd lost all sense of perspective over the last turbulent weeks, and her constantly broken sleep didn't help. A week with her girls and her best friend would sort her out. She turned her head to where Sabine and Elias were sitting in the middle and aisle seats of the opposite row.

Sabine must've sensed her eyes on her because she lifted her gaze from her book and grinned. 'You all right?'

Nicky smiled and nodded. The guilt that Sabine was always checking up on her these days crept across her scalp. She would spend the next week changing that. 'Yep. All good. How's your book?'

'So good,' said Sabine, letting her head roll back and her mouth fall open in an expression of ecstasy. 'You've got to read it when I've finished. It's right up your street. It will break your heart then fix it right back up.' One of the reasons Nicky loved Sabine was her capacity to find joy in everything. She would cry at beautiful paintings and dance unselfconsciously at the first sound of music. Nicky put it down to her Greek roots. Nicky was British through and through and when Sabine salsa-ed to street musicians, Nicky was caught between wanting to hide in shame and wishing she had less of a rod at her own back.

Nicky nodded across at Elias, who was wearing headphones and staring at his phone propped up on the tray table. 'What's he watching?' She wished she hadn't asked when Sabine nudged Elias and he pressed the screen and took his headphones off.

'Eh?' he said, ruffling his dark curls. He raised his eyebrows, making his brown eyes even bigger.

'Nicky wants to know what you're watching.'

Elias leaned forwards to face Nicky. '*Baby Driver*. It's good. Have you seen it?'

Nicky shook her head. 'I haven't, actually.' How did a seventeen-year-old boy manage to make her feel so parochial?

She elbowed Lola. 'Have you seen *Baby Driver*?' She'd tried this tactic in the airport, asking each of the teenagers something in turn, hoping they'd engage then start a conversation of their own. She was terrified Lola and Elias would avoid each other all week and she and Sabine would be left awkwardly making conversation for the group. Sabine laughed when she'd mentioned that when the kids were out of earshot. She told her to relax and give them time. That was easy for her to say; she and Elias had relaxation written into their DNA. She and Lola weren't blessed in the same way.

Lola gaped at her as if she'd asked if she'd ever been to Mars. 'Erm, no.' Her eyebrows knitted in a way that made Nicky certain she was missing something.

'Elias says it's good. Maybe you should look it up.'

Lola narrowed her eyes. 'Okay. It's an eighteen, though.' She cocked her head to the side and pursed her lips in an amused smile.

Heat rushed up Nicky's neck. Naively, she'd thought a film with the name Baby Driver would be as innocent as it sounded. 'Oh.' She'd always been strict about making sure the girls were only exposed to suitable content. It was one of the many things Julian had insisted on. He wanted them to stay decent, saying he didn't want his kids turning into teenage tarts like the ones he saw around town. Nicky had thought that cruel, but hadn't said so.

'It's not that bad,' said Elias. 'Mainly cars and guns.' He gave a quick smile. 'But I'm watching it for the cars.'

'Course you are,' said Sabine, tapping his knee. Elias lifted his mother's gin and tonic from her tray table and drank. She took the plastic glass from him and took a sip before placing it back in front of herself without comment. 'Don't you go corrupting those two innocent girls with your wicked ways this week.' She smiled adoringly at her son.

Nicky felt Lola stiffen beside her and wished she'd never started the conversation.

'Can I watch *Baby Driver*?' said Betsy.

'No,' Nicky said. 'You're only ten. Eat your sandwich.'

'I'm eleven now.'

Elias's mouth twitched up in a smile as he lifted his padded headphones back over his curls and pressed his screen to restart the film. Lola dragged her rucksack out from under the seat in front and found her earphones. She put them in, and it felt to Nicky like a rejection. She racked her brains to think of a way to make things better. The guilt of slicing their family apart sat heavy on Nicky, despite knowing she should have left years ago, before the girls were old enough to be conscious of the dysfunctional dynamic between their parents. Lola had been quieter since Julian moved out and Nicky couldn't bear the thought of either of her girls being unhappy. Bringing up happy, well-adjusted children was her one job. Julian's voice rang in her head: *You're a useless mother. What hope have those girls got with a pathetic role model like you?* She wasn't pathetic. It was her responsibility to shield them from things like inappropriate media until they were mature enough to process them, and that's what she would do. And Lola wasn't interested in cars and guns, was she? They always watched romcoms together, and Lola had never suggested an action movie in her life.

Sabine turned back to her book and Nicky opened her Kindle and tried to read, but the words wouldn't penetrate, and she found herself reading the same line over and over again. She'd been looking forward to this holiday since the moment Sabine suggested it, but now anxiety tightened her shoulders. She'd hoped the girls and Elias would get on, but her daughters were young for their years and Elias seemed worldly and was watching eighteen-rated films with Sabine's consent. She hadn't even commented on him drinking her gin. Julian had instilled it in her that she had to protect their girls from the harsh reality of life for as long as humanly possible. He'd also always told her Sabine was a bad influence.

Maybe a joint holiday hadn't been the best idea after all.

2

SABINE

Sabine watched with amusement as Nicky corralled her daughters and their cases in the arrivals hall as if they were a herd of sheep, likely to set off in random directions, rather than a couple of competent kids with wheely cases in a European airport. She'd always been like that. Though Sabine had to admit she'd benefitted from her friend's need to keep everything under control on more than one occasion. But she hoped Nicky would chill out a bit while they were away. Sabine had waited long enough to invite her back. And now she was free of that rubbery-faced slimeball of a husband, it was supposed to be the start of a new chapter for them all. Not that she'd phrase it like that to Nicky. She was a sensitive soul, bless her. She needed a confidence boost, and Sabine was looking forward to providing it.

She turned to see Elias rolling both their cases towards her. He didn't need shepherding, and she was very grateful for it. She and Elias were more like friends than mother and son and she was proud of that. She hoped some of her relaxed parenting style might rub off on her friend this week. By the way Nicky was sweating and rearranging Betsy's rucksack on her back for no discernible reason, it looked like she could do with learning a thing or two about how to ease up on the helicopter mum crap.

'All good?' Sabine smiled as the group assembled around her.

'I think so,' said Nicky. 'I feel like we must've left something on the plane, but I can't for the life in me think what it might be.'

Sabine wrapped an arm around Nicky's shoulder. 'You're all good. You haven't left anything on the plane. And even if you have, it will be replaceable.' She gestured to the kids. 'And we've remembered all the important things, our darling little angels.' Betsy cupped her chin in her hands and fluttered her eyelashes, making them all laugh. She was a sweet kid. Hopefully Sabine could persuade Nicky to stop hovering above her every move and allow her to be a bit more independent. That would do them both the world of good.

Sabine gave Nicky a squeeze, then took hold of the handle of her case, pointing to the exit with her other arm. 'Onwards, troops.'

The heat outside took her breath away. She loved this moment, stepping from the airport, knowing she was back on the soil of her ancestors. She might have been born and brought up in North London, but her heart belonged to Greece. All the holidays of her childhood tumbled through her memory, her yiayià in her black dress insisting she improved her Greek pronunciation over breakfasts of yoghurt and fresh fruit, her cousins whooping and cannonballing into the pool. She swallowed down the sadness that the extended family had decided to rent out the villa for most of the season, limiting the time it was available for her to use. She'd enjoyed free holidays her whole life, so she could hardly complain. Resentment that this was the only week available, and that Leo was in the middle of an important deal at work, still rankled though. At least Nicky and the girls could enjoy it, and God knows, Nicky needed a lift after finally getting up the courage to ditch that dick of a husband.

As they approached a black people carrier, the surly driver in a dirty T-shirt looked them up and down. Sabine spoke in fast Greek, using local colloquialisms, letting him know she wasn't just another tourist. As she anticipated, his demeanour immediately changed, a smile revealing two missing teeth in his lower jaw.

'I always forget you speak Greek,' said Nicky. 'What did you say?'

'I told him to ignore the speed limit and get us to the villa as quickly as possible.' Nicky's face was a picture. 'Of course I didn't, you idiot. I just told him where we want to go.'

On the road, Sabine tried to imagine what Nicky would make of the scrubby grassland and tatty billboards they sped past. She knew the route so well she didn't usually see the half-finished buildings, but travelling with others made her view it through fresh eyes. 'It might look a bit shabby now,' she said over her shoulder to where Nicky sat in the back with her girls. 'But I promise the village and the house are beautiful.'

'In my memory, this was all pretty scenery,' said Nicky. 'I don't remember a motorway at all.'

'You've probably romanticised it,' said Sabine. 'The infrastructure has changed, to be fair, but I bet your imagination has made it more like the online brochures of Greek islands, all white buildings and domed chapels.'

'Hm,' said Nicky. 'It's certainly been a long time.'

Sabine wondered if that was pointed. It could be a simple acceptance, or it could be an implied judgement. Nicky never asked why Sabine hadn't invited her back after that first idyllic trip when they were in their second year of university, and she'd never told her. She chose avoidance instead, like any sane person.

'I can see the sea!' said Betsy, pointing to the glorious blue-green Ionian Sea beyond a cluster of terracotta buildings.

'Look at the colour,' said Nicky, sounding more excited now.

'A bit different to the English Channel, right?' said Sabine. 'Although you love a dip off the British coast, don't you, Nicky?'

Nicky spluttered out a laugh, as Sabine knew she would. 'You'll never let me forget that, will you?'

'Never,' said Sabine, glad that she'd reminded Nicky of a time when her troubles didn't weigh so heavily on her. She wanted that version of her friend back, for Nicky as much as for herself. She turned to view the girls in the back seat. 'Your mother insisted that it was warm enough to swim in the sea when we took a trip to Brighton one weekend when we were at uni, even though it was raining.'

'It was summer rain,' insisted Nicky, laughing. 'And we were at the seaside. We had to have a swim.'

'It was bloody freezing.' Sabine could see them both now in her mind's eye, Nicky dipping her shoulders under the water, pretending it was refreshing, before giving up and running back to where their towels had got wet in the downpour. 'And we had to go back to this awful B and B we were staying at soaked through and that dragon of a landlady told us off for dripping water up the stairs.'

'Good times,' said Nicky, sighing contentedly.

'Can we go swimming in the sea today?' Betsy pleaded.

The sound of Betsy bouncing on the leather seat made Sabine smile. 'You might prefer to swim in the pool,' she said. She knew she would. She was exhausted. They usually got a later flight and arrived on the island in the early evening. A pang of longing for her calm, competent husband resonated in her gut. They had their pattern when they arrived: he would leave her to unpack while he and Elias went to the supermarket to get supplies, then he would mix cocktails and barbecue huge prawns and halloumi as she sat and basked in the warm air and watched the sun set. This week would be different, but it would be just as enjoyable, she was sure of it.

The familiar guilt of having avoided spending family time with her best friend's children crept over her. She'd had her reasons, but she'd never told Nicky the painful truth about why she'd distanced herself for a time. Lola and Betsy were nice kids, from what she knew of them. She and Leo had lived in the US when Nicky's girls were small, but when they came back to the UK, she could have made more of an effort. It wasn't as if they lived far apart, but seeing Nicky one-on-one became the easier option, and Nicky seemed content with the situation too. It meant they could both avoid the elephant in the room.

When they were at university, they'd planned a life where they would live on the same street in somewhere like Camden with their cool, artsy partners and always be in and out of each other's impossibly trendy houses. Sabine had kept her side of the bargain. She was an interior designer and Leo worked for an auction house dealing in modern art. Nicky, on the other hand, married a city boy who'd persuaded her she didn't need to go back to work as a graphic designer after she had the children. Nicky was the one who'd renegued on the deal.

Now she was single again, Sabine had visions of Nicky re-emerging into the world like a magnificent phoenix from the flames. This holiday would be the start. She watched the scenery as the taxi turned off the motorway and on to the dusty road leading to the village, thinking about how she would show Nicky it was possible to be friends with your child, rather than an anxious mother hen, and how she'd help her find her purpose again.

She turned to Elias in the seat next to her. He was gazing out of the window at the houses on the outskirts of the village, the sun bathing his face in light. Leo insisted their son had a look of Timothée Chalamet, but she didn't see it. Elias's eyes were bigger, his hair curlier. Beyond him through the window, she caught sight of a girl with long dark hair she thought she recognised coming out of a grocery store. A shiver ran through her. It probably wasn't her. This island was entirely populated by people with dark hair. Even so, she hoped they wouldn't bump into that particular girl or her father this year.

Elias had done nothing wrong, she reminded herself. He was perfect inside and out, and that was because of his enviable genes and the way he'd been brought up. If thinking that made her smug, she didn't care. If she compared the effort Nicky put into parenting with her own, then it might seem like Elias brought himself up, but she was always there for guidance, of course. He only had to ask. Everyone was different, she supposed. She was just lucky she had won the jackpot.

Soon the tyres crunched on the gravel of Villa Idalia's drive. She let out a satisfied breath as the square white house came into view. She had so many wonderful memories of this place, and they were about to make more. 'Here we are,' she said. 'Let the holiday begin.'

3

NICKY

The breath stalled in Nicky's throat when she caught sight of Villa Idalia through the dusty car window. Her mind spun back twenty-five years to her first holiday abroad, when the white building had come into view, with its covered terrace and pretty stone paths down to the pool, and she'd thought she'd arrived in heaven. She'd been nineteen then, her whole life in front of her ready to fill with joyful experiences.

But life hadn't turned out like that. She viewed Betsy and a familiar surge of love and gratitude flooded her. The only bright thing to happen since university was her girls. She couldn't boast a glittering career, or a handsome husband. She was approaching forty-five and had nothing but a failed marriage and a heap of regret to her name.

The car drew to a halt at the side of the house with its central door and peculiar stone steps at either side. She reached for her girls' hands and grinned at each in turn. 'We are going to have the best time,' she said, squeezing their fingers then letting go. She owed it to them to make this holiday wonderful, after what they'd been through in the last few weeks. And all the years before, her brain added, as if she didn't already feel guilty enough.

When the taxi reversed out of the drive, the five of them stood at the base of the steps while Sabine dug in her bag for her keys. 'Can I go around the front and have a look?' asked Betsy, her eyes shining with excitement.

'Wait until—' Nicky began.

'Of course.' Sabine peered sheepishly at Nicky. 'As long as it's okay with your mum.'

Nicky didn't know why she'd tried to stop her. She supposed her natural response was to say no until she'd done a mental risk assessment, but she didn't have to do that here. She briefly wondered when she'd stopped trusting her own instincts, but that well was deep and she didn't want to sully this moment by diving in. This place was safe. She'd spent two of the best weeks of her life in the grounds of this house. Not only that, but Betsy was eleven now – not a little girl any more. She had to stop her pesky brain from adding she'd still been ten three weeks ago. That was the problem with having two summer babies; everyone else in their school year seemed so much older and you ended up being overly protective, especially when you'd been told that every move you make is the wrong one for as long as Nicky had. 'Yes, of course. Go on.'

'I'll show you around,' said Elias.

'Thanks,' said Nicky, watching the two of them disappear around the front of the house. She turned to Lola. 'Go on, have a look.'

'It's all right,' said Lola. 'I'll give you a hand with the cases.'

Nicky gave her daughter an appreciative hug and was about to insist they could manage and shoo her off with the others when Sabine said, 'You're a doll. It's good of you to help two old ladies out.' She hunched her shoulders and made her voice waver, then gave the snorting laugh that Nicky had always found infectious.

'Speak for yourself,' said Nicky. 'I'm in my prime.' She lifted her chin and made a show of trying and failing to hoist her case up the steps effortlessly.

Sabine watched with an amused smile. 'Clearly.' She laughed. 'I'm only joking. You are in your prime. You're still youthful and absolutely gorgeous, just like me.' She gave Nicky a loud kiss on the cheek before turning to Lola. 'It's probably a bit weird being thrown together with a boy you barely know. I don't know if it's better or worse for you that Jackson couldn't make it.'

Jackson was the name of Elias's friend who'd been due to join them until his appendix burst a few days before. Nicky realised Sabine was trying to make it easier for Lola. Why hadn't she thought of that, rather than making fruitless attempts to get the teenagers to interact? If she was truthful with herself, she found self-assured Elias a little... not intimidating exactly... but she was slightly in awe of his confidence. There was something enigmatic about him that made her want him to like her. She wanted him to like Lola too, but watching her daughter apologise for getting in Sabine's way, then hoist her case inelegantly up the steps, she couldn't help thinking she and Elias were essentially from different planets. Like her and Sabine really. Even twenty-seven years on, she wasn't 100 per cent certain why her stylish, charismatic friend had chosen her to hang out with out of everyone on offer. She lifted her face to feel the warmth of the sun. She might not understand it, but she wasn't going to complain.

* * *

Two hours later, they were unpacked, and Betsy and Lola were slathered in suntan lotion and in the pool. Sabine and Elias had taken the dusty old Fiat that sat in the lean-to to the supermarket to get supplies, so Nicky took the opportunity to reacquaint herself with the house. She was staying in the same room she had a quarter of a century ago. Those words rang in her head. How could it be twenty-five years, not only since she was here, but since she was young and hopeful? She'd allowed so many years to escape her. No, they hadn't escaped her, they'd been stolen. That's how she was beginning to view her years with Julian now. And time wasn't the only thing he'd taken. Her confidence had never been high, but what little she had, he'd diminished snipe by nasty snipe, until she didn't trust herself to breathe in and out correctly. Not that she'd ever confided that in anyone. Not even Sabine. How did she tell someone as vibrant as her that her husband, the person who was supposed to hold her in the highest esteem, told her she was worthless on an almost daily basis? It was shameful, humiliating. The fact she'd accepted it for the best part of two decades, before that video had arrived on her phone and snapped any resolve to try to keep her family together, made her believe he was right. She was useless and pathetic. The regret threatened to overwhelm her, then she heard Betsy's laughter from outside, and she decided to do her very best to stay above the waves of self-loathing that kept trying to engulf her.

She put her hand on the wall, feeling the rough beige stone. All the interior walls were the same, giving it a rustic farmhouse kind of feel. There was a small window with a view of the path to the pool, which was bordered with pink and yellow flowers, and twin beds made up with plain white linen. Last time she was there the beds were adorned with multi-coloured crocheted throws, but she supposed those had been discarded when the house was prepared for letting. It was a shame. Nicky imagined a long-lost relative with busy crochet needles making the throws to keep generations of her family warm. Not that the beds needed any more covers. Outside, the heat was stifling and she leaned against the stone, glad to feel it cool against her back. She raised her head and saw an air conditioning unit above the bed. That was a relief. It probably cost a fortune to run, though, and she already felt guilty about her and the girls having free accommodation.

Reassured all was well by the background noise of Betsy's incessant chatter, and the sound of splashing, she went downstairs to the kitchen. The freestanding hotch-potch of dressers and cupboards she remembered had been replaced by a smart pale-green fitted kitchen with integrated electric oven. A pristine dining table set with rattan place mats stood where an old, scuffed oak table used to be. She remembered tipsy walks home along the unlit road, the sound of her and Sabine's giggles the only thing breaking the silence, then sitting at that table eating toasted pitta and hummus, dissecting the evening's events, or planning their glorious futures.

The sound of a car approaching lifted her from her reverie. She rushed down the steps at the side of the house to help bring in the shopping. Elias was already lifting carrier bags from the car, and she was surprised at the sight of his defined biceps as he hooked bag after bag over his forearm. Surely they belonged on a man, not a boy? She reminded herself he was almost an adult, although didn't the children of your friends always remain youthful in your perception?

'Let me give you a hand,' she said.

'Don't worry, I've got it,' said Elias, walking past her with several bags, groceries straining against the thin green plastic. She followed him into the kitchen and started to unpack what they'd bought, mouth watering at the sight of grapes twice the size of the ones she got at her local supermarket and tubs of thick Greek yoghurt.

'We'll stick these in the pizza oven tonight,' said Sabine, coming in holding a stack of enormous pizzas in front of her. 'With a nice Greek salad. What do you think?'

'Perfect,' said Nicky, opening the fridge door for Sabine to deposit the pizzas inside. They took up an entire shelf. She stopped herself from checking what kind of pizzas Sabine had bought, hoping there was at least one plain margarita. Betsy hadn't yet grown out of her fussy-eating stage and Nicky was already anticipating the embarrassment that would come when Betsy refused to eat anything, while Elias tucked into octopus tentacles, or something equally exotic, without a second thought. She hadn't been able to bring herself to ask Sabine to buy an industrial-sized bottle of ketchup because Betsy wouldn't eat most meals without huge dollops of the stuff. She hoped this holiday might be an opportunity to offer her youngest child an insight into more sophisticated eating habits. She'd discovered so many new tastes on this island. She was sure Betsy would too. Almost sure, anyway.

She turned to look out of the window at the sound of flip flops approaching and saw Lola walking towards the house. In her peripheral vision, she was aware of Elias taking a step towards the window. In that moment, Nicky suddenly viewed Lola not as her daughter, but as a sixteen-year-old girl in a tiny bikini. She saw the length of her legs, the way the strings tying her tiny bikini bottoms together bounced on the side of her small buttocks, the curve of her stomach and where it hollowed just before her hips. She noticed her daughter's hard nipples, her firm breasts barely covered by the triangles of material.

She glanced across at Elias, but he turned away before she could see the look in his eyes.

4

NICKY

Nicky continued to watch through the kitchen window as Lola neared the house. The blonde highlights threaded through her hair shone like gold, and her pale skin shimmered with droplets of water. Nicky had to admit, that was the body of a young woman, not a girl, and since Elias was a teenage boy, he was bound to notice. But however good she looked in a bikini, Nicky was sure Lola wasn't Elias's type of girl. She expected he knew plenty of girls who would strut around in their swimwear, taking pouty selfies and making sure the boys noticed them. She was glad Lola wasn't like that.

Almost at the house, Lola glanced up and saw them both through the window. She seemed to shrink, her shoulders curling inwards as if she wanted to hide her body. 'Can you find me a towel please, Mum?' she shouted, then turned and rushed back towards the pool.

It was all Nicky could do to stop herself from yelling, 'Don't run, it's slippery,' after her. When she turned, Elias was busy slotting milk cartons into the fridge, quietly humming to himself.

She went off to find Lola's blue beach towel and took it down to her. She found her sitting on the end of a sun lounger. She sat next to her and wrapped the towel around her shoulders. 'It's not too shabby here, is it?'

Lola grinned. 'Not too shabby at all.'

Nicky hugged her, pleased when Lola relaxed against her. They watched Betsy practise wobbly legged handstands in the pool. 'What do you think of Elias?'

'He's okay.'

'Just okay?'

Lola laughed. She turned her face to Nicky, her green eyes full of amusement. 'What do you want me to say?'

That was a good question. Nicky wasn't sure. She felt the familiar low-level hum of danger in her gut, but wasn't entirely sure why. 'We're going to have a lovely holiday.' She kissed the top of Lola's damp head. 'A week with you two is exactly what I need.'

'You all right?' Lola's eyes were serious, and Nicky cursed herself for not hiding her feelings well enough. Lola should not have to worry about her.

'Me? I'm fabulous.' She threw out an arm. Lola laughed again and Nicky hugged her close to her side. She would make sure her girls had the holiday they deserved. 'I'm so proud of you,' she said. 'I know it's been hard since...' She stopped, not wanting to bring the darkness of the last weeks to this sun-shiny moment. 'You are a superstar, Lola, and I am very, very proud to be your mum.'

Betsy swam to the side of the pool and rested her forearms and chin on the ridged tiles. 'And mine,' she said.

'Nah, you're a loser,' said Lola. 'I'm the heir, you're just the spare.' She laughed, mischief sparkling in her eyes.

'You're the loser,' said Betsy, splashing water at Lola.

Nicky leaped up and strode to the side of the pool, scooping up water in her palms and flinging it first at Betsy, then Lola, loving the sound of their surprised squeals. She scrunched her eyes against the water Betsy splashed back, not even minding that her trousers were getting wet. 'I'm proud of both my girls,' she said, standing and shaking the moisture from her hands. And she was. They might be very different, but they were both perfect in their own ways. The thought that they deserved a better mother than her crept into her mind, but for once, she didn't let it take hold.

* * *

Three hours later, Nicky's stomach was full of pizza, and she was lying on a sun lounger next to her best friend in the fading evening light. The underwater bulbs made the pool glow pale blue. Grasshoppers chirruped in the borders and citronella candles gave the air a lemony scent. The kitchen window lit up. A shadow flitted across the room, before the light was extinguished again. She thought it was probably Betsy on the hunt for a sugary snack while she wasn't looking. 'The kids were quiet over dinner, weren't they?' she said. Even Betsy hadn't rambled on in her usual way. It was as though Elias's presence struck the girls dumb.

'Try not to worry,' Sabine said, placing a calming hand on her wrist. Sabine was a tactile person and had always touched her more gently than anyone else, even Julian. It was such an intimate thing, and always comforting. 'They'll be fine when they get used to each other. You're always thinking about other people. Try thinking about yourself for a change. Enjoy a moment's peace and quiet.'

'I feel bad that they're holed up in their rooms,' Nicky said, wishing she could just switch off. 'They should be out here, or... I don't know. Not on their phones, anyway.' At home she usually took Betsy's phone away at 8 p.m. and Lola's at nine. It had been one of Julian's rules, one of the few she actually agreed with. Now it was the holidays, she'd reluctantly conceded to 10 p.m. She had to fight Julian's voice in her head telling her she was a sap for bending. It didn't matter how much they bargained, begged or sulked; she'd read the research and knew how important it was they got enough sleep. It wasn't easy and it didn't help her win any popularity prizes, but it was the right thing to do, and, whatever her husband said, she always tried to do the right thing for her girls. She hadn't the heart to confiscate their phones tonight, though, and suspected the girls were taking full advantage of the extra screen time.

'Try to relax,' said Sabine. 'They're exhausted, we're exhausted, it's been a long day, so we should all give ourselves a break.'

Nicky wished she knew how to follow her friend's advice, but she found it impossible to turn her thoughts off. 'They'll be on their phones till dawn, I bet.' Julian's scowling face occurred in her mind's eye, shaking his head at her weakness.

'Maybe we should let them, they're on holiday after all. Lola's exams are over, she probably needs the downtime. You do too. You worked as hard as she did over the last few months to get her through those exams. Nobody could have done more. You deserve a break from being super-mum.'

'Thanks, love.' Nicky appreciated Sabine acknowledging the effort she'd put into helping Lola with her revision. In truth, she was glad it had given her something to focus on other than the turmoil that was always threatening to overwhelm her.

Nicky imagined Sabine let Elias keep his phone in his room overnight and always had done. Also, she knew her argument would be weakened by the fact that Elias aced his GCSEs last year and played rugby for the county. He wasn't exactly failing at life because he had a phone in his room.

She laid her head back and let out a long breath. 'It's so lovely to be back here. It doesn't feel like twenty-five years since we last lay out here, does it?'

Sabine reached across and squeezed Nicky's forearm. 'It does and it doesn't.' There was a wistfulness in her voice that made Nicky hope she'd say more. In truth, she wanted Sabine to tell her why she wasn't invited back to this villa for over two decades. Not that Julian would have agreed to come. He probably wouldn't have given her the money to bring the girls without him, either, but it would have been nice to be asked. The silence stretched until Sabine spoke again. 'Do you remember how we talked about bringing our children here?'

Nicky nodded, although at the time she'd thought they'd meant when the kids were toddlers. They'd talked about sandcastles and teaching them to swim in the pool. Now their eldest kids could quote Shakespeare and discuss the climate crisis with confidence, and it felt like they'd left it too late somehow.

'And now, here we are. Do you remember what else we said?' Sabine grinned across at her, her eyes glinting with green from the pool lights.

'What?'

Sabine laughed. 'It's mortifying. We were so young and idealistic.'

Nicky remembered the two of them lying out under the stars, dreaming of a future where their lives were intertwined. Instead, Sabine moved to another continent for years when their children were tiny, and now their offspring barely knew each other. 'Which bit?'

'About how our kids would fall in love and get married, then we'd be related and have one massive happy family.'

Nicky laughed. 'God, we were naive, weren't we?'

'I don't know, it could still happen,' said Sabine.

'Erm, I doubt that,' said Nicky. Planning for your future babies to one day get together was very different to thinking about a grown man lusting after your child.

'Why not?'

Nicky bit her bottom lip, wondering how much to say. It wouldn't be acceptable to tell her best friend she thought their kids were just too different. If she did, she'd have to explain why. 'A year is a long time at their age. Elias seems much older than Lola.'

'Didn't we always fancy the older boys more, though?'

That was part of Nicky's concern. She remembered Sabine's free and easy attitude to sex when she wasn't much older than Elias, and since he was a boy and one generation on, she didn't trust him to be careful either with her daughter's tender heart or her body. 'To be honest, I'm more worried the kids aren't going to get on. I had visions of board games and races in the pool, but they're hardly speaking.'

'Have you forgotten what it's like to be a self-conscious sixteen-year-old?' Sabine sat up and lifted the glass of wine from the table next to her lounger.

Nicky sat too. 'Like you were ever self-conscious.'

'I was.' Sabine took a gulp of wine. 'Not as much as you, obviously. You were so meek, which was bonkers because you've always been bloody gorgeous. When I first met you, you skirted around the edges of rooms, hoping no one would notice you. Until you got a drink inside you.' She wagged a finger. 'Then it was a different story. That first night—'

'Stop it.' Nicky covered her face and laughed.

'Well, I'm glad it happened,' said Sabine, grabbing both her hands and squeezing. 'Before that I was starting to think you really were the good little girl you seemed to be.' She let go of Nicky's hands and held her palms up. 'Not that there's anything wrong with that. It's just me and that girl weren't likely to be bosom buddies, if you know what I mean.'

'I can't believe you were going to bypass me as a friend because I was a good girl.' Nicky shook her head and feigned indignation.

'I wasn't going to bypass you. I just thought we were different, and we'd eventually find groups that were more... compatible.' She took a slug of wine. 'And anyway, you showed your true colours and the rest is history.'

'You mean you realised I was suggestible and easily influenced.' Something passed across Sabine's face that made her heart drop. 'Is that really what you thought?' It was something Julian had levelled at her more than once, and not just about her relationship with Sabine. Whenever she introduced a potential new friend, he'd find fault and explain to her how they were trying to manipulate or dominate her for their own ends.

'Oh my God! How could you think that? Of course not.' She paused. 'He really did a number on your confidence, didn't he?'

Nicky couldn't deny it. 'I've heard high self-esteem is overrated. Who needs it?' She attempted a light-hearted laugh, but it fell short.

'When I think of all that confidence you built up at uni—'

'That was you rubbing off on me,' Nicky interrupted. 'I just reverted to type when we stopped living together.' As the words came out of her mouth, she thought they might be true. Sometimes it felt like she wasn't even a person in her own right, but just a reflection of others. The thought made her want to cry.

'That's rubbish. You just needed someone to remind you how wonderful you are. You become the people you surround yourself with. That's what they say, isn't it? Be careful who you spend the most time with because their behaviours and attitudes will inevitably rub off on you.'

Nicky relaxed back against the sun lounger. 'God, heaven help me, then. I've spent two decades with a man who treated me like a doormat.' That word didn't begin to describe what had gone on in their home, but she was too ashamed to tell her friend the truth about her marriage. She was only just starting to admit it to herself.

'Which is why it's ideal that you're here with me and the girls now, because we all adore you, and so you're bound to start to feel better about yourself. It's science.'

'Science?'

'Or philosophy, or something. Either way, it's good.'

'It is good,' said Nicky, trying to hide the fact she was close to tears. Sabine was right. Being here with her was the perfect anti-dote to what had happened at home. 'Thank you for having my back and for saying lovely things. I might not always believe you, but I do appreciate you.'

'No problem. It's my job as best friend and cheerleader.' Sabine shook imaginary pompoms. 'If you can still get your big head out of the door at the end of this week, I will have failed in my duty.'

'I love that you've set yourself that challenge. I'll do my best to be a raging show-off by the time we leave.' Nicky laid her head against the cushion. The sun loungers that were there before were thin, foldable things. These plump, grey padded ones were infinitely more comfortable. She could fall asleep here quite easily. She was on holiday. It didn't matter if she didn't sleep well. There were no school runs in the morning, no games kits to wash or meals for fussy eaters to plan. She closed her eyes.

'Glad we have a plan. You feeling better about yourself will rub off on the girls too. They're absolute darlings. You've done a great job with those kids. I can't believe how much Lola's grown up.' Sabine's voice drifted in through Nicky's half-consciousness, the praise making her tight muscles unknot. 'I genuinely didn't recognise her when I collected her from school a few weeks ago when...' She paused, but not before Nicky saw herself in her mind's eye, six weeks ago. The video had woken her up to the truth about her husband. It arrived the day before Lola's final GCSE exam, and it had taken every ounce of strength and courage for Nicky to behave normally until Lola left for school the next morning. Then she ended her marriage.

Despite the fact it was undeniably him leaning out of the window of their family car, then inviting the woman in the short skirt inside, Julian had been savage when she confronted him. When he couldn't deny it, he tried to tell her it was her fault, turning nasty and asking if it was any surprise he turned to other women for attention with a wife like her. He let her know exactly how unworthy of love and respect she was, and how the girls would never amount to anything with a useless mother like her. She had to prove him wrong. She had to. She would protect them with every ounce of her strength and show them all that she was good enough.

Sabine carried on. 'It was like she'd stretched, and she had long legs and glossy hair like in the adverts. She's got a gorgeous figure on her too.' She giggled. 'Honestly, Elias's eyes were practically on stalks when she came out in those tiny shorts after her shower tonight. They might not be talking to each other much, but the chemistry is there, mark my words.'

Suddenly Nicky was wide awake.

5

SABINE

Sabine was woken by the sound of laughter. She reached for her phone and unplugged it from the charger. Nine o'clock. She should probably have got up earlier to help her guests with breakfast, but when another peal of laughter penetrated the thick walls, she surmised they were happy enough and sank back on to her pillow. It was her holiday too, after all.

It was Betsy's laughter she could hear, and she was glad. Six weeks ago, when she'd arrived at Nicky's house in the immediate aftermath of the split, she couldn't envisage any of Nicky's family ever laughing again. From what she knew of Betsy, she was an exuberant child, full of curiosity and energy. She definitely got her confidence from her father, but even that was rocked when her family disintegrated.

She listened out to see if she could hear Lola's voice. Sabine worried about Lola. She was too much like what Nicky had been like when Sabine had first met her at university: an anxious girl who wanted to go unnoticed, or at least please the people who did acknowledge her presence. Just like her mother before her, Lola had no idea of her own beauty, or how attractive her hard-won giggles were. Even though Sabine had often been told that she had the best and most infectious laugh, making Nicky laugh was Sabine's favourite thing to do when they first met. They had a similar sense of humour and she'd seen it as her mission to bring out the fun side Nicky seemed to repress unless she had a drink inside her. That's why their friendship worked, she'd always thought; they brought out the best in each other. Underneath it all, Nicky wasn't only a wallflower, and Sabine wasn't quite as extrovert as she came across. They knew each other as they truly were. Sabine told herself this, as if she needed to reassure herself the secret she'd kept from Nicky didn't make a difference. Not really.

She imagined her friend's face as she kept an eye on her girls now, always on high alert, as if they were in imminent peril and she was the only one who could save them. She pictured the muscle in Nicky's jaw twitching as she clenched her teeth last night when she tried suggesting her girls needed to hand over their phones before bedtime.

'Will it do them any lasting harm to have them in their rooms when they're on holiday?' Sabine had said.

Nicky gave her a harsh stare.

'I'm only saying. Elias always has his overnight, and he's turned out okay.'

Elias hadn't helped by twisting up his face, dribbling from one corner of his mouth and saying, 'Yeah, didn't do me no harm,' in a strangled, weird mid-west American accent.

Nicky laughed and agreed, albeit with obvious reluctance. Sabine had to try hard not to tell her to chill out. No one ever relaxed because you told them to. You just gave them something else to be cross about, which was annoying because if anyone needed to chill the heck out, it was Nicky.

She stared at the rough plaster of the ceiling, resolving to demonstrate to Nicky how to relax, by being zen as fuck herself. It was the least she could do after she'd finally had the courage to throw that moron out.

She sat up and swung her legs out of bed. The tiles were cold on the soles of her feet and the sensation made her smile. This is what it felt like to be on holiday.

'Good morning, good morning!' she said, marching into the kitchen with her arms wide. She pulled Nicky in for a hug. 'The sun is shining, and I predict a glorious day.'

'Morning,' said Nicky, holding her wet hands out behind Sabine's back as she hugged her. She went back to washing up breakfast dishes in the sink. 'Sleep well?'

'Not bad.' Sabine switched on the kettle. 'Though I miss the smelly old crocheted bedspreads,' she said. 'There was something comforting about knowing there were generations worth of dead skin cells lying on top of you each night.'

'Urgh,' said Nicky. 'I missed them too until you said that.'

Sabine kicked a kitchen cabinet with her heel. 'And I hate all this built-in stuff. I want yiayià's knackered old table and the rickety cupboards with wonky doors.'

'I thought you'd approve of the makeover.' Nicky dried the bowls with a pristine tea towel. Sabine even missed the ancient towels with holes that had been there for decades, the cotton getting thinner year on year.

'Huh. They didn't even consult me,' said Sabine. 'That's how much my family respect my professional opinion.' She scrutinised the kitchen. 'I mean, why choose green? How does celadon say rustic Zante? Answer me that?'

'I might if I knew what celadon was.'

'This,' Sabine said, flicking at the pale-green cupboard. 'They just got the letting company to do a standard refurbishment. Criminal.'

'Not a strong accent of colour in sight,' mocked Nicky.

Sabine laughed. 'Don't you start on my colour accents.' She wagged her finger. 'And when we get back, my first job is to de-beige your house. You're a creative woman with impeccable taste, and it's about time your home reflected that.'

'I can't afford you,' said Nicky, the smile falling from her face.

Nicky had disclosed how difficult she was now finding living on the budget set by Julian, and it made Sabine's blood boil. She'd pretended that she'd used air miles that were about to expire to pay for all their flights to Zante, because she knew Nicky wouldn't have the money, or allow Sabine to pay for them, even though she could afford to. She had no idea why her friend was still allowing that prick to dictate how she lived, especially after what he did. She needed a fire lit under her, and Sabine was standing by with the matches. She would tread carefully, though. Nicky was still fragile.

'Gratis,' said Sabine. 'We'll call it my divorce present.'

'We've already had a free holiday,' said Nicky, stacking the bowls in the cupboard.

'I told you, you're saving me and Elias from a week on our own here. Much as I love my son, I'm in no hurry to watch him play on his phone for seven nights.' She cut a fat slice of crusty bread and put it in the toaster, moving out of the way when Nicky started to wipe up the crumbs she'd made. 'Darling, you don't have to clear up after me. I can mop up my own mess.'

Nicky dropped the crumbs into the bin. 'I know you can. But you won't.'

'I will,' said Sabine, 'eventually.' She winked. 'Not promising to come up to your ridiculous standards though.'

Nicky put on a prim accent. 'And I will not lower my standards to your level just because we are on foreign soil.' She shook her head as Sabine took butter and jam from the fridge. 'I don't understand how you can make houses look so beautiful, then leave jammy knives on counters and beds unmade.'

The toast popped up and Sabine dropped it on to her plate, shaking the heat from her burning fingers. 'That's the wondrous mystery of me. I'm a complicated woman. Hard to fathom.'

Nicky laughed. 'You're a grot-bag.'

'Ha! I've been called worse.' There was the sound of Betsy's laughter again. 'That's music to my ears,' Sabine said. She flung an arm over Nicky's shoulder, making her stop for a second and absorb the wonderful noises coming from outside.

'Hm,' said Nicky. 'Betsy got Lola up at stupid o'clock to go in the pool. Lola wasn't happy.' She pulled away and peered out of the window, but the pool was out of sight beyond the terrace. 'It's already hot out there. I hope they've got enough lotion on.'

'I'm sure they will have,' said Sabine. 'They're clever kids. Just like their mum.'

Nicky blew her a kiss before running Sabine's sticky knife under the tap.

'What do you fancy doing today?' Sabine said through a mouthful of toast and jam. Manners weren't necessary when you were with your best friend.

'Betsy fancies the beach. That okay?'

'Fine by me,' said Sabine. 'But we should go earlier rather than later, because it's going to get properly hot this afternoon. There's a lovely secluded cove, do you remember it? We can come back here for shade after lunch.'

'Okay.' Nicky didn't say anything about remembering the cove, which surprised Sabine. Instead, she said, 'Is Elias up?' She took Sabine's empty plate and rinsed it while Sabine licked jam from her fingers.

'Doubt it. He probably won't be till noon.'

'What...?' Nicky scrunched her nose. 'So... will you get him up to come with us?'

'Nah.' Sabine avoided Nicky's eyes. She knew her son, and he liked a lie-in. She was also afraid her friend would think staying in bed on a beautiful day like this was both idle and wasteful. 'It's his holiday too. I'll leave him to it. I'll leave a note, then if he wants to come down to the beach when he gets up, he can. That's one of the benefits of having older kids, isn't it? Everyone can do what makes them happy.' She was annoyed at herself for feeling defensive. If one of her aims this week was to show Nicky that being a more relaxed parent was beneficial for everyone, she needed to stand her ground. 'Don't you think?'

'Aren't you worried he'll miss half the holiday?'

'Define holiday.' Sabine shrugged. 'If his idea of a holiday is lying in bed, then he's bang on track for a good time.' Defiance lifted her chin. If Elias did get up now, she might just send him back to bed to prove her point.

'But—' Nicky was interrupted by the appearance of Betsy on the path outside the window.

'Morning, my lovely,' said Sabine.

'Morning.' Betsy grinned at Sabine then turned to her mother, water dripping down her body and pooling at her feet. 'Lola got out and now she won't go back in the pool with me,' she said. 'She said she wants to get a tan so she's just lying there like this.' She stuck her arms to her sides and raised her face to the sun.

'I told her not to sunbathe,' said Nicky, a deep line appearing between her brows.

'You're fighting a losing battle there, my love.' Sabine turned to her friend, shaking her head. They were in Zante, for God's sake. A tan was all but inevitable.

'It's bad for your skin,' said Nicky, flushing. 'I'm astonished anyone does it these days, especially with the rates of skin cancer in places like Australia.'

'She's not going to get a melanoma from a week in the sun,' said Sabine as gently as she could. 'And it's not even 10 a.m. yet. The UV won't be that strong.' She wasn't in a hurry for anyone to burn, but surely a bit of a suntan wouldn't hurt the girl? This level of caution was becoming a little irritating, which wasn't a good sign this early in the week. She made herself pause. Nicky was worried about her kids. She was a naturally anxious person and Sabine should try to respect that.

'Tell her to get ready to go to the beach,' Nicky said to Betsy.

Betsy pulled her fists into her middle. 'Yes!'

'And you both need to put factor fifty on and wear a hat,' Nicky called to Betsy's retreating back.

'Right, I'd better get ready too,' said Sabine. 'It will take me ages to get into my burka. Don't want a stray sunbeam to penetrate through to my tender flesh.'

'I'm just trying to be a responsible parent,' Nicky said, not quite snapping, but not far off.

'I was joking,' Sabine said, mollifying her. 'I'll be wearing factor fifty too. Don't want to ruin this beautiful face.' She touched her fingers to her cheeks and pouted.

'Too late for that, pal,' said Nicky, smiling at last. 'That horse has well and truly bolted.'

'Sod off.' Sabine threw a tea towel at Nicky's head, pleased to see the old Nicky was still in there somewhere. She just needed to encourage her out into the open a little bit more and remind her that, if she could just let herself relax, she could have a much better time. She deserved to enjoy herself after everything that had happened, and those beautiful girls did too.

6

NICKY

Walking to the beach felt like negotiating an obstacle course. 'Why are the pavements so high?' Nicky said as the dusty stack of breeze blocks which passed for a pavement came to an abrupt stop, making her step down to road level and avoid a pipe trickling dark liquid on to the ground. She could already feel damp patches under her armpits and beads of sweat trickling down her spine. She'd forgotten how hot this place was in the height of summer.

'A lot of the island had to be pretty much rebuilt in the 1950s, after some massive earthquakes. I feel like they're still catching up on the rebuilding.' Sabine turned left down a narrow alleyway in front of what appeared to be a derelict building but on closer inspection had washing hanging over crumbling balconies. Nicky didn't remember the random pavements or the decrepit buildings from her first visit. Maybe time had whitewashed all the grubby parts from her memories. She watched Betsy and Lola strolling alongside them and wondered whether they noticed the sporadic exposed pipework on the ground, or if they just felt the sun on their faces and heard the chirrup of cicadas. She hoped the latter.

They all tucked into the side as an open-topped buggy rushed past followed by a speeding motorbike. 'Why are they driving so fast on this narrow path?'

'Oh, darling,' said Sabine, hooking her arm through Nicky's. 'They're just young and reckless, like we were once upon a time.'

'Mum, reckless?' said Lola, peering at them over the top of her sunglasses. She'd been chattier since they set off for the beach, making Nicky wonder if Elias was the reason she'd been more reserved than usual so far. 'Photos or it didn't happen.'

'You've got me mixed up with someone else,' said Nicky, letting her jaw drop. She lowered her voice. 'And thank the Lord camera phones weren't a thing back then.'

'The stories I could tell,' said Sabine. She mimed zipping her mouth and throwing away the key.

Nicky cleared her throat. Sabine might just be playing along, but it still made her nervous. She was a different person to the one she'd been at university. Julian would have called her all kinds of names if he'd seen her and Sabine on a night out back then, especially if he'd seen her drunk and careless. Why was that the first thing that occurred to her? He wasn't here. Instead, her best friend's arm was through hers and her gorgeous girls were by her side. That was what she should be concentrating on.

'Go on,' said Betsy, dancing around Sabine, her rucksack bouncing on her back. 'Mum acts like she was an angel when she was younger. Was she?'

'I was,' said Nicky. 'Can't you see my wings?' She tried to poke out her shoulder blades.

'What are you doing? You look like a deranged chicken,' said Sabine.

'I'm an angel!' said Nicky, feigning indignance, as Betsy and Lola made clucking noises.

'Okay, whatever you say.' Sabine laughed. 'She was better behaved than I was. That's all I'm willing to say.'

Of course Sabine wouldn't expose Nicky to her daughters. She was so used to being belittled, she expected it, but Sabine didn't want to diminish her. She did everything she could to build her up and always had. Her natural cheerleading was one of the things Nicky loved most about her. She should try to be less defensive.

'Down here, then over those rocks,' said Sabine, taking another even narrower path and pointing to a line of boulders ahead. 'Only locals know about this little cove.'

Nicky was glad she'd worn trainers instead of flip flops as she attempted to navigate the enormous rocks with seaweed and rubbish in the cracks in between. She had a vague recollection of coming this way before, but in her mind, she'd stepped from boulder to boulder as effortlessly as a mountain goat. Now she wobbled on unstable ankles and had to use her hands to steady herself. She glanced up and caught Betsy leaping the chasm between two rocks. Her pulse soared. She could slip and fall and smash her head on a stone. She took a breath. Betsy hadn't fallen. She was standing on the sand, jiggling with excitement, waiting for the others to catch her up. Sweat trickled into Nicky's eyes. As soon as she was safely on the sand, she took out her water and gulped, thankful it was still cool from the fridge.

Ten minutes later, they'd laid out their towels. Betsy threw off her shorts and T-shirt and moaned about how long Lola was taking.

'You need to put more lotion on your shoulders before you go in the sea,' said Nicky.

'I've got loads on,' said Betsy. 'And I don't like the sliminess. It's gross.'

'If you want to swim, you'll do as I say. And put your hat back on.'

'I can't swim in my hat.'

'She'll lose that hat if she goes in the sea with it,' said Sabine. 'It's choppier than usual.' It was breezier there than at the villa and Sabine's dark curls whipped around her face as she spoke.

Nicky gazed out to sea. Most waves frilled at the shoreline, but the odd one gained momentum, rolling and frothing before running out of steam and creeping up the sand. She glanced around, wishing they weren't the only ones in this secluded spot. It might look idyllic, but if something went wrong, how long would it take to get help? She imagined Julian picking up the phone back in England, listening as his worst fears were confirmed, proof that Nicky wasn't an adequate mother coming in the most deadly form. 'Is it even safe to swim here? There's no lifeguards.'

'It's fine, darling. I've been swimming off this beach for my whole life,' said Sabine. 'And they won't go out far, will you, girls?'

'I'm not sure I want to go in the sea,' said Lola, resting back on her elbows and lifting her face to the sun.

'Lola,' said Betsy. 'You said you'd swim with me.' She stamped her foot like a much younger child and Nicky's toes curled. She was usually happy Betsy was young for her age – it meant she could still baby her – but at times like this even Nicky could see she was acting like a spoiled brat.

'I'll go in with you, if you stop throwing a toddler strop,' Nicky said. When Betsy's cheeks coloured, she felt mean. She'd only said it so Sabine didn't think she was blind to her daughter's faults. But, if she was honest, she didn't want to go in the sea either. She wanted to read the book which had been sitting unopened in the bottom of her bag since they'd left the UK.

'Come on, then.' Betsy wiggled her toes in the sand, like worms churning up earth.

Nicky sighed and tugged off her shorts, feeling self-conscious about how white her legs were. A year ago, she would have been anxious about exposing the fat that had begun to cling to her thighs and buttocks and made her stomach soft. Julian had mocked her about it so much that she'd only ever undressed in the dark for years. But the welcome side effect of the distress of the last few weeks was that it had clamped her stomach shut and she'd lost more than a stone. Beside her, Sabine stripped down to her bikini. 'How, at forty-five, do you still manage to have abs?'

'Gimp-room Pilates,' said Sabine, folding her clothes on top of her bag. 'I told you, it's brilliant.'

'What's a gimp room?' said Betsy.

'She means Reformer Pilates,' said Nicky, tightening her lips to stop the smile. 'Doing stretchy things on a machine.'

'Can I start that?' said Lola. She looked from Nicky to Sabine, and Nicky wanted the sand to suck her and her pasty, untoned body under. It was no wonder she wanted to emulate Sabine rather than her.

'It's expensive,' said Nicky. She'd looked into it when Sabine first mentioned it, but it was almost thirty pounds a session. Way beyond her current budget.

'You don't need it,' said Sabine, assessing Lola's slim, youthful body. 'You've got your mother's excellent genes, you lucky thing. Just make sure you're active and you'll be fine. Don't give up sports like lots of girls your age do.'

'Like swimming.' Betsy put her hands on her narrow hips and let her head drop to the side.

Lola lay back, adjusting her sunglasses and ignoring her sister. Nicky gathered all her energy and ran across the hot sand towards the sea. She was rewarded by a whoop of delight from her youngest daughter, who overtook her in a few strides and was soon galloping into the waves. The splash of water on Nicky's shins made her stop. It wasn't as cold as she expected, but the feel of sand swilling over her toes and the swirl of water around her ankles made her feel unstable. 'Not too far,' she shouted to Betsy, who was leaping up and down a few yards ahead. The water was already up to her middle. 'Don't go much further. There might be a shelf. You need to be able to stand up.'

'I can stand up,' said Betsy, turning and waving her arms in the air. 'Look.'

Nicky forced herself to stride on, eyes flitting between what she hoped was just seaweed tickling her thighs under the green-blue water and her daughter. She was up to her waist now. Ahead of her, Betsy's shoulders dipped in and out of the water. 'That's far enough.' A wave pounded against her stomach, taking her by surprise. Betsy was swimming now, giggling as the water lifted her and dropped her back down. The next wave took Nicky's feet from under her, and she fell, struggling to find her footing under the water.

She rose, spluttering, just in time to see Betsy, mouth open, laughing and pointing. But she didn't see the enormous wave at her back, and before Nicky could shout to her, it collapsed over Betsy's head, submerging her, then swallowing Nicky whole. Nicky struggled against the water tumbling over her head, into her ears and eyes. She gasped and salty liquid burned her nose and throat. With a monumental effort, she found her way back to the surface. Through stinging eyes, she searched the water for Betsy. But her daughter was nowhere in sight.

7

NICKY

'Betsy!' Nicky screamed. Then, there she was, flailing, then standing and stumbling, mouth contorted, eyes wild with fear. Nicky plunged forwards and grabbed her daughter. She pulled her upright and dragged her back towards the shore, the sound of her crying overtaking the rushing of water still pulsating in her ears.

Sabine and Lola were sitting up, watching, eyes wide with concern as they staggered back then dropped on to the towels. 'What happened?' Sabine stood and wrapped her towel around Betsy's shoulders.

'She went under. I thought...' She was close to tears herself. It felt like she'd made it happen by imagining the devastating phone call to Julian. 'I thought she was drowning. That was scary.' Betsy's crying was quieter now. When Nicky put a hand on her leg, it was trembling. 'You're alright, poppet. You're safe now.'

'I couldn't stand up,' Betsy snivelled. 'The water was in my mouth.'

'I told you not to go out of your depth.' Nicky's voice was sharp, but it wasn't Betsy she was angry with, it was herself. Once again she'd proved she wasn't up to the job of keeping her children safe. She had to try harder.

* * *

Elias was lounging by the pool with his headphones on when they arrived back at the villa after a subdued lunch. Betsy was unusually quiet, and Nicky didn't feel like she'd quite recovered from the shock of thinking her daughter might drown. Lola stayed close by her sister's side. She might find Betsy annoying now and again, but she was a protective, caring older sister and Nicky was proud of that.

Standing near the sunbeds, Nicky couldn't help but notice the patch of dark chest hair between Elias's pecs and the line leading down from his navel to the waistband of his navy swimming shorts. He could easily pass for twenty, definitely more man than boy. An empty bag of Doritos sat beside him on the grey cushion. Sabine had messaged him to see if he wanted to join them for lunch at the beach-side café where Lola and Betsy ate burgers and Nicky and Sabine shared an enormous Greek salad. He hadn't replied, but it hadn't seemed to bother Sabine.

'Were those crisps your lunch?' said Sabine, poking Elias's toned stomach with a finger.

Elias jumped and took off his headphones. 'You could have given me a heart attack, sneaking up like that.'

Sabine nodded towards the empty crisp packet. 'Ahem, you clearly intend to harden your arteries all on your own.'

'You're right,' said Elias. 'I should definitely have eaten one of those greasy burgers down near the beach. Much healthier.'

Nicky tried to imagine Lola answering her back like that. Julian never allowed backchat. If any of them said something he didn't like, they would be met with days of silence. The atmosphere had been better since he wasn't around, but the habit of watching what they said didn't seem to have left them. She turned to see Lola watching, but she couldn't read her daughter's expression behind her huge sunglasses. Was she wondering why they rarely had that kind of exchange, or did she already know? Their dynamic was still very much mother and daughter. There was plenty time for a mature relationship when Lola was older, Nicky reassured herself. Despite her outward appearance, she was still legally a child for two more years.

'I thought you'd be longer,' said Elias. 'I was going to come down in a bit.'

'Looks like it,' said Sabine.

'I was.' Elias sat up, the skin on his stomach creasing over his muscles. 'Did you have fun?' He directed the question at the girls, and Nicky was struck again by his easy manner.

'I went in the sea,' said Betsy, 'and I nearly drowned.'

'Don't be dramatic,' said Lola, laughing and rubbing Betsy's head. 'You only went under for a second.'

'It felt longer than that to me,' said Nicky, shuddering. 'Would not recommend.'

'Safer here,' said Elias. 'No nasty waves in this pool.' He stood and poked an inflatable ball, which was bobbing on the surface, with his toes. He kicked it to the centre, then did a sleek dive after it, his body hardly making a splash as he entered the water. He bobbed up and pushed his hair out of his eyes. 'Anyone coming in?'

'Me,' said Betsy, seemingly recovered from her earlier trauma.

'Have a shower first to get the sand off,' said Sabine, pointing at the shower under an olive tree at the other side of the pool.

'Then put more lotion on,' said Nicky, ignoring Betsy's groan.

The two women went into the kitchen. Sabine poured two big

glasses of water from the five-litre bottle. She handed one to Nicky. 'You might prefer gin after this morning.'

'Tempting,' said Nicky. It really was. 'I just keep thinking of what could have happened.' She rubbed her hand over her face. 'I should have been right by her side.'

'Oh, love. You did nothing wrong,' said Sabine, placing a warm hand on Nicky's arm.

'That's not what Julian would say.'

'Well, he's not here, is he? And the sooner you stop thinking about what he would or wouldn't say, the better, in my humble opinion.'

There was nothing humble about Sabine's opinion, and Nicky bristled at another person telling her what she should and shouldn't do. And it wasn't as easy as she made it sound. Sabine hadn't spent years trying to second-guess his reactions. She hadn't had to live with the silences, or the scathing put-downs.

'He doesn't think much of my parenting.' That was the simplest way she could think of putting it, and it only told a tiny part of the story. She hadn't told anyone how he really spoke to her, or about his controlling behaviour. She was starting to realise that's what it was. She'd been in an abusive relationship and was only just beginning to process that herself.

As far as Sabine knew, she'd thrown Julian out after she was sent an anonymous video of him soliciting a prostitute. She hadn't disclosed that the woman who covertly filmed it had been having a long-term affair with Nicky's husband, and had been following Julian after she became suspicious he was cheating on her. It was too humiliating to admit. The whole episode had been sickening, and staying strong for the girls had been near to impossible. Sabine had never asked for details and she was grateful for that. She'd come around as soon as Nicky made the distressed call after Julian slammed out of the house, listened to what she was able to share and held her as she fell apart. If it hadn't been for Sabine holding her together emotionally, she wouldn't have survived.

'Well, I don't think much of him full stop. And he's wrong,' said Sabine. 'You're a lovely mum and the girls are lucky to have you. You're kind and funny and generous and you always put them first.'

Nicky couldn't help but smile. 'Thanks.'

'He was a fool not to appreciate what he had.' Sabine waved a finger down the length of Nicky's body. 'He should have treated you like a queen. Look at you. You're hot.'

Nicky almost laughed. 'Hm. We'll have to agree to disagree on that. And Julian didn't exactly boost my confidence on that front.' That was the understatement of the century.

'He's an idiot. He always—' Sabine stopped speaking at the sound of wet footsteps slapping up the path.

Betsy appeared at the door and said, 'I feel sick.' Then threw up all over the kitchen floor.

8

SABINE

'Where are Lola and Elias?' Nicky asked, coming into the kitchen looking more like she'd done a difficult shift as an Accident and Emergency medic than a woman on a relaxing holiday. Strands of damp hair stuck to her neck. She wiped sweat from her top lip.

'Out by the pool,' said Sabine. 'How's Betsy?'

'She's okay.' Nicky sat at the table and yawned. 'Feeling very sorry for herself for being sick on her holiday.'

Sabine felt quite sorry for herself too for having to clean up Betsy's sick on her holiday, but knew that was uncharitable. At least the floor was freshly tiled. Trying to dig chunks of vomit out of the cracks in the old flagstones would have been a monstrous task. 'Poor lamb.'

'Thanks for clearing that up. That's above and beyond.'

'You're right, I should have left it for you.' She winked. 'I'm sure she'll be right as rain tomorrow.'

'I think she might have had too much sun.' Nicky wrinkled her nose, clearly feeling guilty for Betsy getting sick. There was nothing that poor woman couldn't blame herself for.

'It was more likely to be a burger on top of sea water, then swimming on a full stomach. You couldn't have seen that coming.' She lifted a damp strand of hair off Nicky's face and tucked it behind her ear. 'Try not to beat yourself up. You take excellent care of those girls.' She didn't want Nicky worrying about the girls getting sunstroke on top of everything else. Betsy already resembled a zombie most of the time, she was so smothered in thick white gloop. Sabine had only ever put that stuff on Elias when he was tiny, and even then, his cousins laughed at him. She remembered his little face all scrunched up with indignance as he insisted on putting on the same oil his Greek family wore when they weren't fully clothed. He'd been so cute, and so wilful. It was easier to let him get on with it. And he hadn't come to any harm.

Nicky didn't reply.

'I've asked Elias and Lola to make dinner so we can have the night off.'

Nicky raised her eyebrows. 'Can Elias cook? Lola's never made anything more taxing than beans on toast outside food tech lessons.'

'She's sixteen.' It came out with more disbelief than Sabine intended. But surely Lola could cook the basics at her age? Elias often made dinner for the three of them when she and Leo were working late. 'Sorry, that came out wrong.'

Nicky raised her arms then let them fall. 'I haven't had a job since I had the kids, have I? I make the food, that's the way it's always been. Lola has homework in the evenings.' She scanned the kitchen as if searching for something to bolster her argument. 'She makes cakes sometimes.'

Sabine saw a way to make Nicky feel better. 'Oh, God, that's the one thing I won't let Elias do. The mess! Honestly, the last time he tried baking there was batter on the handle of the fridge door, on the taps, all over. Gross. It took me ages to clean up.'

'You cleaned up?'

Sabine pursed her lips, but couldn't keep it up and burst out laughing. 'You got me. All right, it took Sue ages. And don't look at me like that. I work hard. I deserve a cleaner.'

Nicky nodded. 'No judgement from me. I'd love a cleaner.'

Sabine wondered if that was true. For most of the years Nicky was married, they didn't seem to be short of money, but either Nicky didn't want a cleaner or Julian hadn't thought it necessary since Nicky didn't work. She wondered whether to double back to the conversation they'd almost had before Betsy had deposited the contents of her stomach on the floor. But Nicky sagged like a deflated balloon. Sabine couldn't add to her troubles now. Nicky was like a sister. Perhaps that's why they were still here, together, despite how different they were. They'd bonded so completely early on, they were like family to each other. And you did what you could to protect family.

'Are you sure Lola agreed to cook?' Nicky said, resting her hands on her hips.

'She was hardly going to say no, was she? She may have known me all her life, but she's not comfortable enough with me to tell me to sod off.'

'I hope she never would, however well she knows you.'

Sabine snorted. 'Elias tells me where to shove my bright ideas all the time. You know where you stand with that boy.'

Nicky picked up a cloth and started wiping, and Sabine got the feeling she'd said the wrong thing again. Why did Nicky always make her feel like they were in some kind of parenting competition? She pulled back her shoulders. If they were, she'd win. Her son was self-assured and self-reliant. She felt bad as soon as the thought occurred to her.

'It's only seafood ravioli and salad,' she said. 'What could go wrong?' She took the cloth from Nicky. 'Now, try to remember you're on holiday too. You don't have to look after us all. You deserve to be a princess yourself some of the time. Not all the time, obviously. I need my princess time too.'

'Princess time?' Nicky cocked an eyebrow.

'Yeah, baby,' said Sabine. 'Full-on Disney princess shizzle.' She pouted and fluttered her eyelashes, and they both laughed.

'I honestly can't remember a time when I didn't feel more like Cinderella, before her glow-up,' said Nicky.

'All the more reason to let other people do the work for a change, starting right now. I'm going to get us a couple of beers, and we're going to go and sit in the shade by the pool.'

'That sounds divine,' said Nicky. She took Sabine's hand and held it for a moment. 'Thank you.' She let go and pushed her hair back from her face. 'I'll just check on Betsy then see you down there.'

When Sabine sauntered down the path, two bottles of lager sweating in her hands, Lola and Elias were sitting on adjacent loungers. She smiled inwardly. She knew if they just left them alone for long enough, the two of them would get on. The beers she'd allowed them earlier probably helped.

'Are those for us?' Elias called as she approached the opposite side of the pool.

'No, they're bloody well not,' said Sabine. 'You can get your own.'

'Do you need something from the house?' Nicky's voice came from further up the path.

'You're all right,' called Sabine. 'I've told him he can get off his lazy arse if he wants another beer. We're not his servants. We're princesses.'

Nicky's footsteps paused, then started up again. Surely she wouldn't have an issue with the kids having a beer? Lola was only a year younger than Elias, and he'd almost matched his dad drink for drink when they were here last summer. She firmly believed the Mediterranean attitude to alcohol was far healthier than the British one. If she allowed Elias to drink with them, then he wouldn't see booze as this exotic, forbidden and therefore enormously desirable thing. He'd only been drunk a few times as far as she knew, but what boy his age hadn't got messy now and again? She pushed away the memory of the numerous times she'd smelled the unmistakable stink of marijuana coming from his room a few months ago. When it became too regular for comfort, she'd asked him about it. He'd lied and she didn't challenge him on it. She'd patted herself on the back for doing the right thing because she hadn't smelled it again since.

She observed her friend's face as she reached the poolside, noting her eyes dart over to where Lola and Elias were sitting. Her jaw was tight, but when she sat beside Sabine it seemed to relax. Sabine turned her gaze to the teenagers and saw both beer bottles were tucked together right next to Elias's sunbed. *Clever girl, Lola*, she thought. *You know what your mother needs to believe.* She handed a bottle to Nicky, who took a swig then let out a long sigh. She lay back and Sabine was pleased to see her look like a woman on holiday, for the first time.

Fifteen minutes later, Betsy sauntered along the path, carrying a towel and a book. 'How are you feeling?' Nicky asked.

'Better,' she said. She sat in the shade and lay on her side, tucked the towel under her head and opened the book. Nicky watched her daughters. She seemed content they were both safe and eventually closed her eyes.

Nicky was breathing deeply and steadily, her mouth slightly open, when Elias and Lola went inside to begin prepping for dinner. Sabine could hear their laughter and the banging of cupboard doors along with the sound of her best friend's breath and the chirp of cicadas. All was well with the world.

She decided to celebrate the calm with another beer, so quietly climbed off her sun lounger and made her way along the path. Elias's deep voice and Lola's laughter coming through the open kitchen door made her smile. She reached the door just in time to see her son take a step towards Lola. Lola dropped her eyes to the tiles. Elias put a finger under her chin and lifted her face to his, staring deep into her eyes. A gecko scurried out of the shrubbery to Sabine's left and darted across the path in front of her foot. Startled, she shifted out of the way, and when she looked back up, the teenagers had parted, Elias now at the sink and Lola studiously searching in the cutlery drawer.

'Fancied another beer,' she said, marching to the fridge. 'All going okay in here?'

'All good,' said Elias.

'Fine, thanks,' said Lola, still raking through the drawer as if everything wasn't easily to hand.

Bless your little hearts, thought Sabine as she made her way back outside, the bottle satisfyingly cool in her hand. She was half tempted to wake Nicky up to tell her what she'd just witnessed. But her friend appeared so peaceful, the furrow between her eyebrows relaxed and smooth at last. And it wasn't her news to tell. She'd let Elias and Lola take their sweet time. A holiday romance was magical. They didn't want adults stepping in and spoiling it. Nicky would find out in the fullness of time, and she would be as excited as Sabine that their children were fulfilling the dreams they'd once talked about, when they were not much older themselves.

9

NICKY

Nicky had woken regularly in the night, hot despite the noisy air conditioning unit blowing cold air into the room. As soon as she'd woken, the sweaty sheets seemed to absorb the chill and turn to ice. At 1 a.m., she'd crept along the corridor to check on Betsy. The girls had still been on their phones, and it was hard not to snatch them out of their hands. Instead, she'd growled a reminder that they needed their sleep, waited for them to turn them off, then went back to toss and turn in her own bed, trying to shut out Julian's voice telling her she was weak for not taking the phones, a poor excuse for a mother. When would his voice quieten in her head?

The following morning she was exhausted. She sipped on a strong coffee and eyed the jar of Nutella on the counter. Predictably, Betsy hadn't eaten the pasta Lola and Elias made, and Nicky eventually allowed her to have toast smeared with a thick layer of chocolate and hazelnut spread. She thought she could feel Sabine's disapproval. She didn't know how lucky she was having a child who was happy to eat everything put in front of him.

She'd kept those thoughts to herself. She had to stop comparing their offspring. The thought that if there was a competition, Sabine and Elias would win slithered into her brain, dragging in shame behind it. Nicky's mother had hammered home the need to always be seen to be humble. The phrase 'No one likes a show-off' accompanied every childhood memory Nicky had of being momentarily proud of her achievements. It never stopped her mother crowing about how impressive other church members' offspring were, though. Bigging up someone else's child while denigrating your own signified piety, apparently.

Lola was just as good as Elias, Nicky reminded herself, just not quite as confident. At least the two of them were getting along now. The conversation had been easier at the dinner table and they had even insisted on doing the clearing up. One less thing to worry about.

Now, Betsy wandered into the kitchen, her skin pale. 'It was too hot to sleep last night.'

Nicky knew the heat wasn't the problem; the lure of the internet was. She should have taken their phones. Betsy was too young to make good decisions, so Nicky should have insisted. She tried to cover her guilt with levity. 'Is that why you were on your phone – the unbearable heat? If only there was an invention that would make rooms more comfortable... Oh, wait.'

Betsy smiled her acknowledgement, then curled her thin arms around Nicky's neck and slumped against her. Nicky breathed in her daughter's scent of fabric conditioner and sweet-smelling sweat. She understood why people who lost loved ones slept with items of clothing they'd worn. There was something primevally comforting about the smell of your child. She tugged her on to her knee, hugging her as her bony backside dug into her thighs.

'Aw, look at you two.' Sabine sauntered into the kitchen and stuck out her bottom lip. 'I miss having a child small enough to cuddle on my knee.' She came over and wrapped her arms around the two of them.

'You're not exactly small enough, are you?' said Nicky to Betsy, when Sabine let go. 'But I won't let that stop me.' She wondered if Sabine thought she babied Betsy, but decided she didn't care if she did. Her girls were all she had left.

'How are you feeling?' Sabine asked Betsy, pinching her elfin chin.

'All right,' said Betsy. 'A bit tired.'

'You're still pale.' Nicky examined Betsy's face. There were purple smudges under her eyes. New freckles spread across the bridge of her nose and scattered her cheeks. A rush of love swamped Nicky. She kissed her on the end of her nose.

'Like a ghost?' said Betsy. She wiggled her fingers and drew down her bottom jaw. 'Whooooooo!'

'Now I'm scared,' said Nicky. 'Really scared.' She tickled Betsy's ribs until she jumped off her knee. 'And quite reassured that you're perfectly all right. Ready for breakfast?'

'Not yet.'

'Okay. Let me know when you're hungry.' That wasn't like her. Betsy was always ready for food, as long as it was something in her limited repertoire. Despite being smaller, Nicky generally gave Betsy the same portion sizes as Lola because Betsy seemed to burn more energy by just being her effervescent self. 'I think we'll stay close to home today.' She looked up at Sabine. 'That okay for you? I mean, you could do whatever... I just think we might stay here.' She waited for Betsy to argue, but she didn't. That confirmed it.

'Fine by me,' said Sabine. 'My book isn't going to read itself. I might pop to the supermarket later.'

'If you do, could you get a margarita pizza and some plain

pasta? And ketchup and some bananas.' Betsy's eating habits might be annoying, but she still had to make sure she got the calories she needed. She should stand up for her more. Advocate, that was what it was called, wasn't it?

'No problemo,' said Sabine. She picked up her phone. 'I'll put it in the notes app.' She pretended to type. 'Octopus pizza and spicy salami pasta.'

'Urgh,' said Betsy, laughing. 'No thank you very much.'

Sabine grinned. 'Don't worry. I've got it. Sorry I didn't check what you like before the last shop.'

'It's okay,' said Betsy. 'I'm sorry for being annoying about food.'

Nicky wanted to immediately jump to her defence but stopped herself. Her little girl was growing up. She was speaking for herself and that was a good thing. If Nicky had learned to do that, maybe her life would have turned out differently. Yes, it was a good thing. Betsy wasn't as weak and pathetic as her, even if it meant her littlest girl didn't really need her any more.

* * *

Nicky sat on the terrace under the slatted canopy with her second coffee, trying not to check the time on her phone every five minutes. It wasn't easy. Sabine was clearly happy for Elias to lie in until noon, but she was struggling to allow Lola to do the same. She concentrated on the taste of the strong, smoky coffee, fighting the urge to rush into Lola's bedroom and insist she got up to enjoy the glorious day. And it was glorious. The sun was bright in the sapphire sky and the temperature seemed a little less stifling than yesterday. They'd be back in London's unpredictable weather before they knew it and it seemed a shame that Lola wasn't making the most of this break from the gloom.

She remembered sitting exactly where she was now twenty-five years ago, looking out at the two paths which led from either side of the house and merged together on the approach to the pool. It occurred to her that she and Sabine had rarely emerged from sleep until late morning. When and why had she decided things had to be different for her daughter? She knew the answer: it was because Julian's views had poisoned hers. The sooner she could wipe her brain clean of that man, the better. She tried to distract herself by comparing the view to that in her memories. The garden was better tended now, although it appeared drier and less rustic with its neat beds of greenery enclosed by grey and beige stones. She supposed that was because the house was being managed by the holiday lettings company rather than Sabine's family. It was better before.

She gulped the last of the coffee, musing that everything was better before. Did everyone feel like the best of life was behind them when they reached their mid-forties? Sabine didn't seem to have lost her *joie de vivre*. But she had a nice husband and a great career and access to a beautiful villa on a Greek island. She also had her unshakable self-esteem. Nicky envied her friend, and she didn't like herself for it.

A gecko scurried along the tiles near the edge of the terrace, stopping for a moment in the narrow strip of sunshine burnishing the ground through the slats. It raised its head as if relishing the moment. Nicky smiled to herself. She should be more gecko. She was luckier than most. She had a roof over her head, two wonderful children and a life-embracing best friend with a villa in Zante.

The scrape of lazy footsteps made her turn. Lola rounded the corner, and Nicky was struck again by how gorgeous her girl was. She wore a white vest and denim shorts, the string of her red bikini top tied around her neck. Despite the constant re-application of suntan lotion Nicky insisted on, her slim arms were already evenly tanned in a way that only seemed possible for people under the age of thirty. When Nicky examined her own tan line in the mirror last night, she'd barely changed colour, other than patches of pink on her chest and thighs.

'Morning, sleepy head.'

'Morning.' Lola dropped into a chair beside her and yawned. She lay her head on Nicky's shoulder. Nicky dropped a kiss in her hair, breathing in the familiar scent of her daughter first thing in the morning just as she had with Betsy. Lola smelled of suntan lotion mixed with minty toothpaste. 'Sleep well?'

Lola yawned. 'Betsy snores like a rhino.'

Nicky laughed. 'Have you heard many rhinos snoring?'

'Loads,' said Lola. 'And they all sound exactly like Betsy.'

Her head jiggled on Nicky's shoulder as they both sniggered. 'Well, we're just chilling out here today, so it won't be too taxing. Betsy the rhinoceros is still not 100 per cent.'

'Oh, I—'

'What do you want in your sandwich, Lola?' Sabine appeared at the corner of the house. 'Elias wants mozzarella and tomato. That okay for you?'

Lola lifted her head, and Nicky missed the weight of it. 'Yes, that's good for me, thank you.'

'For breakfast?' Nicky turned to Lola. 'Or are you having an early lunch, like a brunch?'

Lola opened her mouth, but Sabine spoke first. 'They're taking it down to the beach. There's no point those two hanging around here with us, is there? They're going to explore the island.' She disappeared back around the side of the house.

'You and Elias?' Nicky said. She toyed with the handle of her cup, her fingers suddenly needing to be busy.

Lola shrugged. 'Yeah. I mean, if it's okay?'

Nicky's brain started to run through all the potential scenarios in which Lola could be harmed. It hadn't occurred to her she might be out of her sight this week. They were abroad. Surely she should keep an eye on her? 'Where are you thinking of going?'

'A walk around, then maybe the beach where we went yesterday.'

Nicky worked to keep her voice level. 'You won't go swimming, will you? You saw what happened yesterday. There's no lifeguard there. It's too remote to be taking risks.'

Lola laughed. 'Elias is an actual IRL lifeguard. Didn't you know that? He's got a qualification and everything. He works at the gym Sabine goes to.'

Nicky did know that. She'd just forgotten. It was hard to keep up with all the ways Elias was better than the average kid. 'That doesn't mean you should take risks.'

'Risks?' Lola shook her head. 'Like swimming with a qualified lifeguard? God, Mum, I'm sixteen, not six. Just because Betsy the drama queen swallowed a bit of water yesterday, it doesn't mean I should be banned from ever going in the sea.'

'Now who's being dramatic?' Should she refuse to let her go?

Lola stood, her lips tight. 'I'd just like to be able to do something, anything, without you stressing about it.' Her hands curled into fists at her sides.

'I'm not stressing. I just want to—'

'Stop me living so you don't have to worry?'

'That's not fair.' She had no idea what it was like to have sole responsibility for two young lives when you couldn't trust yourself to make the right choices. 'I—'

'Sandwiches are ready,' called Sabine.

Lola turned to leave and Nicky realised there was nothing she could do to stop her. Nothing reasonable at least.

'Keep your phone on,' said Nicky. 'Text me and let me know

how you're getting on.' She tried to make her voice light, despite the knowledge her relaxing day was about to morph into long hours of trying not to text her daughter to make sure she hadn't drowned or been abducted by men in open-topped jeeps, or... She needed to get a grip of herself.

'Will do. See you later.' Lola sounded weary, as if her mother's requests were a burden. They probably were. She started to walk away. 'Love you,' she said over her shoulder.

'Love you. Have fun,' said Nicky, when really she wanted to say, *Don't go.*

10

NICKY

'What time did the kids say they'd be back?' Nicky asked, unpacking the bags of groceries Sabine brought in from the car. Lola hadn't mentioned a return time to her before she left, and she could kick herself for not asking for specifics. She'd carefully composed a message which she sent an hour and a half ago to check if they were having a good time. In truth it was to confirm Lola hadn't drowned or been kidnapped, and Lola probably knew that, so sending another text would be viewed as nagging. She knew the rules, even if she found it hard to stick to them. But it was almost dinner time, so surely they'd be back soon?

'They didn't say,' Sabine said breezily, as if the whereabouts of their children was of no real concern. She dropped a bunch of enormous bananas in a bowl. 'Look at the size of those.'

'Impressive. Does everything grow bigger here?' said Nicky.

'Not everything,' said Sabine. 'Otherwise I would have married a Greek man.'

'You have a one-track mind.' Nicky laughed. She picked her phone up and frowned at the screen. 'I only ever get one-word answers from Lola.'

'One word?' Sabine put a margarita pizza in the fridge. 'You're winning. I get one letter. Usually a K. KK if I'm lucky. You'd think they were charged by the letter, the way they ration them. I wouldn't mind, but I pay the bloody phone bill.'

That wasn't what Nicky wanted to hear. She wanted Elias to have given explicit details about what they were doing and when they'd be home. Her finger hovered over the tracking app Julian had made them all install. After a week, Julian had switched his tracking off. *I'm not vulnerable, am I? It's women and girls who need to be protected by this software, not men.* Even then, she'd wondered whether that was just an excuse to cover up his real reasons for not wanting her to know where he was. She hadn't argued, though. She was too exhausted by then and couldn't face being sneered at then ignored for days, or longer.

She felt Sabine at her shoulder. 'You all right? You look worried.' Her breath tickled Nicky's cheek as she spoke.

'I've just realised Julian can still track my phone on this app.'

'He can do what?' Sabine peered at the screen, then at Nicky. 'Seriously? After what he got up to, you're still letting him stalk you?'

'I'm not letting him. I'd forgotten he was on there. I only use it to check on Lola if she's out late. It didn't occur to me he might still look at it, but he could if he wanted.'

Sabine blew out her cheeks. 'Time to kick that loser into the virtual long grass, my friend.'

Nicky felt a buzz of excitement. She might not yet have succeeded in cutting Julian out of her thought processes, but she could stop him tracking her movements any time it took his fancy. She tapped into settings, then into 'Location Sharing'. She slid the button next to her name to the off position. 'There,' she said. 'Done.' She pushed down the thought that now the girls wouldn't be able to see where she was either. They didn't need to. She was never far from home. The fact that Julian would be angry with her crossed her mind. *Let him*, she thought. His moods were no longer her concern. She felt an inch taller.

Sabine high-fived her, then grabbed her for a tight hug. 'I'm so proud of you.'

The words made tears spring to her eyes. 'I'm proud of me too.' She clicked the side button to send the screen to sleep. If she started to watch Lola's movements on the island, she'd find it hard to stop, and this bright feeling would sink under the weight of her anxiety. Since she'd been living alone with the girls, she found herself checking Lola's whereabouts almost compulsively. If she saw she was on the bus, she'd keep checking until she got off, then watch the app's footsteps icon move until she was at the front door and the location registered the same as her own. Nicky kept imagining someone snatching her slightly built daughter off the street when she walked between the bus stop and home. She could visualise it so clearly it felt inevitable, somehow, as if she was manifesting it by just thinking about it. Then it would be her fault if it did happen. It was all she could do not to rush out and escort Lola safely to their front door. But that would mean leaving Betsy home alone, sometimes after dark, and who knows what could happen if she did that? She knew that level of vigilance wasn't healthy. But at least it meant she was watching out for her girls, and that kept them safe.

Sabine glanced at the clock on the oven. 'I gave Elias some money to get dinner out if they wanted, so they might be a while yet.'

Nicky looked at her and blinked. The lightness she'd felt a minute ago left her as a belt of anger tightened around her stomach. Surely she should have been consulted on whether her sixteen-year-old daughter went out all day and all night? She was trying to think of how to temper what she wanted to say when Betsy came into the kitchen.

'Lola's back.'

'Is she?' Relief loosened the belt a notch.

'Yeah, they're—'

Betsy stopped as Lola and Elias appeared in the doorway. Nicky turned, the smile on her face freezing when she saw their hands locked together by their sides. They were actually holding hands. 'You're back.'

'Yeah,' said Elias. 'This one wanted a shower before we went for dinner.'

This one? The phrase sounded ridiculously over familiar to Nicky. She kept her eyes on their faces, despite the temptation to drop her gaze to their intertwined fingers. Lola's cheeks were flushed, and her eyes shone bright. Whatever had gone on between them today had made her happy. Excited. What had happened? Her brain started to invent what might have gone on, on that secluded beach, between her innocent daughter and this worldly boy. Despite herself, her mind went back to Julian. He didn't think girls should have boyfriends until at least university. Not his girls, anyway. For the millionth time, she replayed the clip of him leaning out of his car window to talk to a woman in a clingy short dress who was standing on the street in town, notorious for its sex workers. She lifted her hair to allow air to her neck.

'That's not fair if you go out again,' said Betsy, pouting. 'I've been on my own all day.'

'Thanks,' said Nicky. 'That's the last time I play fifteen rounds of Uno with you.' Betsy sounded petulant even to her ears.

'Sorry,' said Betsy. 'I just meant it's not the same with only grown-ups.'

Lola pursed her lips. Usually she'd come back with something biting about not wanting to babysit a brat, but Nicky could see she was managing her behaviour in front of Elias.

'Why don't you stay in tonight and maybe go out another evening?' said Sabine. Nicky could have kissed her. It wasn't just that Betsy would be placated. It would take time for her to get her head around this new development, and while she did, she wanted Lola in her sights.

'Okay by me,' said Elias. He turned to Lola. 'You?'

Lola shrugged. 'Fine.' The light in her eyes dimmed and Nicky could tell she was disappointed. She probably regretted wanting to get clean for her date now.

'Yay,' said Betsy. 'Will you swim with me now?'

'Race you.' Elias dropped Lola's hand and rushed off down the path. Betsy squealed and followed him. Lola trailed slowly behind.

'Oh my God!' Nicky said to Sabine when she was sure the kids were out of earshot.

'I know,' said Sabine, gripping Nicky's hands. She bared her teeth in an excited grin. 'I'm wearing red to the wedding, remember.'

Nicky forced herself to smile as widely as her friend, but inside her stomach churned. 'I honestly didn't think they'd get together.'

'I saw it coming yesterday,' said Sabine, letting go of Nicky and opening the fridge. 'Where's that bottle of bubbles? I think this calls for a toast.'

'It's bit premature to be talking about weddings and toasts,' Nicky said, forcing a laugh into her voice. In truth, her throat was tight. 'How did you see it coming?'

'I saw them getting a bit smoochy in the kitchen last night. They sprang apart when they noticed me.'

'A bit smoochy?' Sweat trickled down Nicky's back.

Sabine flapped her hand, then went back to prising the cork from the dark green bottle. 'Not actually snogging.' She put the bottle down and moved close to Nicky. 'Elias was all like this.' She put a finger under Nicky's chin and gazed into her eyes.

Nicky stepped away and took the cloth from where it hung over the tap. 'He's got the moves.' She wiped the worktop, feeling the air between them thicken.

'What does that mean?' Sabine's voice was clipped.

Nicky kept on wiping. 'Just... that seems like something from a film, don't you think?'

'What do you mean by that?'

Nicky rubbed at a splodge of mayonnaise that had dried and hardened on the counter. 'All the boys I knew in sixth form were clumsy. They mumbled and fumbled about, then tried to stick their tongues down your throat. They didn't do romantic staring into eyes stuff... It feels...' She wanted to say contrived and manipulative, but that sounded too brutal, even in her head.

'That's from your vast experience, is it?'

Nicky swallowed. 'I didn't mean... I'm not saying—'

'Because from what I remember, you'd only had one teenage relationship, so you were hardly the expert on what was usual.'

Heat rushed up her neck to her cheeks. 'That's a bit harsh. And I think it's okay to have some reservations. I remember what you were like too.'

11

TWENTY-SEVEN YEARS AGO

Nicky

Nicky hated herself for being so insipid in her second tutor group meeting. Once again, she'd allowed herself to be intimidated by the two confident boys who'd asked all the questions. The cool-looking girl called Sabine, whose curly hair bounced on her shoulders and who wore dungarees baggy enough for another person to climb in with her, was equally alarming. What did someone called Nicola have in common with someone called Sabine? She imagined her mother's face if she told her she had a friend with such an exotic name. Her lips would pinch and even if she didn't say it out loud, Nicky knew she'd be thinking that girl's parents had notions of grandeur. There was nothing self-effacing about having a name that stuck out from the crowd. Nicky's parents had no such notions. They prided themselves on their humility, and Nicky was encouraged to do the same, despite silently believing the whole concept of pride in piety was deeply ironic.

Sneaking an admiring glance at the sleeveless black hoodie

under Sabine's dungarees, Nicky cringed at her own cotton dress with its flowery pattern. She looked like some kind of throwback: a prairie girl visiting the big city. Growing up, she'd been taught that thinking too much about appearance was vanity, and it wasn't as if they had money to burn on fashion, but since arriving in London she'd noticed people's styles said something about their personality. Now she couldn't unsee it and wished her clothes announced something about her other than she was homely and behind the times. Was it any surprise no one had paid her much attention since she'd arrived on campus a week ago? No one went to university to hang out with people who dressed like their mothers.

'You doing the pub crawl tonight?' Sabine said as they left the tutor's study.

'Oh, erm, I don't know.' Nicky held the material of her dress in her hands, then let go when she realised she probably looked like a toddler grasping a safety blanket. 'Are you?'

'Dunno yet. Fancy a pint now? We could see who turns up and decide then.'

Nicky bit her bottom lip. She'd never been invited for a pint before. Her friends at sixth form all drank berry-flavoured cider or cocktails from cans when they drank at all. Her parents didn't drink at home, and they never went to the pub. 'All right.'

The garishly decorated student bar was fairly empty when they arrived. Only first years were on campus this week and there was a poster on the door advertising the end-of-fresher's-week pub crawl, which started at six-thirty. Nicky checked her watch. It wasn't even six o'clock yet. She followed Sabine to the bar and nodded when she asked if she wanted a pint. She took the enormous glass of amber fluid and smiled her thanks, then followed Sabine to a seat at the side of the cavernous room, feeling like a sheep and trying desperately hard to find something interesting to say.

'Cheers,' said Sabine, knocking her glass against Nicky's. Nicky wasn't prepared, and liquid slopped over the side and on to her hand. 'Ah, sorry.'

'It's fine.' Nicky put the drink on the table and wiped her hand on her dress, then glanced up to see Sabine watching her with a confused expression.

'No tissues in there?' She nodded to Nicky's faux leather bag.

Nicky glanced from her bag to the battered canvas tote sitting next to Sabine. Even her bag was mumsy. 'Just the kitchen sink. I should've used that.'

Sabine snorted with laughter and Nicky tried not to show how pleased she was to have caused the inelegant noise coming out of this extraordinary girl's mouth.

'You're funny,' said Sabine.

'So I've been told.' She hadn't been told that, but she was desperate to make the snorting sound happen again. 'Although I'm not always in on the joke. These shoes, for example. Someone found them hilarious yesterday.' She lifted her foot to show off her old brown brogues. She'd seen a couple dressed all in black pointing at them and sniggering. It was humiliating, but she sensed laughing at herself was a quick route to get this girl with cherry-red Doc Martins to snort again.

'Those are some hilarious shoes.' Sabine nodded. 'Vintage?'

'If you mean did the family of an old dead lady with poor taste in footwear leave them at the charity shop for my mother with equally poor taste to find? Then yes, vintage.'

'Preloved.' Sabine laughed.

'By a dead grandma.' Nicky shrugged. She took a sip of her drink to stop the broadness of her smile from showing. The dry, bitter taste did the job. It was disgusting. She grimaced. 'What is this foul concoction?' She used a Shakespearian tone to hide the fact she actually meant it.

'Lager. Surely you've had lager before?'

Nicky shook her head. 'I prefer my alcohol to be three parts sugar, like any other self-respecting girl from the suburbs.' She put the drink down. 'You city types with your fashionable clothes and your lager drinks have no idea what you're missing. Where I come from, if your vomit doesn't smell of blackcurrant at the end of the night, you're doing it wrong.' She'd never been sick on alcohol in her life, but the successive snorts coming from Sabine told her the lie was worth it.

By the time they arrived at the third bar on the pub crawl, Nicky felt like a different person. She was beginning to understand that the private, self-deprecating thoughts that naturally occurred to her were hilarious to Sabine. She had her own previously untapped brand of comedy. The more outrageous the things she said were, the more Sabine laughed. Initially, she'd waited for her to get bored and wander off to find other like-minded people in big boots and dungarees, but she didn't. She stuck by Nicky's side, making that extraordinary laugh every time Nicky opened her mouth. It was exhilarating. It made her feel like someone else entirely.

When the long-haired young man leading the pub crawl came over to the pair of them at the last pub, Nicky had to squint to see him clearly. She'd moved from lager to sweet cider after the first drink, but when she'd asked for halves, Sabine brought back pints anyway. All the liquid was sloshing in her stomach, and her vision swam in and out of focus.

'Evening,' he said. 'How's your first week been?'

'You're somebody important, aren't you?' slurred Sabine, poking him on the shoulder with a black-painted nail.

The man's chest expanded under his Def Leppard T-shirt. 'I'm Charlie, vice-president of the student union.'

'Nice to meet you, sir,' said Nicky, sitting up straighter, mortified to be in this state when meeting such an influential member of the student community.

'Sir,' said Sabine, guffawing.

The man laughed hard too. Nicky looked between the two of them, then started laughing along, although she wasn't quite sure why.

'A few of us are going back to mine at chucking-out time. You coming?'

'All right,' said Sabine.

'Great. Grab a couple of takeouts before last orders.' He wandered off to talk to another group.

Nicky stared at Sabine, her eyes wide. 'We can't go back to the president's house.'

'Vice-president,' said Sabine. 'And why not?'

'Because I'm the drinkest I've ever been.'

'The drinkest?' said Sabine, before collapsing in a giggling heap.

An hour later, Nicky found herself sitting on the floor in the corner of a dingy room, her thighs butted up to Sabine, whose head rested heavily on her shoulder. 'You can't judge a book by its flowery cover,' said Sabine, lifting the material of Nicky's skirt then letting it fall.

'Eh?'

'I thought you were a bit mumsy when I first met you. But I've had the best night. I can't remember when I last laughed this much. My stomach actually hurts like I've done sit-ups. Knowing you might give me abs. Imagine that.'

Nicky's eyes filled with tears. This was the best night of her life. But she'd been pretending to be someone she wasn't and there was no way she could keep it up for the whole three years of her degree. 'I am mumsy,' she said, a tear dribbling past her nose. 'I'm boring and I'm called Nicola.'

Sabine lifted her head. 'You don't like being called Nicky? I thought it was you who said... Are you crying?' Her face scrunched up in confusion.

'No, I mean, I'm not called Sabine. I'm just boring old me.'

Sabine dropped an arm around her and clumsily pulled her close. 'That's crap, mate. You've made me snort lager out of my nose twice tonight.'

'I've never even been drunk before.' Nicky rested her cheek against Sabine's shoulder, wishing she could stay there forever.

'Well, you should do it more often, you're fucking good at it.' Sabine sniggered, making Nicky's head jiggle. 'I know, let's play Never Have I Ever.'

'Huh. I'll be rubbish at that. I've never done anything.'

'You're not going to be one of those maudlin drunks, are you? Come on. I'll start. Never have I ever... had a threesome, but it's on the list.'

Nicky's jaw dropped. 'A threesome? Really? I've only had sex once.'

'Once? Like, one guy?' Sabine shifted and Nicky sat up, the liquid in her stomach slopping with the movement.

'Nope.' She held a finger aloft. 'Once. One time only. And he was so ashamed afterwards he confessed to his mother, who goes to the same church as my parents, and she told my mum and there were' – she pressed her palms together and closed her eyes – 'prayers.'

'Fuck me!' Sabine's eyes were wide. 'Prayers? Are you serious?'

'Deadly.'

'Whoa.' She shook her head. 'That's messed up. I told my

mum I was going on the pill at sixteen and she didn't blink an eyelid.'

It was Nicky's turn to look startled, although she couldn't keep her eyes wide for long because her eyelids kept drifting closed. 'Have you done it loads, then?'

'Loads,' said Sabine. 'I'm shagging for feminism. Up the sisterhood.' She punched the air. 'I refuse to be judged differently to a man.' She staggered to her feet. 'Come on, let's dance.'

They joined the group of students in the middle of the floor swaying to 'Come As You Are' by Nirvana. Nicky watched in admiration as Sabine lifted her arms above her head and moved her hips provocatively. The movement made the cider climb up Nicky's gullet. Saliva flooded her mouth and sweat broke out on her face.

She elbowed her way out of the room, searching for a toilet. She found herself in a kitchen and launched herself at the sink just in time for the flood of liquid to splash into the aluminium basin.

When she woke the next day, her eyelids scratched like scouring pads across her eyeballs. Her throat was parched and her head pounded. Then she remembered the night before and her entire skin stung with shame at having vomited in the vice-president's kitchen. She'd humiliated herself, and everyone who was anyone had witnessed it. She shrank under her covers and willed the world to stop turning.

She ignored the hollow knock on the plywood door of her room at 6.30 p.m. She hadn't left her bed all day.

'Nicky.' It was Sabine's voice. Nicky groaned and gripped her cover under her chin. She'd had one chance at having a cool friend and she'd blown it. 'Nicky,' Sabine said again. 'Let me in right now.'

Nicky shuffled to the door with her quilt wrapped around her, opened it and peeked out. 'So, so sorry about last night.' She squinted at Sabine. She looked fine. How?

'You need to start drinking fruity cider again.' Sabine pushed the door and stepped inside.

'Why?' She needed to never have another drink again in her whole entire life.

'Because you said blackcurrant cider puke smells better.'

Nicky couldn't help but smile. 'I lied.'

'Come on, get dressed.'

'Why?'

'Because everyone is asking where you are.'

Nicky blinked. 'What do you mean?'

'I went down to the student bar, and all anyone said was, "Where's your mate?"'

Nicky slumped on the bed. 'Oh, God.' She covered her face with her hands. 'Everyone thinks I'm a nightmare. I'm never leaving this room again.'

'Everyone thinks you're a legend. You were hilarious last night.'

Nicky peeked between her fingers. Her mother's voice resounded in her head. *No one likes a show-off.* 'I'm sure they were laughing at me, not with me.'

'They were laughing because you were funny.' She put a warm hand on Nicky's back. 'Seriously, mate. Come on. Face your fears and come with me. Everyone wants to see you.'

For the first time in her life, Nicky decided to be brave. She pushed away the image of her mother's disapproving face, brushed her teeth and her hair, slapped some concealer under her eyes and a touch of mascara, then followed her new friend out to the bar.

12

PRESENT DAY

Nicky

Sabine huffed, took a flute from the cupboard and poured herself a glass of fizz. 'I was a slapper, so my son must be one too. Is that what you mean? God, how are we even having this conversation in 2025?'

Nicky blanched. 'That's not what I meant.' It kind of was what she meant, but when Sabine threw it back at her like that it sounded brutal. Sabine waited for the bubbles in her glass to subside before filling it to the rim, her lips so tight fine lines appeared around the edges. The lines reminded Nicky of her mother. That brought her up short. There was a risk she was acting exactly like her mum would have in this situation and that wasn't what she wanted. Sabine had been the person who helped her escape from that world of judgement and shame, until she met Julian, at least. Her friend deserved better. 'I'm sorry, that's not what I meant.'

'Didn't you?' Sabine continued before Nicky had chance to

reply. 'And it's not as if you were Little Miss Perfect yourself back then.'

'We don't need to—'

'You were a savage drinker. I could hardly keep up with you.' Sabine raised her glass as if making a toast, then drained half of it.

Nicky saw herself sitting on her sofa at home night after night, empty bottle of wine on the floor in front of her, and shame curdled in her stomach. It had become her crutch, the only way to blur the grimness of the life she was living. 'That's not—'

'Are you going to deny it? Have you whitewashed your past since having kids? Do you pretend you were never the kind of girl who threw up in sinks?'

'That was one time.' The kitchen door was open and the heat that had been building all day seemed to creep into Nicky's mouth and dry her throat.

'Only because you made it to the toilet the other times.'

'We were students. That's what students do.' Yes, she'd gone a bit wild in their first year, but the drink helped her be the person Sabine had brought out that first night. After a few months, she was more secure in the knowledge people liked her and found her funny even when she wasn't propped up by booze. She could stop pretending and just be. Where had that girl gone?

She knew the answer.

'Yeah, well, our kids are just kids, doing what teenagers do. Elias might come across as confident and, how did you put it... "worldly", but he's just a seventeen-year-old boy trying to find his way on this broken planet, just like we were at that age.'

Of course he was. That was the problem. He was going to make mistakes like everybody else; Nicky just didn't want him to make them with Lola. She pointed at Sabine's glass. Beads of condensation glazed the outside, adding to Nicky's thirst. She should probably drink water, but that wouldn't do the more important job of taking the edge off this conversation. 'Can I get one of those?'

'I might still be too cross with you to share. This is nice Crémant,' Sabine said sulkily, picking up the bottle and hugging it to her. She stuck out her bottom lip, and Nicky could see it was an attempt at peacemaking.

'I'm really sorry. This is about me, not Elias.' Nicky lifted her hair again to try to cool her neck. It made little difference.

'Huh! You don't need to tell me that.' Sabine put the bottle down and reached into the cupboard for another flute. 'You have this image of Lola that's... I don't know, like this pure and innocent Disney character and you think big bad Elias is going to sully that, but they're not Beauty and the Beast. Elias is a good kid. It hurts me that you don't see that.'

'I know he is. I do know that.' That wasn't entirely true, if she was honest with herself. 'I just know how fragile my heart was at that age. We do what we can to keep our kids safe from heartbreak, don't we? That's our job as mothers.'

'I don't believe it's just heartbreak you want to protect her from. You know keeping them safe could be as simple as neither of us piling on the shame and guilt or praying for their immortal souls, if they happen to do what every other kid their age is doing.'

Guilt and shame: the two main tenets of Nicky's life, drummed into her from an early age. Was it any surprise she wasn't in a hurry for her daughter to enter that world too soon? She gave an involuntary shudder at what Sabine was implying. 'You don't think they're...'

Sabine laughed. 'Your face.'

Nicky tried to adopt a neutral expression. 'She was still only fifteen a couple of weeks ago. Fifteen. She's a child in law for another two years.'

Sabine started to pour. The liquid fizzed. Bubbles rose and popped. 'Don't do that.'

'What? It's true.'

'You're infantilising her. She's turned sixteen now. Old enough to make most of her own decisions. That's a fact, and harping on about her being fifteen a few weeks ago just allows you to keep her young inside your head.'

'I know she's legally allowed to have sex.' Even saying that made her feel odd. 'I just don't think she's ready, physically or emotionally. I'd rather she waited until she was more mature.'

Sabine plonked the glass down in front of Nicky. 'What, twenty? Thirty?'

'Would twenty be so wrong?'

Sabine laughed. 'Not if it was her choice, rather than yours. Seriously, why would you want to deny your child one of life's greatest pleasures?'

Was that what sex was meant to be? Nicky had never experienced it that way.

'Don't hate me for saying this, but I think you see your girls as' – Sabine waved her arms around – 'as uncontaminated, and you can't bear the thought of them having any kind of sexual experience. If they do, then they're adulterated in some way, which is obviously appropriate for Betsy, but Lola is growing up, whether you like it or not. You know what's behind it, don't you? It's generational trauma passed down by your mother to you.'

'That's not true.' Sabine didn't have a clue. Her mother's voice in her head had been replaced by Julian's a long time ago. If Sabine had been party to half of the things he'd said about the difference between his beautiful, sweet girls and the ones he saw as tarts and sluts, she'd get it. But she would never have put up with that kind of cruel talk in the first place. Now Nicky knew what a hypocrite he was, she didn't know how he lived with himself. She felt sullied by association. How she wished she'd been strong enough to throw him out years ago.

Sabine was still in full flow. 'Time to break the cycle, mate.' She stopped flailing and topped up her glass. 'We're animals with urges. Sex is fun. As long as they do it safely, let them get on with it without judgement, that's what I say.'

Nicky gripped the stem of her glass. Sabine was the one whitewashing the past now. 'But it's not always fun, is it?'

Sabine's flute paused momentarily on the way to her mouth. She took a drink, then placed it on the worktop. 'Not always, no.' She raised her gaze. Her brown eyes bored into Nicky's. 'But you can't save your kids from harm by stopping them from ever taking a risk just in case something bad happens.'

They stilled. Nicky lowered her voice. 'If I can save her from something like what happened back then, then surely I should try?' Her mind went back to the one night in their second year at university, when she'd found Sabine sitting, crying in the dark. 'You acted like it was nothing.'

'You think Elias—'

'God, no.' She reached out and held Sabine's wrist. 'I don't think that for a second. I just mean we both have good reasons to want to keep our children safe.'

'But we can't keep them in a gilded cage.' The muscles in her jaw tightened. 'And I haven't let what happened stop me from living my life the way I want to.' Sabine lifted her arm, making Nicky's hand fall away. She breathed in through her nose. 'But, contrary to what you seem to believe, I'm also in no hurry for our kids to make sweet music together this holiday.'

Relief flooded through Nicky, partly at what Sabine said, and partly because she was bringing the conversation back to the present. 'Good. Me neither.'

'You don't say.' Sabine cocked an eyebrow. 'Why don't we talk to them later and establish some ground rules?'

'Good idea.' Nicky smiled at Sabine, hoping this was the end of the argument and they could get back to normal. Sabine nodded, but the smile she returned didn't reach her eyes.

13

NICKY

When Betsy was in the bath that evening, Nicky and Sabine asked Lola and Elias to gather at the table on the terrace.

'What's this about?' said Elias, leaning back and knitting his fingers behind his head. 'I feel like I've been summoned to the head teacher's office.'

Nicky couldn't ignore the way his biceps bulged from the sleeves of his T-shirt. Dark hairs crept out from under his arms. He was a man, there was no denying it. She moved her gaze to Lola, who sat with her shoulders curled inwards, hands on her lap, picking at her nails like she always did when she was nervous. It didn't matter what Sabine said, she was clearly still young for her age. 'We just wanted to talk to you about... about—' She gawked at Sabine for help.

Sabine tutted. 'It looks like you two are together so, whatever that means, we thought we should lay down some ground rules.'

'Kill me now,' said Elias, laughing and dropping his hands on to the table. He sneaked a glance at Lola, whose face was bright red.

'Betsy is still very young and impressionable,' said Sabine. 'It's down to you two to set a good example.'

Nicky didn't know what Betsy had to do with it. The ground rules were so these two didn't get carried away with their holiday romance. Still, it was less mortifying to go down the good influence route than the sex one. 'Yes, Betsy is only ten, and—'

'She's eleven. She's going to secondary school in September,' Lola corrected her. Nicky remembered Sabine's comment about her intentionally keeping her girls younger in her mind, and colour rose in her own cheeks. 'And I'm starting sixth form. We're not little kids any more, whatever you and Dad think.'

Julian's scowling face loomed into Nicky's mind's eye. He was thousands of miles away, but he still had the power to make her shrink back. 'I know that,' she said. 'Which is why we're sitting down as adults to discuss this.' The sun bore down between the slats, burning a slice of skin on her thighs below the hem of her shorts. She shifted in the seat, sweat making the chair under her legs slippery.

Lola crossed her arms. 'This is so embarrassing.'

'It needn't be embarrassing,' said Sabine. That felt pointed. 'I prefer to be open about all things sex and relationships.'

'Oh, Mother,' said Elias, blinking slowly, a look of deep amusement on his face. 'Are we really doing this?'

'Nicky and I respectfully ask that the two of you keep the doors open when you're in rooms alone.'

Elias shook his head. 'We literally only just decided we liked each other yesterday. What do you think we're going to do, jump into bed? It's a small villa and there are five people around all the time.'

Nicky wanted to ask if that was all that was stopping him.

'We were young once,' said Sabine. 'We know what hormones are whizzing around your systems right now.'

Lola covered her face with her hands.

'Make it stop.' Elias laughed.

Nicky bit her bottom lip, trying to find something that might make this moment less excruciating. 'So, we're agreed?'

'I will literally say anything to make this end,' said Lola through her fingers.

'Open doors, all the way,' said Elias, still laughing and shaking his head. 'Can we be dismissed now, please, Miss?' A smile played on his lips, making Nicky certain he wasn't taking this seriously at all. But what could she do, ask him outright not to attempt to have sex with her daughter? Tell the two of them they weren't allowed to continue this relationship? On what grounds? The grounds that Nicky didn't want Lola to grow up, or that she thought Lola's dad would use this as another reason to call her an unfit mother? That's how it felt, like the situation was getting away from her and she didn't have the skills to stop Lola from getting hurt. She was failing again.

'Off you go, you little sod,' said Sabine, who seemed equally as amused as her son. 'And remember, we're watching you.' She pointed two fingers at her own eyes, then turned them to Elias, who laughed again and scraped back his chair. Lola followed him, her head bowed on her slender neck.

Sabine slapped her hands on her knees. 'Well, nothing awkward about that, was there?'

'Nope. I could have had that conversation all day long.' Keeping her voice light was a monumental effort.

'I think they got the point, anyway.' Sabine stood and stretched. 'Hopefully we won't both be grandmas by Easter.' She laughed. 'Imagine.'

As she walked off the terrace and around the corner, Nicky couldn't stop her mind from doing exactly that.

14

SABINE

Two full days had passed since the uncomfortable talk about ground rules and the teenagers had been acting completely appropriately as far as Sabine was concerned. She was proud of the way her son was conducting himself. Elias and Lola were cute together, holding hands and always smiling or laughing when she glanced their way, which she tried to do as little as possible. They deserved some space.

'Stop spying on them,' she hissed when Nicky stood up and walked to the edge of the terrace, looking through the trees to where Lola and Elias were sitting by the pool. She was always on the edge of her seat, ready to leap up to catch the kids doing something they weren't supposed to, like live their bloody lives. She tried to be tolerant and see it from Nicky's perspective, but there was no denying it was now getting on Sabine's nerves.

'I'm not spying.' Nicky came back to the table and sat. She picked up her coffee mug and drank. 'They were very quiet. I was checking they haven't drowned.' She said it with a smile, which made it hard for Sabine to be annoyed. Instead, she funnelled her irritation into her hatred of the cream coffee mugs they were both drinking from. She missed the chipped, heavy terracotta mugs she'd used since she was old enough to drink coffee, which was probably about the age of five now she thought of it. Elias was addicted too. That was another thing Nicky picked up on that felt like a criticism.

'Are they snogging?' The word sounded silly when Sabine said it out loud. 'Do people still say snogging? God, I'm old.'

'They are not kissing,' said Nicky, primly. 'They're lying on the same lounger, though. Oh, to be thin enough to fit, eh? They look almost like they are asleep.'

There was a splash and a whoop. Both women turned their heads towards the pool. 'They'll be awake now,' said Sabine, grinning. 'That's the sound of a Betsy bomb, if ever I heard one.' She'd got used to the noise Betsy brought with her everywhere she went. If she was brutally honest with herself, she preferred Nicky's younger child. She had a bounce about her that seemed to be missing from Lola. She secretly worried Nicky's anxious parenting might quash Betsy's energy when she was older. At this age, it was appropriate that Betsy was carefully managed by her mother. But she seemed like a kid who would want to party hard when she was in her teens, and Sabine envisaged conflict on the horizon if Nicky couldn't find a way to lighten up.

Elias's voice rumbled, followed by another splash, and she imagined him jumping in after Betsy. That was another reason she was proud of her son; he'd made an effort to make sure Betsy didn't feel left out, despite his and Lola's burgeoning relationship. That was kind. Lola hadn't made the same effort, but then siblings were different. Sabine had an older brother herself, and he was the least interesting thing about her childhood holidays on the island. Her cousins and local kids were far more fun to hang around with than the boy who relentlessly teased her and always seemed to be mooching close by when she didn't want him to be.

'Shall we go out for lunch?' Sabine asked. 'We could go down to Porto Mela. It's a restaurant on the beach, so the kids could swim afterwards.' She leaned forwards. 'And we can have cocktails and keep an eye on them at the same time.'

'You had me at cocktails,' said Nicky.

Sabine grinned. That was more like it. 'That's my girl!'

An hour later, they were all ready to go. Betsy's hair was still wet from the pool, and she looked cute in her shorts and T-shirt, her face tanned now and peppered with hundreds of freckles. Nicky arrived in the doorway with an enormous bag. 'What have you got in there?' Sabine's bag was light on her shoulder. She had the essentials – suntan lotion, keys, phone and money – but the size of Nicky's bag made her think she must've forgotten something.

'Towels, lotion, water, snacks... Just stuff we might need.'

Sabine glanced at the girls. Neither was carrying a bag. Elias's rucksack hung over his shoulder. She hadn't asked him to bring a towel and swimmers, she'd just presumed he would. She opened her mouth to ask why Nicky was the family carthorse but thought the better of it. 'Off we go then.'

Porto Mela was busy when they arrived, but the owner, Georgiou, was an old family friend and after kisses and introductions, he found them a table on the raised section above the sand, with a clear view of the sea. Sabine sat down in a green canvas deckchair under the canopy of dried palms with a satisfied sigh. This place never changed. It still had red checked tablecloths and the table numbers painted on to rocks next to the olive oil and vinegar dispensers in the middle of the tables. She remembered the feelings from her childhood when she peered out to the blue-green waves; the sense that she was exactly where she was meant to be.

She watched Georgiou flit about in his creased white shirt, pot belly pushing against the buttons. She'd had an enormous crush on him when she was a little older than Betsy. Back then he'd been a striking man in his mid-twenties. Now his long hair was grey and thinning. He'd tied it back in a straggly ponytail and Sabine wondered if he was trying to cling on to his youth. She remembered her plans to come back to the island when she was an adult and wow him with her sophistication. He would fall in love with her immediately and she would move to Zante, and they would run the family restaurant together and live happily ever after.

He wiped sweat from his forehead and poured water for an unsmiling customer. Sabine thought of Leo. His hair was greying at the temples, but he was still a deeply attractive man. He moved through the world with calm assurance. Their life in London was made up primarily of work, but they always had time for gallery trips, and still felt young enough to occasionally go to gigs in dingy venues in North London. It was a world away from what she'd thought she wanted back then. That's one of the reasons she thought Nicky should stop worrying about her girls the way she did. Everything changes. Once, Sabine was a girl who wanted to run a restaurant on a Greek Island. Now she was an interior designer living her best London life. 'I used to fancy the pants off him.' She nodded to Georgiou, who was carrying a tray of drinks to a table on the sand.

'Aw, I could have been a little Greek baby,' said Elias.

'You already are a little Greek baby,' said Sabine, pinching his cheek.

'Half Greek,' said Elias. 'I could have inherited all of this.' He gestured out to the restaurant.

'It was never going to happen,' said Sabine. 'I was about Betsy's age, and Georgiou was far too old and already married. It was just one of my many childhood fantasies.' She sat back and let out a wistful sigh. 'You lot have no idea how lucky you are to have it all in front of you.'

'You sound like you think the best is behind you,' said Elias. 'That's not what you usually say. What happened to, "There's no way I'm turning invisible just because I'm in my forties"?'

They all laughed at Elias's exaggerated impression of his mother.

'Has being back here made you wish you'd done life differently?' said Nicky. She leaned forwards, like she was invested in the answer.

Sabine grinned. 'Not at all. How could I?' She took Elias's face in her hands and kissed his cheek, tasting suntan lotion and salt. 'I'm very happy with my lot, thank you very much.' The grin fell from her face when she scanned the table and saw Nicky staring at her hands in her lap. She probably wished she'd made different choices in her life. How terribly sad. Sabine was trying to think of something to change the subject when there was a gruff shout from the beach. A man she vaguely recognised was marching towards their table. His round, slack-jowled face was red and he was ranting and pointing at Elias.

Soon he was standing over her son, spit exploding from his mouth as he snarled words in Greek. Sabine tried to keep up, but it was hard to translate at that speed. She stood, her arm raised, palm out. A teenage girl appeared behind the man, tears on her cheeks. She was imploring him to leave Elias alone. Sabine recognised the girl. She was the one she'd glimpsed from the taxi on their way from the airport, the one who'd been hanging around Elias and his cousin Demitri last summer. And this was her father, just as angry now as he had been when he said those terrible, untrue things about her son last year.

'Stop,' she said in Greek. 'Leave him alone.' She moved to stand between the man and her boy.

'How dare you bring him back here?' the man shouted.

Georgiou rushed towards them. 'What's going on?'

The girl begged her father to leave, pulling on his thick arm, but he shook her off. 'You shouldn't allow this boy in here,' he spat.

'It's my restaurant, Andreas,' said Georgiou. 'I'll decide who I serve. Now kindly leave.'

'Papa,' said the girl. 'Please.' She was crying and looking around at all the faces watching them, clearly distraught and humiliated.

Elias turned pale. He glanced between the adults with fear in his eyes. 'I said sorry last year,' he hissed to Sabine in English. 'It wasn't even that bad.'

'I know,' said Sabine. She turned to the man. 'You need to leave. Listen to your daughter.'

The man raised a meaty finger and pointed close to Elias's face. His daughter tugged at his other arm again and he let her pull him back towards the beach as all heads in the restaurant turned to follow him, then back to their own groups, talking in low voices and flicking glances back in the direction of their table.

'What the hell was that about?' said Nicky, patting the sweat on her face with a paper serviette.

'Just a misunderstanding last time we were here,' said Sabine. 'Nothing to worry about.' She didn't want to go into it. It was a painful enough experience back then, but she thought it had all been dealt with at the time. She hadn't anticipated a fallout when they returned to the island.

'It didn't look like nothing,' Nicky said.

'Can we just leave it and enjoy our lunch?' said Sabine.

'He was furious. Why was he pointing at Elias like that? What was he saying?'

Sabine watched Elias take Lola's hand. He whispered something in her ear and Lola nodded. Betsy watched them all with big, round eyes. It wasn't like her not to ask questions. Sabine could imagine how frightening that scene must've been for her. She was shaky herself. 'It's all right, sweetheart.' She patted Betsy's hand. 'Nothing to worry about.'

'What was his problem?' Nicky clearly wasn't going to leave it.

'I'll tell you later,' she said quietly. 'Not in front of Betsy.' She thought that would be enough to make Nicky leave it for now, but when her friend's eyes widened, she knew she'd made a mistake. Instead of downplaying it, she'd made it into something so bad it couldn't be discussed in front of a child. 'Honestly, it's nothing terrible.'

But she saw Nicky's gaze move to Lola and Elias's intertwined hands, and Sabine could see a new distrust in her eyes.

15

NICKY

'Why don't you three have a game of Uno by the pool?' said Nicky when they arrived back at the villa.

'Yay,' said Betsy at the same time as Lola groaned.

'Go on,' said Nicky. 'There's not much of the holiday left, and you two need to beat Elias at least once before we go home.' She couldn't care less if her girls beat Elias at Uno. She just wanted the kids occupied while she quizzed Sabine on what the hell had gone on down at the restaurant. Her thoughts had been on overdrive since that angry man and his daughter were ejected from the premises.

When she was certain the game was in full swing, she went upstairs to find Sabine. Her bedroom door was closed. Nicky wasn't going to be put off by that. She knocked. 'All right if I come in?'

'Yeah,' said Sabine. She was sitting up against the headboard of her bed, scrolling through her phone. She glanced up and gave a brief smile when Nicky came in, then turned her attention back to the screen. 'Are you okay?'

She could act as nonchalant as she liked. Nicky still had questions. She sat at the end of the bed, ignoring the breath Sabine let out when she lay her phone next to her. 'Go on, then.'

'Go on, what?'

Nicky tried not to roll her eyes. Sabine knew perfectly well what. 'Why was that man yelling at Elias?'

Sabine shrugged. 'He was overreacting. It's no biggie.'

'Overreacting to what?' Sabine was being intentionally evasive. All the reasons why that might be paraded through Nicky's mind.

Sabine closed her eyes and took in a deep breath through her nose. 'Last summer, Andreas's daughter took a shine to Elias. More than a shine. She started to follow him around. She'd turn up wherever he was and do things just to get his attention.'

'What kind of things?'

'She'd pretend she was struggling in the sea and call for him to help her. Stupid things like that. He'd drop what he was doing and rush into the sea, then she'd drape herself all over him like a fainting maiden. As if someone brought up here needs an English kid to help them out of the water.' She blew out her lips.

'So, she had a crush on him?' Nicky wished she'd paid more attention to the girl now. She tried to visualise her, but all she came up with was her father's snarling face.

'Yeah. He didn't feel the same, but she wouldn't take no for an answer, so he ended up asking her to leave him alone.'

'They didn't... kiss or anything?'

Sabine's mouth tightened. 'No, they didn't kiss or anything.' She said the last part of the sentence deliberately slowly, making Nicky feel like she was being salacious.

Nicky crossed her arms. Sabine must be trying to make her feel foolish for a reason. She clearly had something to hide. Nicky cocked her head to one side. 'Why did Elias turning her down make her dad so angry? It's been a whole year. Weird to hold a grudge about your child being rejected by a sixteen-year-old lad for that long.'

'You saw them. They're not exactly a rational family.' Sabine sounded defensive. 'She must've told her dad some cock and bull story about him, or something.'

'You think she might have, or you know she did?' Nicky narrowed her eyes. She knew Sabine, and she was holding something back. Why?

Sabine let her hands fall heavily on the bed. 'All right. The girl – I can't even remember her name, that's how insignificant what happened was – she told her dad Elias bullied her.'

'How?'

'Jesus, what's this, twenty questions?'

Nicky tensed. 'I'm not being funny, but Elias is now in a relationship with my sixteen-year-old daughter. If another girl has accused him of something, I think I have a right to know.'

'There you go with the age again.'

Nicky shook her head, frustration mixing with a darker feeling swirling in her abdomen. 'What exactly was he accused of?' How many times had Julian told her that teenage boys were only after one thing? He should know. He'd warned her to keep an eye on Lola, to make sure she wasn't taken advantage of, but instead, she'd brought her here, right into the lion's den.

Sabine raised an eyebrow and glared at Nicky. 'You heard the word "accused" in that sentence, did you? Because you seem to have already held a trial and found him guilty of something, even though you know nothing about it.'

'Tell me, then.' She sounded shrill, but what did Sabine expect when she skirted around the subject like this?

'I will, if you calm down.'

Nicky made a show of letting her shoulders relax. 'I am perfectly calm.' She gazed at the beige and cream stone wall, trying to manage her rising anxiety by tracing her eyes along the pattern of pale cement holding the rocks in place.

'All right. Her dad has a temper. Everyone on the island knows that. You saw how Georgiou responded to him. When Elias tried to give the girl the brush off, she wouldn't get the message. She was a pain to be honest, and he was pretty irritated by the end of it. Elias ended up saying some hurtful things to her. He was only sixteen and he acted rashly, and the girl didn't react well. She told her dad he had bullied her, and Andreas went off the deep end. Elias apologised and we thought that would be the end of it, but Andreas acted like it was a slight on the family name or something. Leo ended up having a word with the police about him. Thankfully it was near the end of the holiday, so we didn't have to face him again.'

'The police were involved?' Nicky desperately wanted to point out that Sabine had mentioned Elias was sixteen as a defence. It suited her to see sixteen as young when it supported her own argument.

Sabine raised her eyes to the ceiling. 'Yes, because Andreas's reaction was out of all proportion. It was just one kid telling another kid he wouldn't touch her with a bargepole.'

'Is that what he said?'

'I can't remember exactly' – Sabine's voice was an octave higher now – 'because it was over in a flash, it was a year ago, and I hadn't given it a single thought until that madman came charging over to our table today.'

Sabine wasn't looking directly at her, and that made Nicky both nervous and suspicious. 'Maybe I should ask Elias what he remembers?'

'Why?' Sabine flung her arms out to the side. 'What is it you're really asking here, Nicky?' Her eyes flashed dark.

Nicky paused. What was she really asking? All she knew for

sure was what happened at the restaurant made her even more uneasy about Lola and Elias's budding relationship.

She wished they'd spoken in English in the restaurant because she knew in her gut that Sabine wasn't telling her the whole truth. Her friend was usually the most honest person she knew, but she didn't always face up to the truth when it related to her. Nicky knew that. When things were too hard to face, Sabine was capable of telling herself the story that worked best for her. She'd done it before. What if she was doing it again?

16

TWENTY-SIX YEARS AGO

Nicky

When Nicky turned the overhead light on in the small snug of their student house, she put her hand to her chest, startled. Sabine was sitting on the sofa in the dark, her legs tucked up, arms folded around her shins, her face resting on her knees. She didn't move when the light went on.

Nicky stepped into the room. 'You scared the life out of me. Why are you sitting in the dark, you weirdo?' Sabine didn't lift her head. 'Sabine?' Her friend's shoulders were shaking. Nicky rushed to sit next to her. 'What's happened?' She put her arms around her and felt her shuddering breaths. Needles of fear pricked her skin. Sabine was usually so self-assured. They'd been friends since Fresher's Week and even now, in their second year, Nicky had hardly ever seen Sabine drop her armour of confidence. This was new and frightening.

'You were out with Toby tonight, weren't you?' She pictured Toby with his lop-sided grin and gelled-back hair. He was in the third year and Sabine had been hanging around with him and his friends a lot recently. They weren't Nicky's kind of people. She felt they looked down their noses at her because of her state school education and matching accent. Sabine told her she was allowing herself to be diminished when she'd said that group made her feel small. Sabine said she hung out with them to prove she was just as good as they were. When Nicky told Sabine what she'd heard about how they didn't treat girls very well, she laughed and all but patted her head and told her to stop being so parochial. They slept around, she slept around. Equality, see?

Nicky secretly thought Sabine had exactly the same hang-ups as she did, just a different approach. Nicky avoided them to make herself feel better. Sabine infiltrated the group, then had sex with some of them to show she could behave in exactly the same way they did. But part of Nicky didn't believe for one second that those entitled boys admired Sabine for her ability to treat sex so lightly. She suspected they were using her friend, and Sabine unwittingly saw it as liberation and equality. But what did Nicky know? She might be Sabine's best friend, and she tried not to judge, but inside she was still controlled by the morals her parents drummed into her.

'Talk to me,' she said into Sabine's curls. 'This isn't like you. What happened?'

'It's nothing.' Sabine lifted her head. Her eyes were bloodshot and the slick of eyeliner which was usually applied with precision to her top lid was smeared halfway down her left cheek.

'Come on.' Nicky squeezed Sabine's shoulders. This change in dynamic made her anxious. She was the weak, emotional one, not Sabine. 'I've never seen you in this state. This isn't nothing.' Different scenarios flitted through her head. Maybe Sabine had bad news from home. Perhaps she'd had an argument with Toby, and he'd said something hurtful.

'Did you argue with Toby? Is that it?'

Sabine shook her head. She pulled a tissue from her sleeve and blew her nose, then gave up when it disintegrated in her fingers.

'I'll get some loo roll.' Nicky rushed upstairs to the bathroom they shared with the other three girls in the house, none of whom seemed to be around. She didn't know if that was a good or bad thing. Sabine was her best friend, so it should be her comforting her; but she felt something was seriously wrong and was painfully aware of her inexperience. She was out of her depth and wanted backup. She peered into the bathroom mirror and a young, foolish face with wide eyes stared back at her. She needed to grow up.

When she arrived back downstairs, Sabine was sitting with her head resting on the back of the sagging sofa. She reminded Nicky of a Pierrot, black makeup staining her pitiful expression. She handed the wad of paper to her and was rewarded with a tiny smile. Nicky sat, picking the cuticle on her thumb, wondering whether to ask more questions or just sit quietly. Why didn't she know what to do? Sabine would know if it were the other way around. After an excruciating minute of listening to Sabine's jagged breathing, she tried again. 'If you want to tell me what's upset you, I'm here. If not, I'm here.'

Sabine spluttered into the tissue, making Nicky think she must've said completely the wrong thing. 'You're so bloody lovely,' Sabine said through her tears. 'I have no right to be making this kind of fuss.' She shook her head.

Nicky waited for Sabine to say something that made sense.

'I mean, what did I think would happen?'

Nicky hoped that didn't mean what she thought it might.

'And I don't even know why I'm so upset.' Sabine rubbed her eyes, smearing the eyeliner even further. 'It's not like I'm some kind of heavenly virgin or something. I've done it before, and he knew that, it's just that I didn't...' She trailed off into sobs.

Acid gurgled in Nicky's stomach. 'Are you saying what I think you're saying?' She laid a hand on Sabine's arm. She was shaking.

'I don't know,' she said. 'I mean, I didn't want to, so...' She lifted her shoulders then let them fall.

'Did Toby have sex with you when you didn't want to?' Nicky spoke slowly and deliberately, her heart thumping against her ribcage. This was bad. This was very bad.

Sabine shrugged again. 'I don't know... It wasn't as if he dragged me down a dark alley or anything. He didn't drug me or tie me up. It was just sex,' she said, as if trying to persuade herself.

'You said no, and he had sex with you anyway?' Nicky wanted to be clear, but she also wanted Sabine to hear the words, because for some reason she seemed to be minimising what happened.

Sabine nodded. 'But we were kissing, you know, and we were in his room, and we were messing about on his bed. I suppose I thought we might have sex. It wasn't off the cards or anything, but then he said something horrible.' She stopped and blew her nose. Tears tumbled down her cheeks. 'And I thought, I don't even like this boy. What am I doing?' She hugged her knees in tighter.

'What did he say?' Nicky regretted the words as soon as she said them. What he said wasn't the point.

Sabine didn't seem to notice her clumsiness. 'He was talking about this boy on his course and said he was "a fucking queer".' She half laughed. 'It wasn't just that that's an offensive thing to say, it was the way he said it, all superior and sneery. I told him that was homophobic, and he laughed and said I sounded like a lesbian which, from what he'd heard, I was clearly not. Then he started to tug at my knickers, calling me a dirty bitch and saying he knew how much I liked dick.'

The breath left Nicky's lungs. 'Oh, God. That's awful.' She felt like she should be recording this conversation for evidence to give to the police, but she couldn't stop Sabine so she could go and get a pad and pen. What was the right thing to do?

'I tried to push him off, but he was laughing and saying he didn't know I liked it rough, but he'd play along. After a bit I gave up struggling. I just let him do it. I don't know why I didn't do more to stop him. It seemed easier, somehow. I know that sounds mad.'

'It doesn't sound mad.' Nicky pulled Sabine in towards her. 'No one knows how they'd react in that situation. I'm so sorry that happened to you.' She paused. Language mattered. 'I'm so sorry he did that to you.' Sabine's ribs rose and fell under her hand. She waited until their breathing was in sync, then said, 'I'll come to the police station with you.'

Sabine sat up. 'I don't know whether I want to report it—him, I mean.'

Nicky's cheeks were hot. Of course Sabine would be hesitant. It was a huge thing to undertake, and the repercussions were scary, but it had to be done. If Sabine was scared about going to the police, then she would support her. 'I'll stay with you, I promise.'

Sabine shook her head. She slashed at the tears on her cheeks then wiped her hand on the pink throw covering the old sofa cushions. 'I don't know. Think about it. What's my case, really?'

'It looks pretty cut and dried to me. He had sex with you without your consent.' Fury built in her chest. It made her bold. She was up to supporting her friend. She would be strong when Sabine couldn't. She imagined Toby in the stand, having to face up to what he'd done. She'd be a witness, straight backed and clear voiced, making sure justice was meted out for hurting her precious friend.

'I'd been drinking. I was lying, half-dressed on his bed. We'd been kissing.'

'None of which gives him the right to have sex with you.' Why was Sabine trying to defend the indefensible?

Sabine covered her face with her hands. 'I know, but I can't help imagining the reaction of any police officer listening to all that.' She let her hands drop and stared at Nicky with wet eyes. 'And what if it did go to court? Imagine my family sitting in a courtroom hearing I'd already slept with two of his friends, from the mouth of some hotshot lawyer his loaded family would pay through the nose for. I'd be obliterated and they'd be mortified.'

'Your parents are relaxed about that stuff, though. That's what you told me.'

'Relaxed, yes, but seeing your nineteen-year-old's sex life judged by the tabloids isn't on any parent's wish list, is it?' She screwed her eyes tight. 'I don't think I can do it to them.'

'They'd want what's best for you,' said Nicky. She pushed away the certainty her own mother would prefer her to suffer in silence than put the family through a rape case like that, then felt guilty for having the thought.

'I'm thinking about what's best for me.'

'You're not going to let him get away with it?' Nicky gripped Sabine's arm. 'You have to go to the police. Even if it doesn't go to court, at least he'll be brought in for questioning and it might make him think twice before he rapes someone else.'

Sabine stiffened. 'Please don't start to guilt trip me into doing what you think I should. Rape is a... I didn't say it was rape.'

'I'm sorry, but that's exactly what you described.' Nicky's scalp tightened. This wasn't right. Sabine was strong and righteous. She always stood up for women's rights. 'Sex without consent is rape.' She didn't understand why Sabine was backtracking. 'I'm not trying to guilt you into anything. I'm trying to help.' Nicky's throat constricted. Surely Sabine could see going to the police was the right thing to do? 'You're probably in shock. I'm just trying to help you see how serious this is.'

'I was there.' Sabine's voice was cold. 'It happened to me. You don't get to tell me how to react to this.'

Nicky sat back. 'That's not what I was trying to do.' Tears collected behind her eyes, and she swallowed hard to keep them at bay.

'I'm going to have a bath, then I'm going to bed. I'll sleep on it and decide what to do in the morning.'

'You shouldn't have a...' Nicky stopped talking when Sabine glared at her. She was going to destroy whatever evidence she had. They'd both seen enough crime dramas to know the score. But the look on Sabine's face told her she'd said enough. Sabine would do whatever she wanted to do. She always did. It occurred to Nicky that that was what got her to where she was now, then despised herself for allowing the thought to enter her head. 'Want me to bring you up a hot chocolate?'

'Thanks,' said Sabine. She stood, arms hugging herself. 'Sorry for—'

'No, I mean, it's fine. You do what... Sleep on it and we'll talk in the morning. I'm always here for you.'

'I know. I do know that.' Sabine smiled weakly and Nicky listened impotently to the creak of the stairs as she walked to her room. Sabine spent a long time in the bathroom, then was already asleep, or pretending to be, when Nicky put her head around the door to check on her an hour later.

The following morning, Sabine came down late, the traces of last night's make-up still dark speckles around her eyes. When they were alone in the kitchen, she quietly said, 'I'm sorry for overreacting last night.'

'You were understandably upset. That's not overreacting.'

Nicky had hardly slept a wink, fury at that entitled monster running hot through her veins all night long.

Sabine shook her head. 'I'd drunk too much. I was just being a drama queen.'

'That's not what—'

'I'm not going to the police.' Sabine's voice was firm. 'You said you wanted to help, so support me on this. Toby and I both made mistakes last night. I honestly don't think he knew I wasn't up for it. He's just an idiot boy, not a rapist. I don't want to ruin either of our lives, and that's what would happen if I tell anyone else. Please don't say anything. This is just between you and me, okay?'

Nicky opened her mouth to speak, but no words occurred to her that Sabine would want to hear. Instead, she opened her arms. Sabine stepped in and they held each other tight.

17

PRESENT DAY

Sabine

Sabine sat on the terrace with her book open in front of her. Her eyes were reading the words but the sense of them was lost before they reached her brain. She closed it and gazed up at the vivid blue through the slats above, casting her thoughts back over the last twenty-four hours. She'd had to work hard to slap a smile back on her face after being quizzed by Nicky following that cretin Andreas's outburst yesterday. She understood Nicky being curious, but she gave the distinct impression she thought Sabine was hiding something, which was downright offensive. Not that Sabine could say that. Nicky wasn't strong enough yet to hear Sabine's inner thoughts.

Sabine had hoped this holiday would bring the two of them closer together, but the opposite seemed to be happening. She felt strangely untethered by that. Even when she'd lived abroad, their friendship had been one of her solid foundations, especially after her parents died. She wasn't close to her brother, so other than Leo and Elias, Nicky had been an important touchstone.

Naively, she'd secretly thought the split from Julian would allow Nicky to become herself again, the kind, funny girl she'd met twenty-seven years ago. Without the anxieties of a floundering marriage, and that jumped-up husband hovering in the background, she could shed the skin of wife and mother and get back to being an individual in her own right. But instead, she'd become hypervigilant about the girls and more uptight than ever. It had only been a matter of weeks since her marriage ended, so she should probably cut Nicky more slack, but now Elias and Lola were together, both Sabine and Elias were under the microscope, and she wasn't enjoying this new scrutiny at all. If she was honest, Sabine was glad this was the last full day of the holiday. She hadn't achieved any of her objectives and she was ready to go home. The realisation of that sat like a weight on her chest.

Betsy bounded up the path from the pool. She was a ray of sunshine, at least. Spending time with Betsy had been the best thing about this holiday. 'Can we go to the big beach this afternoon?' She clenched her hands together and gritted her teeth, adding, 'Please,' as an afterthought, then, 'Pleasey squeezy.'

'Pleasey squeezy?' repeated Sabine, raising her eyebrows.

Pool water collected around Betsy's bare feet. 'Double pleasey squeezy with a cherry on top.'

Sabine laughed. 'Well, if there's a cherry on top, how could I say no?'

Betsy punched the air. 'Yes!'

Nicky rounded the corner from the house. A smile brightened her tired eyes when she saw her grinning daughter. 'What's making you so happy?'

'Sabine said we could go to the big beach this afternoon, the one with the umbrellas and the ice cream hut.'

Nicky nodded and Sabine waited for her to come up with a reason why they couldn't. When no excuses for why they had to stay in the safe confines of the villa came, Sabine felt bad. She'd become defensive. She needed to relax. 'Why don't you go and tell Elias and Lola,' Sabine said to Betsy.

Betsy's smile fell. 'Can you? They were whispering to each other and kissing, and they wouldn't come in the pool when I asked. And Lola will just say I'm being annoying if I go and talk to them.'

'I'll tell them.' Nicky set off towards the pool, as if rocket propelled. What did she think was happening down there, with their mothers only a few metres away? Sabine remembered the signs by the side of the leisure centre swimming pool when she was a kid – *No running, no diving, no heavy petting* – and hid a smile.

Sabine stood and gave Betsy a hug. 'We're going to have a fantastic last day. I'll make sure of it.'

Poor Betsy. She'd been very tolerant most of the week. Hopefully there'd be more distractions for her down at the main beach. Sabine decided to try to make this a memorable day for her. It was the least she deserved.

18

SABINE

They were all hot and sweaty when they arrived at the beach. Despite Nicky's protestations, Sabine insisted on paying for sunbeds and umbrellas for all of them. She chose five in the first row so Nicky would be able to keep an eye on the kids when they were in the water. Nicky tried to argue that the girls could make do with towels on the sand, but Sabine refused to listen. 'It's our last day,' she said. 'We're going to live like kings.'

'Let me pay for our beds, then,' said Nicky, opening her purse.

'Absolutely not,' said Sabine. 'Today is on Leo, anyway. He messaged this morning to say we should push the boat out today, whatever the cost. He said it's raining in London, so it will cheer him up to think of us sipping cocktails in the sunshine. He insisted on paying. What can you do?' She lifted her hands, palms up, as if helpless.

Nicky hesitated, then closed her purse and tucked it back in the side pocket of her beach bag. 'Well, tell him thank you. That's very kind.'

Sabine smiled and lay down on her sunbed, relishing the heat of the early afternoon sun on her skin now there was nothing to do but relax. Leo hadn't said anything about paying for them. He'd told them to have a good day, but certainly hadn't mentioned financing them to treat themselves. It would have been weird if he had. They both had their own bank accounts, with a joint one for the household stuff, and Sabine was able and willing to pay for them all to have whatever they wanted today. During that awful period after she told Julian to leave, Nicky admitted her husband managed all their money during their marriage, and she was on a tight budget now. Despite that, her pride would've stopped her from allowing Sabine to pay. If she thought Sabine was being treated too, then it was more palatable. Sometimes you had to tell people what they needed to hear.

She turned at the sound of Betsy's voice. She was sitting on the edge of her sunbed talking to a girl in a yellow bikini. The girl looked to be about Betsy's age and was chatting away, making patterns in the sand with her toes as she talked. Sabine glanced at Nicky and saw she was watching the girls. She hoped that if Betsy made a friend, then Nicky might finally find it easier to relax. To her credit, Nicky had put her back into making sure Betsy didn't feel left out while the older kids were doing their thing the past few days.

'Can I go in the sea with Flick?' Betsy said to Nicky.

'Hello, Flick.' Nicky smiled at the girl. She turned to the water. It was practically still today, hardly rippling on the shore. 'It's calm today, at least. You'll still need to be careful though. Paddling only, please, no swimming without an adult.'

'I'm called Felicity, but I like Flick better,' said the girl.

'I like Flick too,' said Nicky. 'Let me just put a bit more lotion on Betsy's shoulders before she goes in the sea.'

A woman in mirrored sunglasses on the next sunbed along lifted herself on to her elbows. She was deeply tanned and soft rolls formed on her stomach as she sat up and smiled at them.

Sabine immediately liked her. She admired women who exuded confidence in bikinis, especially if they weren't stick thin. It was something she tried to pull off herself, hating that her eyes insisted on returning to the dimples in her own thighs and the stubborn pocket of fat on her lower abdomen, despite how hard she worked on her core. It was a woman's curse, finding fault with her own perfectly good body, despite her best intentions to be body confident.

'Hello,' the woman said. 'You're British, right?'

'Yes,' said Sabine. 'I'm Sabine. Good to meet you.'

'Nice to meet you. I'm Claire. I take it you've met Felicity?' Her daughter turned her head and glared at her mother. 'Sorry, I meant Flick.' She lowered her sunglasses and raised an eyebrow at the women, an amused expression on her face. 'Must get it right.'

'Hi, Claire,' said Nicky, rubbing gloopy factor fifty into Betsy's shoulders. Betsy wobbled under her mother's firm hands. 'This is Betsy, I'm Nicky.' She gestured towards the sunbeds where Lola and Elias were lying, sharing headphones so they could listen to the same music. 'That's Lola and Elias.'

'They're in love,' said Betsy. She pretended to gag, and Flick giggled.

'Right, that's you done,' said Nicky, releasing Betsy, now the colour of a corpse. 'Please stay where I can see you, and do not go out of your depth. Do you hear me?'

Betsy nodded.

'I chose this spot because it was between the two lifeguard towers,' said Claire, pointing both arms out at the flags.

'Wise woman,' said Nicky. 'Elias is also a lifeguard, aren't you, Elias?'

Elias raised his head. 'Sorry?'

'I was just telling Claire here that you're a trained lifeguard.'

'Yeah,' he said. 'Hi.' He waved before repositioning the earbud and lying back down.

'Even less reason to worry, then,' said Claire. 'And more reason to be glad the bar is directly behind us.' She winked.

'Good spot,' said Sabine, laughing. 'I'm thirsty, now you come to mention it. Anyone fancy a drink? I'm thinking cocktails. Who's in?'

'Go on then,' said Nicky. 'Just the one. Would it be too cheesy to have a pina colada? I haven't had one for years.'

Sabine grinned. Maybe today they could turn the holiday around and make some good memories after all. 'Urgh, too sweet for me,' she said. 'What about you, Claire?'

Claire's sun-burnished cheeks made two round apples as she smiled. 'Do you know what, I fancy a pina colada too. Thanks. The next round is on me.'

The first drink went down faster than Sabine intended. She'd chosen a frozen margarita. The lime and tequila melting in her mouth in the heat of the afternoon was like heaven. She watched Betsy and Flick throwing an inflatable ball to each other in the shallows and, for the first time that week, all felt good with the world.

'I think I'll be sick if I have another of those,' said Claire, downing the last of the thick yellowy liquor. 'What was the margarita like?'

'Divine,' said Sabine. 'I could definitely go again. What about you, Nicky?'

'I'm all right with this, thanks.' Nicky lifted her half-full glass.

Sabine viewed her through narrowed eyes. She'd drunk less last night, too. Just when she was starting to worry that Nicky might have a problem, she decided to rein it in. It occurred to her that it might be because she no longer trusted Elias with Lola and wanted to keep a clear head in case her daughter was in danger, but she didn't want to think about that. Nicky drinking less was a good thing. One less thing to be concerned about.

'Okay. Will you watch Flick for me while I get the drinks?' Claire stood and pushed her feet into pink flip flops. A few minutes later, she returned carrying an enormous jug full to the brim with pale lime-coloured liquid. Ice clinked against the sides as she put it on the table beside the sunbed along with three plastic glasses.

'Whoa, that's a lot of margarita,' said Sabine. She was all for day drinking, but that amount of margarita was surely for six people, not two?

'Save us getting up again,' said Claire, pouring out two large glasses. Sabine could imagine being friends with Claire back in the UK. She looked from her to Nicky, who was nursing what was left of her pina colada, her gaze flitting between her offspring as though if she allowed herself to drop her guard for a moment, one of them would immediately be in mortal peril. Sabine changed her mind. That woman needed another drink.

'Try this,' she said, holding out her glass to Nicky.

'I'm all right,' she said.

'I insist. I can't allow you to miss out on something so damn delicious. It would make me a bad friend. Refusing it would make you a bad friend. Drink it for both our sakes. For the sake of our friendship.' Maybe she'd laid that on a bit thick.

Nicky shook her head and laughed. 'Masterful emotional blackmail, there, Mrs.' She took the glass from her. 'That is very nice,' she said, after taking a sip.

Claire took that as a cue to pour a third glass. 'I'll just pop that there for when you're ready.' She placed it on the table next to Nicky.

Nicky tipped the last of her pina colada into her mouth. 'This tastes like pure sugar after a sip of that.'

'Let's call it a palate cleanser,' said Sabine, lifting Nicky's margarita and handing it to her.

'You're a pair of enablers, you two,' said Nicky, taking the glass with a wry smile.

Sabine wasn't proud of how relieved she was when Nicky started to drink, and the effects showed in the loosening of the muscles in her jaw. 'Cheers,' she said, deciding to dismiss the fact she was a hypocrite and a bad friend. 'To margaritas, sunshine and friendship.'

Nicky raised her glass and smiled, and Sabine saw the girl she'd been when they'd last been on the island, and her heart lifted with love for her friend. They could find their way back to each other, she was suddenly sure of it. It was all going to be okay.

19

SABINE

Claire could drink. She could talk too. Sabine's thoughts were woozy after the second cocktail, so she lay back in the shade of the umbrella and let Claire's chatter flow over her. She imagined being on holiday with just a ten-year-old for company must be hard for someone so sociable. Clearly, now she had some adults to communicate with, she was going to make the very most of it. They'd already heard about what she thought of the apartment she and Flick were staying in and what they'd done on the island in more detail than Sabine needed to know. She pulled her legs up out of the sun, checking for red patches on her shins. She used to tan by just looking at the sun; now her skin began to tingle uncomfortably after ten minutes' exposure. It was quite annoying; it felt like an insult to her heritage.

'Is Flick your only child?' asked Nicky. She was sitting up facing Claire, a wide-brimmed hat shading her head and shoulders. The hat regularly turned to where Betsy and Flick were sitting in the shallows, where they seemed to be conversing as avidly as Claire.

Claire took a swig of margarita then shook her head. 'I've got a twenty-year-old from my first marriage.'

'Girl or boy?'

'Girl.' Claire took another drink, then leaned closer. 'I keep looking at your teens and shuddering.'

'Why?' Sabine could imagine Nicky frowning as she asked.

'You've got it all to come. How old are they? Sixteen, seventeen?'

'Lola's sixteen and Elias is a year older.'

Sabine glanced at the two of them as Nicky answered. They'd migrated to the same sunbed and were lying on their sides facing each other talking in low voices. She envied the even tan and youthful glow of Lola's skin. She could only see the side of her face. Her eyes were bright, and a smile was never far from her lips. Elias lifted his hand and stroked Lola's cheek. She remembered Nicky's comment about his moves, and a swell of indignance grew in her chest. Her boy was treating Lola beautifully. She was a lucky girl, and Nicky should be able to see that.

Sabine would never admit it, but she didn't really understand what Elias saw in Lola. Yes, she was beautiful and had a great body, but she didn't have her sister's effervescence or positive energy. Everything she did seemed measured, which gave Sabine the feeling she was playing a part, not being entirely herself. Sabine admired authenticity in a person above anything else. But it wasn't her job to query who her son found attractive. The feeling that Nicky disapproved of Elias came back like a sting. Would Nicky prefer Lola was dating some bumbling, inexperienced teen who blew hot and cold, because he wasn't mature enough to know what he wanted? Nicky should be grateful Elias had chosen Lola. It occurred to her none of these thoughts were kind.

'Gah! I'm dreading Flick getting to that stage. If I had the money, I'd send her to boarding school when she got to fifteen and not let her back until she's nineteen, so I don't have to deal with all the shit again.'

'What shit?' Nicky's voice was anxious.

Sabine sighed inwardly. 'Elias hasn't been any bother,' she said, sitting up so she could see both women's faces. She didn't want Claire giving Nicky more to worry about. They all watched as Lola and Elias climbed off the sunbed and walked, hand in hand, towards the sea. Sabine watched Lola's perfect behind in just a tiny triangle of blue bikini swaying as she walked, and couldn't help imagining the sagging, creased skin of her own buttocks in comparison. She missed being young and beautiful.

'It's the girls that are the problem,' said Claire. 'I wouldn't wish a teenage girl on my worst enemy.'

'Lola isn't difficult, to be honest,' said Nicky, her eyes on her daughter's back. 'I suppose I've just been lucky.'

Claire's eyebrows arched over the top of her sunglasses. 'That's what you think.'

Shut up, thought Sabine. *Stop talking right now*. She visualised slapping a hand over Claire's face. Those margaritas were strong.

'What do you mean?' said Nicky, her face etched with concern. She pulled the towel around her, shielding her exposed back from the glaring sun.

'I thought my Evie was an angel.' Claire took another drink, and Sabine resisted the urge to take it from her hand. 'She did her schoolwork, never got in trouble, but then, when the shit hit the fan, I found out I didn't know her at all.' She waved her drink around as she spoke. 'Turned out that when she told me she was staying at her friend's house, she was really at parties, going back with boys to God knows where. In my defence, I was exhausted because I was working full time and my second marriage was going up the spout, and I had Flick to look after, but I took my eye off the ball with Evie, and she took full advantage.' She swigged the last of her drink and poured herself another, slopping much of it on to the table. 'Anyway, it all came out when she ended up in hospital.'

'Hospital? What happened?' Nicky was rigid. Sabine was pretty tense herself, but not because of this woman's errant teen.

'She had a bad reaction to something she'd taken. They were all doing it, but she has allergies, and I think—'

'What was it? What were they taking?' Nicky glanced at the shoreline and back.

'Ket. Ketamine. They're all at it.'

'Well, not all,' said Sabine. She didn't care if she sounded smug. Her son didn't take drugs like ketamine. He had the odd spliff now and again, but that wasn't a big deal.

Claire huffed. 'You keep telling yourself that.'

Sabine was quickly going off this woman.

'What reaction did she have?' Nicky said, her voice tight.

'God, it was awful. She frothed at the mouth, her eyes were rolling back in her head. It was like a scene from a horror movie, I'm not joking. Her idiot friends rang me rather than ringing an ambulance because they were scared they'd get arrested or something. Anyway, I got to where they were holding this party and saw the state of her and called an ambulance. All the others scarpered. It was the scariest night of my life, I'm not gonna lie.'

'And you didn't know what she was up to until then?' Nicky said. She held the towel tightly against her. Her eyes darted to the kids in the sea, then back to Claire.

'Not a clue. It all came out then, though. As soon as she was well enough to talk, it was like she was purging herself of every bad thing she'd done. It was like she was a different person when she was out of the house, and I didn't know a single thing about it. She was moody and hormonal when she was at home, like all teenage girls, but I thought that was just normal. Turns out I didn't know her at all.'

'God,' said Nicky. 'How is she now?'

Claire flapped her hand and lay back on the sunbed, resting her drink on the soft mound of her stomach. 'Oh, she's fine. No lasting damage. To be honest, it's probably a good thing she had that reaction. It made her cautious about taking anything else.' She laughed. 'At least, that's what she's told me. She's in her second year at uni, so she could be up to all sorts again and I wouldn't know a thing about it, would I?' She closed her eyes. 'Anyway, all I'm saying is, it doesn't matter how well you try to parent them. They'll do what they want to, and there's bugger all you can do to stop them. It's hard work, this parenting malarkey. Especially when you've got girls.'

Her breathing slowed and soon her cheeks slackened. After a short while, the glass wobbled in her hand and Sabine took it before it fell on to the sand. A minute later, she was snoring.

Sabine and Nicky stared at each other, mouths agape. They looked at Flick, kicking at the waves with Betsy, oblivious to the fact her mother had downed four strong cocktails in an hour, then fallen asleep.

'It doesn't matter how well you try to parent them,' whispered Sabine, her mouth close to Nicky's ear.

Nicky spluttered with laughter. Claire shifted. Drool seeped from the side of her mouth as the two other women kept an eye on her child.

20

NICKY

'It doesn't matter how well you try to parent them,' said Sabine once again, wagging her finger at Nicky, then bursting into laughter. There was a welcome breeze on the terrace. Since they'd got back from the beach they'd been chatting like the old days and Nicky's limbs loosened for the first time in as long as she could remember. Such a shame they were going home tomorrow.

'I can't believe she didn't see the irony of telling us that so vociferously, whilst getting royally pissed at the same time as ignoring her ten-year-old child, who was in the actual sea.' Nicky was breathless at the end of the sentence. She didn't mind keeping an eye on Flick, but she did worry for the girl's safety when there weren't two benevolent strangers around to make sure she didn't drown.

'And the snoring!' Sabine slapped her leg. 'Then pretending she'd only closed her eyes for a minute when we woke her up to say we were leaving. Christ.'

Nicky nodded. 'I can't believe I was a bit worried initially, you know, when she was telling us about her eldest. I started to think, what if Lola has some kind of secret life I know nothing about?

Then I saw how she actually parents, and...' She held out her hands. 'Far be it from me to judge, but...'

'I'll drink to that,' said Sabine. 'I've been saving a nice bottle of Crémant for our last night.'

Nicky grimaced. 'Isn't it a bit hypocritical to drink more, after what we've just said about Claire?' In truth, the buzz of the cocktails was wearing off and she was dying for another drink. She wasn't proud of that.

Sabine raised an eyebrow. 'Claire drank twice as many margaritas as we did! Also the kids have had a great day. They're exhausted from being in the beautiful sunshine and swimming in the sea and now they're on their phones in the sitting room. They are safe and sound. Us having a few drinks now is not bad parenting.'

'Go on then.' She was glad Sabine was pushing for it. It was their last night so why not have bubbles? She'd be back in the real world tomorrow. She stopped that thought before it could take hold. Instead, she closed her eyes and breathed in the lemony scent of the citronella candles and listened for the chirrup of grasshoppers and the breeze ruffling the leaves of the olive trees.

She opened her eyes at the sound of footsteps. Sabine popped the cork, and the liquid fizzed as it hit the glass. She handed one to Nicky. 'Thank you for coming away with me this week.'

Nicky was surprised to feel tears collect in her eyes. She clinked the top of her glass against Sabine's. 'Thank you for having us. It's been an absolute treat.' She took a sip. 'I'm not sure I've been the best company, though.'

'Don't be daft.' Sabine didn't meet her eye.

'I know I can be... uptight.' There was so much more she wanted to say. She wanted to tell her friend about how Julian's voice was always louder than her own inside her head, how she didn't know how to live alone. There were so many decisions, and she never trusted herself to make the right one. If they'd had an evening like this earlier in the week, perhaps she would have, but now it seemed too late. She would enjoy tonight, then work on herself when she got home. Then there would be nothing to share.

Sabine let out a long breath. 'I just worry about you, that's all. You're coiled tight. It's difficult to watch, so I can't imagine what it's like to... to find it so hard to relax.'

Nicky took a drink. It was cold and delicious. 'I'd rather be an anxious parent than a neglectful one, though,' she said. She sounded defensive, so added, 'God knows what could happen to Flick if Claire regularly acts like she did today.' She needed to remind Sabine why she personally acted like she did. It was to keep her girls safe. Sabine had no idea what it was like to have girls. Julian was wrong about plenty of things, but she thought he was actually right about how much more vulnerable they were. Elias was tall and strong. She knew male on male violence was a worry, but Julian was always telling her their daughters were more at risk on a day-to-day basis. Sabine would have a different take, and that was her prerogative, but she didn't want to talk about that now. She just wanted to sip her bubbles and enjoy the last evening with her friend. 'Enough about the kids, anyway.' She lifted her glass. 'This is delicious.' She sighed. 'It really is beautiful here. I'd forgotten about all the sounds in the evening before we came back out. Do you remember that night we fell asleep by the pool?'

Sabine grinned. 'And we both woke up at the same time and thought we'd heard wolves or something.'

'What was that noise?'

'God knows. It might just have been you snoring.'

Nicky snorted. 'Or you.'

They sat quietly for a while. Nicky wondered if Sabine was recalling how the two of them had been so unnerved they'd slept in the same bed that night, talking until the early hours, then waking in the sweltering heat as the midday sun glared in through the window. She opened her mouth to talk about it, but something stopped her. They were so close back then. More like sisters than friends. There was no filter when they spoke; they just had stream-of-consciousness conversations knowing they could say anything to each other without fear of being judged.

Nicky remembered how she'd told Sabine more about her strict upbringing, and about the boy she'd lost her virginity to and her mother's extreme reaction. She'd felt understood, freed by Sabine's tenderness when she asked how that made her feel. But this week, Sabine had thrown that back in her face, saying she was repeating her mother's behaviour, just because she was anxious her daughter might get hurt.

She couldn't help her thoughts spiralling. Despite the lovely day they'd just had, she had to accept that she and Sabine had grown apart. Nicky had hoped this week would fix it, but instead it was like the cracks in their relationship had been baked in and made permanent by the sun. Chinks of their old relationship had shimmered through the gaps, but not enough to put them back on track, and that left a void almost as big as the one waiting for her at home. Her husband had gone, somehow leaving his critical words behind, and she didn't feel understood, respected, or even liked sometimes by her best friend. Thank God for her girls. Without them she might fall into the gaping hole inside herself and never climb out.

She wondered if things might have been different this week if Lola and Elias hadn't started this holiday romance. The more she thought about it, the more certain she felt that's what the problem was. It wasn't kind of her, but she couldn't help thinking

Elias moved in on Lola simply because she was the only girl available. She'd watched him stroking Lola's face and staring into her eyes like some kind of leading man in a romance movie. Elias had honed his craft and when he got home, he'd have a plethora of other girls to try it out on. She'd already started practising what she'd say to comfort her poor girl when Elias inevitably ditched her.

'I think I'll call it a night,' she said, tipping back the last of her drink.

'Aw, don't go to bed yet,' said Sabine. 'It's so nice sitting here with you.' She started to pour another glass. 'I've missed spending time with you.'

Nicky sat back in the chair, winded by how elated those words made her feel. She was on a permanent roller coaster of emotional extremes. 'Have you?'

Sabine filled her own glass. 'Yes. Of course I have. You're my best friend.'

Nicky took a sip to hide that she was trying not to cry. She'd been convinced she was just an irritation to Sabine, that their friendship had run its course, and she realised she'd been trying to steel herself to cope with that by being hypercritical herself. The fact she wanted to sob with relief at Sabine's words showed her that any defence she'd put up was flimsy at best. 'You don't wish I hadn't come along this week?'

'What? No. Of course not.' Sabine narrowed her eyes. 'Is that what you've been thinking?'

'A bit.' She couldn't fight the tears. She wiped them as they fell on to her cheeks. 'Sorry. I can't believe I'm crying again. You've had enough of this since Julian left.'

Sabine grabbed her hand. 'You cry all you want. You've had a shit time.'

The strength of Sabine's grip made her think that perhaps

the cracks could be mended after all. She hoped so. She didn't know who she was any more. She had been Julian's wife for so long and now she was alone. She was a mother to her girls, but she could feel Lola drawing away and that frightened her more than she cared to admit. Sabine had always been there for her: her strong, funny, brilliant friend. As the tears rolled down her cheeks, she realised some of her anxiety this week was because she didn't feel as connected to Sabine as she had before, and that was like one of the most important foundations of her life crumbling away.

'I love you,' she said through her tears.

'I love you too,' said Sabine, gripping her hand even harder.

The sound of footsteps came from around the corner of the house and she let Sabine's hand drop so she could wipe the tears from her face. Lola and Elias appeared. Nicky was glad the only light was the candle in the centre of the table.

'We're off to bed,' said Elias, lifting his hand in a weak wave.

'Night,' said Lola.

Sabine let her head fall to the side. 'You're voluntarily taking yourselves off to bed? Who are you and what have you done with our teenagers?'

Elias laughed. 'I'm knackered. We did a lot of swimming today.'

'Is Betsy still up?' said Nicky, equally as astounded as Sabine at this turn of events.

'I'm making her go to bed too,' said Lola. 'I don't want to put up with her whining about being tired on the flight.'

Betsy appeared at Lola's side. 'It's not fair. I'm not tired.' She yawned and everyone laughed.

Nicky held out her arms. 'Give us a kiss.' Betsy gave her a sulky cuddle and they all sauntered back into the house, leaving Nicky and Sabine looking at each other, eyes wide.

'Wonders will never cease,' Sabine said. 'Maybe the kids are getting more responsible.'

'I'll drink to that,' said Nicky, touching the top of her glass to Sabine's. This sudden feeling of connection made her brave. She listened until she couldn't hear the children talking any more, then took a deep breath. 'I haven't told you everything that went on with Julian,' she said. 'What it was really like living with him.'

Sabine sat up straight, and Nicky knew she had her full attention. It was time to share the truth with her friend. 'The video, and the cheating, was just the tip of the iceberg.' She took another drink, hoping it might calm her wavering voice. 'He... he didn't like me seeing you, for a start off.'

Sabine snorted. 'I worked that out.'

'He didn't like me seeing anyone. More than that, he made it very difficult for me to spend any time with anyone other than him and the girls.'

'How? What did he do?' Sabine squinted at her, her expression serious.

'At first, he dressed it up as being hurt that I wanted to spend time away from him, but that turned into sulking, then sniping... He'd say horrible things.'

'God, Nicky. Like what?'

So many tiny cruelties paraded through Nicky's mind. 'He'd accuse me of wanting to meet other men.'

'Huh. That's rich.'

'I know. It's so messed up, and I'm only just realising the extent of it now. He'd put me down in front of other people, even the girls.' The shame of what witnessing that must've been like for her girls brought heat to her cheeks.

'Shit, mate. That's awful.' Sabine took her hand. 'I can't believe I didn't know. Why didn't you say anything?'

The gentleness of her friend's touch and the concern in her

eyes brought Nicky's tears to the surface. This was how people who loved you touched you. 'I didn't see it for what it was for a long time. He painted it as love. I know that sounds stupid, and I'm a gullible fool for falling for it.'

'No.' Sabine's voice was firm. 'None of it is your fault. You have to see that.'

Nicky was grateful, but it was hard to truly believe what Sabine said. Julian had done that to her. He'd made her believe she was worthless and that she deserved every bad thing that happened to her. But that wasn't true, because Sabine, her incredible, admirable friend, cared about her. 'He made me completely reliant on him. He encouraged me to stay at home after I had the girls, and then he chipped away at my confidence until I didn't feel like I could get a job if I wanted to. I had to ask him for money, even for groceries, and even then he made me feel like I was profligate with his hard-earned cash.'

'Jesus.' Sabine ran a hand over her face. 'I'm so sorry you went through this. I thought he was just a dick, but this is coercive control, pure and simple. The bastard should be locked up.'

Nicky's shoulders tightened. 'He's still the girls' dad.' Any gratification she felt at the thought of Julian being made to pay for the way he'd treated her was countered by imagining Lola's and Betsy's reactions to her getting their father arrested. The thought of what it could do to them made her stop herself from telling Sabine any more. 'And it's over now. Nothing could compel me to let him come back. It's done, thank God, and I'm here, in beautiful Zante, with beautiful you.' She forced herself to smile.

'I'm so proud of you,' said Sabine, taking her hand and gripping it. 'I want to kill him. I wish I'd known what was happening. I feel awful for being so oblivious.'

'You saw what I wanted you to see,' said Nicky, thinking of all the times she'd put on a brave face and pretended she was okay. 'I wasn't ready before. But now I just want to put it all behind me and look forward.' She wiped the tears from her face and tried to steady her breathing.

'Okay. If you're sure I can't take a hit out on him?'

'No hit.'

'Understood. Then I'll just have to settle for doing everything I can to help you rebuild your life, since you thriving will probably piss him off more than anything else.' Sabine raised her glass. 'To a gloriously happy future for you and your beautiful girls.' She spoke fiercely, as if this was a challenge she was taking on, and Nicky loved her for it.

'I'll drink to that,' said Nicky. 'Let's hope the best is yet to come.' As she knocked her glass against Sabine's, hope lifted her chest. With her friend by her side, she suddenly felt like she could conquer the world.

21

NICKY

Nicky's head pounded when her alarm went off the following morning. She and Sabine had finished the bottle of Crémant last night, and she hadn't drunk anywhere near as much water as she should have. Her eyelids scratched across her eyeballs when she blinked. She fought the self-loathing that usually came along with a hangover. Last night was different; she wasn't sitting alone, ruminating on her miserable existence. She'd been bonding with her best friend. Telling her the truth about her marriage had been the right thing to do. She'd felt properly close to Sabine for the first time this holiday, and it was timely and very welcome indeed. This holiday might not have been the dream she'd anticipated, but it had been respite from the realities waiting for her at the end of today's flight. She'd been avoiding thinking about what life would look like for her when they arrived back in the UK. It was too bleak.

Closing her eyes against the light pushing its way through the edges of the blinds, she saw an image of Julian waiting for the girls at the airport, impatience written all over his face. They were due to spend a few days with him when they returned home so he was collecting them, and if the flight was delayed, she was sure he'd make it her fault. Even if it wasn't, she'd be made to feel how inconvenient it was that he had to waste his valuable time driving to the airport and standing waiting, as if he was just some kind of chauffeur, rather than the girls' father. He had never been contrite about what he'd done to her, or their family. He'd gone on the defensive and stayed there. Being caught out made him angry, instead of ashamed, and her having the audacity to ask him to leave the house that he paid for made him angrier still.

Second-guessing his reactions was a hard habit to break. When he used to come home from work, she'd listen for the way he closed the door, and the weight of his tread on the floorboards. A slam, or a sluggish gait, would tell her that she would need to do a lot of tiptoeing and cajoling to avoid annoying him further. It rarely worked. He'd come into whatever room she was in and point out something she'd done wrong. He'd let her know how much harder she made his life, how other men didn't have to put up with what he did. If that was the case, she failed to see why he was so furious when she eventually called time on their relationship. Although, she did. She'd read up on coercive control and knew that he couldn't stand losing his power over her. Intellectually, she knew that he had systematically diminished her. She understood his tactics and could recognise that it wasn't her fault she was under his spell. She hadn't allowed it to happen. She wasn't the one in the wrong. But even though she'd heard it from Sabine now too, what she knew and what she felt were two different things, and despite her best efforts, he still sat like a poisonous toad in her head, and she didn't know how to get him out.

In her mind's eye, she watched Betsy run towards her daddy, her freckled face full of excitement to see the man she adored most in the world. Nicky hadn't ever criticised their father to her daughters. No matter that they'd grown up hearing how useless and pathetic she was, he painted himself as their protector. He told the girls and the rest of world what a brilliant father he was, and as far as Nicky could see, the world believed him. There was nothing she could do to change the narrative, because she'd been complicit in propagating it for years. She'd played the part of devoted wife right up until he cheated on her so blatantly, and in such an ugly way, that even her suffocated self-esteem said, *No more.*

When they arrived back in the UK, she would have no choice but to stand by, helpless, as he led her girls away to his car, to his new apartment and his new life, while she got into Sabine's Range Rover to be dropped off at her empty house. She could already feel the stillness of the air in her hallway, the silence only broken by the sound of her case rolling along the wooden floor.

All the tasks she'd put off until after her holiday lined up in her mind now, jostling to be at the front of the queue. Getting a job was at the top of the list. It had been so long since she'd done any graphic design that the software had changed beyond recognition. She should've kept her hand in. Julian told her the girls needed her more than they needed the money. What a fool she'd been not to push back. She'd become a dinosaur in the world of design, and now she'd be lucky to get an admin job on minimum wage.

She threw off the covers and sat upright. Her stomach lurched. She sat still for a moment, then forced herself to stand, then showered and dressed, keeping her eye on the time.

'Come on, you two,' she said, turning the light on in Lola and Betsy's bedroom. She was glad to see Lola's hair trailing along her pillow, highlights bleached blonder from the sun. Each morning since Lola and Elias got together, Nicky's insides had clenched in preparation for finding Betsy alone in the room. She didn't really think Lola would be brazen enough to sneak into Elias's room in the night, but she was afraid he might have influenced her enough to take the chance. As Sabine kept reminding her, she was legally old enough to share his bed.

She hadn't, thank goodness. 'Wake up, sleepyheads. We need to pack.'

Lola kicked out her legs and pulled the covers over her head. Nicky laughed. 'We have a flight to catch. There's no time for a lie-in this morning.' She pulled at the covers, but Lola held them tight.

'Morning,' said Betsy, yawning. 'Is Daddy picking us up?'

Nicky thought she'd prepared herself for this question, but it was still wounding. 'Yep, he'll be waiting at the airport. Come on. Brush your teeth and wash your face.'

'Yay.'

That hurt. She watched Betsy rub her eyes with curled fingers like a character from a cartoon then slope off towards the bathroom. 'Lola,' she said firmly. 'You need to get up and help to pack.'

'Five minutes.' Lola's voice was muffled.

'Five minutes,' Nicky conceded. 'Not a second more. And remember to pack everything you both need for your dad's into your case. Put all the washing in Betsy's for me to take home.'

She headed back to her own room and threw her case on the bed, unzipping it with a sigh. This was it. Back to the real world. She heard the creak of a door along the corridor opening and Elias's deep voice speaking in quiet tones. Something made her feet move quietly to her open door. She peeked down towards Lola's room in time to see the door pushed closed. The temptation to tiptoe along the tiles and put her ear to the wood was almost overwhelming. It was too risky. And also, completely bonkers. What could they possibly be saying she should be privy to? Sabine was right; she needed to leave them to it. She checked her watch. She could go and interrupt them in a few minutes anyway because she said she'd be back in five.

She took her light summer dresses from the hangers in the wardrobe and folded them into the case. It felt like saying goodbye to old friends. The weather in the UK had been dismal when they left and the forecast for the next few weeks wasn't much better. She was reaching for the last hanger when a door slammed and she heard Lola's raised voice followed by Betsy's.

Nicky marched to their room. 'What's going on?' She glanced around but there was no sign of Elias.

'Nothing,' said Lola. Her face was red, and she glared at Betsy with bloodshot eyes.

'Betsy?' said Nicky.

Betsy's bottom lip jutted out. 'Nothing.'

'Come on, I wasn't born yesterday,' said Nicky. She turned to Lola. 'What's wrong with you? You look like you've been crying.'

Lola pulled the covers over her head. 'Nothing's wrong. I'm just tired,' she growled.

The aggression in her voice grated. Nicky was feeling pretty fragile herself this morning so she could do without a hormonal teenager treating her with disrespect. 'We're all tired,' she said. 'But that doesn't change the fact we have an hour and a half to pack everything up before we have to leave. You want to be treated like an adult, so do some of the work that comes along with that.' She checked her watch. 'I'm going to come back in here in twenty minutes and I'd better see progress. Understood?'

Betsy nodded. There was no movement from under Lola's covers, but instead of ranting, Nicky made the choice to lift her chin and stride off to the kitchen to get a shot of caffeine.

22

SABINE

Zante airport seemed hotter and busier than it had when they arrived, so Sabine was glad when they eventually boarded the plane. It wasn't just the humidity that was making her tetchy; something had felt off all morning. After Nicky's revelations about Julian last night, she'd been hoping to get her on her own to check she was okay, but packing had been fraught and since they'd left the villa Elias had been pinned to Sabine's side, following her everywhere she went. Lola was acting strangely too.

'Do you want to sit with Lola?' Sabine asked Elias as they made their way to their seats. 'I could sit with Nicky and Betsy.' She didn't really want to. Her head was pounding and her tongue felt furry in her dry mouth. Ideally, she'd love to ignore everyone, close her eyes and try to sleep off her hangover, but she felt it was only right to offer.

'You're all right,' said Elias, not catching her eye.

'Has something happened?' Her boy was unusually quiet and he and Lola hadn't said a word to each other all morning. It looked very much like the holiday romance was over. Sabine didn't want either of the kids to be hurt, but she couldn't force herself to be sad that their relationship wasn't coming home with them. She couldn't believe she'd ever joked about them getting married. Their fling, if that's what it was, had added an extra layer of complication to her friendship with Nicky, and the last thing she wanted was for Julian to be part of their lives, especially after what Nicky had disclosed.

'Nah, it's all good.' His voice was flat.

'Sure?'

'Sure.' She didn't believe him for a second, but he was seventeen, and she had no right to demand more information from him. She wasn't even sure she wanted to know.

She watched as Nicky fussed about, shoving rucksacks in the overhead locker, then dragging hers out again. A man with a sunburnt nose squeezed past her too closely and Nicky closed her eyes, her lips an angry tight line. Poor Nicky. She'd had to put up with enough crap in her marriage; she didn't need strangers acting like dicks around her too. 'Arsehole,' Sabine muttered as the man passed her seat.

'What?' said Elias.

'Nothing.'

He took out his headphones and put them on, his curls squashing to his head under the band. She gazed at him when he closed his eyes. His face was inscrutable. She glanced over at Nicky and Lola across the aisle. Nicky was angled in, talking urgently to Lola, who seemed to be resolutely staring out of the window. Sabine was about to lean over and ask what was going on when the safety announcement was called and the cabin crew stood in the aisle, asking for their attention. It was for the best, she thought as she watched a woman wearing a tight hair bun and claret lipstick slip a life-vest over her head. Elias and Lola were almost adults. Her son had made it clear he didn't want to talk about whatever had gone on, and that was his prerogative. She would respect that, and she wouldn't broach it with Nicky either.

When the safety announcement finished, she opened her book and tried to lose herself in the words on the page.

she would have done, and she couldn't read it without
more.

When the plane began its final descent, she shut her
book up tight, terrified her secret might slip out into the

23

NICKY

Nicky's stomach was still churning when the plane touched down. Her eyes kept returning to the mark on Lola's thigh. Lola hadn't moved her gaze away from the window. Every so often she pulled the sleeve of her sweatshirt over her hand and wiped tears from under her eyes. Nicky needed to do something. She couldn't just sit there and watch her daughter suffer, but whenever she tried to speak to her, Lola made a performance of taking out her ear buds and screwing up her face as though it was the greatest inconvenience, until eventually she had no choice but to give up. She tried to stop her brain creating ugly scenarios to explain the fresh bruise, the graze on her shin and Lola's obvious distress, but she seemed to have lost control of her thoughts.

Betsy was quiet too. That was a very bad sign. At least she still had a ready smile, showing Nicky the tiny red bobble clinging to the white stick, which was all that was left of the lollipop Nicky gave to her as the plane descended. As she waited for the seatbelt sign to be extinguished, her mind went back to what Claire said yesterday afternoon about never really knowing what went on inside your child's head. The thought made her throat close. Something was seriously wrong, and Lola had shut her out.

Her fingers itched to grab Lola's hand and insist she shared what had happened. She needed to fix it before they left the airport, but she didn't know how. She couldn't exactly demand to know Lola's private thoughts and experiences. Lola was making it patently clear she didn't want to talk. She was losing her, and in another few years, Betsy would pull away too. Teenagers didn't show you the progress of their lollipops. Teenagers didn't show you what was going on inside their heads. If she'd been a different kind of mother, maybe they'd be close enough to discuss everything. But she wasn't, and she continued to fail her daughters.

She shot a glance at Elias. At the very least, he'd done something that had seriously upset Lola, that much was clear. They'd been love's young dream yesterday and now they couldn't even look at each other and Lola couldn't stop crying. What had he said in Lola's room earlier? She was desperate to know. If she didn't have the details, how could she make it better?

By the time they got to arrivals, the inside of Nicky's head stung. She had half an hour at most to find out what went on before she had to hand her precious kids over to Julian. She needed to help Lola before that happened. She had to get her to speak to her. Another awful thought slammed into her mind. What if Julian found out that Nicky had been drinking with Sabine instead of taking care of their girls? He'd already hinted at a custody battle. She hadn't been too concerned since she had the video of him soliciting and the evidence of his infidelity sitting on her phone, but if he could prove she'd been neglectful, he could use it for his case. The thought drained all moisture from her mouth.

Lola and Elias stood at opposite sides of the baggage carousel, both with their eyes trained on the various shaped bags and cases paraded in front of them. Elias leapt forward and retrieved Sabine's sleek black case.

'Please tell me what's wrong,' Nicky said quietly to Lola, hoping she'd masked the desperation she felt. 'I want to help.'

'I told you I don't want to talk about it,' said Lola, huffing and taking a step away.

'But...' *But what? I need to know what happened because I am not in control of my own thoughts and my imagination is taking over? I'm scared something terrible has happened to you and I'm not coping? I'm worried your father will take you away from me because he doesn't believe I'm capable of looking after you?* 'I'm your mum. Talk to me.' Despite her best efforts, her tone was urgent. She was running out of time.

'You can't help. No one can.'

Nicky shuddered. She was about to reply when she saw her old, battered case approaching and leaned in, tugging at the handle, trying to lift it before it moved out of her reach. She caught her little finger in the handle and gave a yelp of pain, then managed to drag it to the ground, hardly able to shake the pain from her finger before having to do the same with Betsy's pink case. At least Lola lifted her own from the carousel. That was something. Her pinched lips and death-stare told Nicky it might be dangerous to ask her anything more. She might end up pushing her even further away. She glanced across at Elias to see if she could guess what he was thinking, but his down-turned mouth and sad eyes didn't offer any clues.

'What's going on with those two?' Nicky said, following Sabine into the toilets, thinking maybe Elias had confided in his mother. It was the only time she'd managed to get her alone since they'd left the villa. Elias had stuck by her side since the minute they'd got in the taxi. She thought about mentioning the bruise on Lola's thigh but couldn't think of a way without her worst thoughts and fears about Elias becoming clear.

'Dunno,' said Sabine. 'How are you doing?' She rubbed Nicky's arm and peered into her eyes.

'I'm fine. It was good to get it all off my chest, to be honest.' Nicky moved out of the way of a woman exiting the bathroom. 'But I'm a bit worried about Lola. Has Elias said anything?'

'Not a thing,' Sabine said lightly. 'And I don't want to pry. None of our business, is it? Such a shame. I had high hopes for those two.' She shrugged. 'Looks like we won't be fighting over who gets to wear red for the wedding after all.'

'Lola's...' Nicky didn't get to finish the sentence because a cubicle became free, and Sabine ducked inside. She wanted to tell her Lola was hurt, genuinely upset, and Julian was picking the girls up so she wouldn't have the opportunity to find out what happened, but she was next in the queue and when she emerged from the toilet, Sabine had already gone. It was probably for the best. Sabine's comment about not prying was probably pointed. It was all right for her, though. Her son was going back to their family home with her. And he wasn't the one in tears.

Eventually they trailed under the green 'nothing to declare' sign and out to where expectant faces watched for those arriving from behind a flimsy barrier. Nicky didn't see Julian at first, then Betsy shouted, 'Daddy!' and left her side, just as she had in Nicky's imagination that morning. When Julian came into view, Betsy tucked under his arm, Nicky wished she'd at least run a brush through her hair and put some lipstick on. He would be judging her and finding her lacking, just as he always did. Julian looked like a thinner, more polished version of the man she'd been with for twenty years. He wore a fitted shirt that showed he'd lost weight and perhaps started working out since they'd split up. His slim-cut jeans and chunky boots were new too, as was the neatly shaped stubble on his chin. He'd made an effort. Who for? Maybe he wanted to show her what she was missing. Typical of him to think he was still desirable, even when he made her skin crawl.

She watched Lola approach her father and wrap her arms around his neck. He hugged her back and when he closed his eyes, a flash of white-hot rage consumed her. How dare he absorb all that love from her girls? How could they offer it? It felt like a betrayal. Where was her heartfelt embrace from Lola? Julian was a disgusting excuse for a father. He had destroyed their family. More than that, he'd destroyed her. Why did he get the love when she was the one who did all the work to make them know they were safe and loved? The love belonged to her. They belonged to her.

He looked up and she saw him appraise her. She wanted to roll into a ball and hide. How did he manage to make her feel so small with just a look? 'Julian.'

'Nicky.' His voice was curt. 'Enjoy your break?' The implication that she didn't need a holiday because her life was one big holiday was there, under the words, even if she was the only one who could hear it. It had been one of the central tenets of their marriage; she should be grateful to him for working so hard, so she could lounge around the house all day.

'Yes, thank you, it was lovely.' She kept eye contact, even though she wanted to look down at her sandals. She wouldn't be diminished by him any more. She would be civil and courteous in front of their children, as she promised herself she always would be.

Sabine walked straight past. Julian had never been her favourite person, and now Nicky had disclosed how he really treated her, her refusal to acknowledge him was no surprise. She automatically started to make up excuses for her friend in her head. She hadn't meant to be churlish, she'd just had a bad flight. She was tired. She'd been grumpy all day. Nicky gave her head a shake. She didn't need to mitigate for Julian's moods now. He wasn't her problem. Added to which, he didn't even seem to notice. He hugged the girls into his sides. 'I've missed you two.'

A waft of his aftershave reached Nicky's nose. That was different too. Everything had changed and now her daughters were huddled against the man who used to be the centre of her orbit. She was a meteor, broken off and hurtling away from the planet that had been her home, heading for what felt like a massive black hole. 'Give me your case,' she said to Betsy. 'Everything you need is in Lola's.' She took hold of the handle of Betsy's case, annoyed she couldn't send them back to Julian's with all their washing. There was no point; he would use it as a weapon to show how lazy she was, how she didn't care for the girls properly. And it wouldn't be done, so she'd just have more to get through when the kids came back home.

'Right then, say thank you to Sabine.' She turned her head and searched for her friend. She was standing with Elias near the sign for valet parking. Betsy ran over and hugged Sabine around her waist. Sabine dropped kisses on her head. Betsy and Elias gave each other a limp high five. That wasn't Betsy's usual way. She'd loved spending time with Elias. Nicky expected her to hug him too. Betsy knew something. That made it worse. She flicked a glance at Julian to see if he had any questions about the interaction, but his face was impassive. She had to stop second-guessing his reactions. What he thought shouldn't be her primary concern.

'Thanks, Sabine,' Lola called. She gave a tight smile and waved. Ordinarily Nicky would have insisted her daughter went to say a proper thank you, but since Elias was standing right next to Sabine, looking miserable and unusually awkward, she let it go.

'I'll drop them back on Tuesday,' said Julian. 'You're getting a holiday after your holiday. All right for some.'

Typical of him to make it seem like he was doing her a favour by having the children. Was that how he felt when he dropped the children home, like he was having a holiday from them? It was the opposite to how Nicky felt. She was bereft. Hollowed out. Pointless. She didn't answer him; instead, she reached for her girls, saying, 'I'll miss you two.'

Lola gave her a quick hug and Betsy squeezed her tightly. She tried not to show she was breathing them in, trying to absorb their essence to see her through the coming empty days. Then the three of them walked off towards the short stay car park, leaving Nicky standing all alone.

'Nicky,' called Sabine. 'Come on.'

She wasn't all alone. She had her friend, and in that moment she felt more gratitude to Sabine than she had felt for anyone in her life.

'He looked like a prick with that stubble,' said Sabine when Nicky reached her. She linked her arm through hers and led her out of the terminal. 'Who does he think he's impressing with those clothes? Such a try-hard.' She squeezed Nicky's arm, and with Sabine by her side, she could almost manage a smile.

But then she studied Elias, whose gaze was on the floor ahead of him, and the questions started up again. What had happened between him and Lola? What were the two of them hiding, and why?

24

NICKY

'I could sleep for a week,' said Nicky, yawning and laying her head against the passenger side window of Sabine's car. 'What did we think we were doing, drinking that much booze when we had to travel today? I'm broken.'

She hoped that was a good enough excuse not to have to chat on the journey home. Being in a confined space with Sabine and Elias felt wrong when she was convinced he'd hurt Lola in some way. Even if the injuries to her leg were nothing to do with him, her emotional state was. She glanced at him through the car's enormous wing-mirror. He was staring down at his phone, his face blank. If she knew him better, she would have asked what was going on between him and Lola. Surely most best friends are close enough to each other's children to have honest conversations? But Sabine's time abroad, plus her and Julian's dislike of each other, meant that, even after a week away together, Nicky was still on polite terms with the man-boy in the back seat. She certainly couldn't come right out and say what was on her mind.

She watched the cars to her left as Sabine overtook them on the motorway, wondering about all the people inside and what their lives were like. A woman driving a BMW was laughing. The man in the passenger seat stared at her with what looked like adoration. Then she watched an elderly couple, the bespectacled man leaning towards the windscreen, the woman sitting by his side with a contented expression, and grief that Nicky would probably grow old alone settled over her.

As they drew into her road, the sight of her lovely house through the rain-splattered windscreen made her want to cry. If she had the girls with her, coming home to a house in darkness wouldn't have affected her. But she was alone, and she was dreading the emptiness. Sabine stopped the car outside and said, 'Home sweet home.'

Nicky leaned across and hugged Sabine. 'Thank you so much, for everything.'

'You going to be all right?' Sabine said quietly into her ear.

''Course,' Nicky lied.

'Okay.' Sabine released her. 'Look after yourself, you hear me?' She wagged a finger. 'See you soon, lovely. Enjoy the peace and quiet.'

How little anyone understood what it felt like to go home to a house filled with nothing but silence. Tears collected behind her eyes as she put her key in the lock and turned. The case's wheels sounded just as loud on her hallway's wooden floor as she'd known they would. Despite her protestations, Elias insisted on bringing her bags in and she surveyed the room, imagining seeing her house through his eyes. Sabine's family home was a modern, open-plan house filled with light. They had a huge kitchen extension with bi-fold doors, and every ceiling had some kind of skylight, showing off huge pieces of artwork to their best advantage.

Her own house might be terraced, and have neutral decor, but she loved the high ceilings and original fireplaces. She loved everything about it. Now she was home and had to face all of the realities she'd been trying to avoid thinking about when she was on holiday, like how she could afford the enormous utilities bills. She waved at Sabine and Elias from the doorway, trying to read Elias's expression as the car pulled away, but he was obscured by the window wipers slashing at the rain that was now falling in spears.

Closing the door, she turned to face the stillness. Goose-bumps rose on her skin. The house was cold and lifeless. She wanted Betsy to throw her school bag down on the floor, run into the kitchen and open the cupboard, searching for a snack. She wanted Lola to wander in and complain Betsy had eaten all the prawn cocktail crisps and left the cheese and onion, and everyone knew she hated cheese and onion. She would do anything to be able to remind her children to turn the lights off when they left a room, not to eat any rubbish because they were having dinner in half an hour. Her house should smell of toast, laundry and that sweet perfume Lola insisted on spraying all over her clothes, not this dank, musty, unlived-in smell that hung in the motionless air.

She imagined the girls at Julian's. Despite his insistence she should feed them nutritious, homemade food and limit their screen time, she knew in her bones that he'd order them greasy takeaway pizza and ice cream and let them watch whatever they wanted on the streaming channels he could still afford to pay for. He'd be on his phone whilst the TV blared, and the girls would see that as their cue to multi-screen too. The apartment would be warm and noisy, nothing like the voided-out house Nicky stood in now.

She lifted the chilled bottle of cheap white wine from the fridge door and turned the screw top. She'd promised herself that she'd cut down on her drinking when she got home, but it was still the final day of the holiday, wasn't it? She poured a large glass and carried it into the sitting room, then slumped on the sofa. Her phone beeped with a text from Julian.

> What's wrong with Lola? She's got a face like a slapped arse. Jesus, you can't even give the girls a good holiday, can you? I knew I should never have let them out of the country with you. I won't make that mistake again.

She fought the shame that welled as she read the message. She shouldn't have opened it, but when he had the girls, she had to. They might need something, or be hurt, lying in a hospital bed, or worse. But this was just another jibe designed to hurt her. It was like the venom he used to spit at her when they lived in the same house was still building inside him, so he had to put it into cruel messages, reminding her what a waste of space she was.

He had a point, though. What was wrong with Lola? If she was still distressed now, then something significant must've happened on Nicky's watch. She typed out one response after another, but nothing seemed right. Lola clearly hadn't disclosed her relationship with Elias. Why would she, after sixteen years of having Julian's hypocritical, sexist version of morality shoved down her throat? Lola wasn't stupid. She knew her dad needed her to present as an innocent little girl for him to accept her. But that meant she had no one to talk to and was suffering alone. Nicky couldn't bear it. She took another slug of wine, then went into the kitchen to refill her glass. This time she didn't bother putting the bottle back in the fridge.

She had to reply to Julian. If she didn't, he'd send message after message about how neglectful she was, how she didn't care about anyone except herself and how the girls would be better off without her. She typed:

Give her a big hug from me.

She composed a long text to Lola, then deleted it, instead just sending a couple of kisses to both girls' phones, letting them know she was thinking of them. Any more and she might push Lola further into her shell.

She imagined Julian's face contorting when he saw her non-committal reply. That wasn't her biggest concern, though. However hard she tried, she couldn't stop her brain from pulsing with images of Lola's face as she'd stared out of the aeroplane window and the ugly patch of red on her thigh. Her expression was haunted. Something bad had happened to her girl, and it was her fault. She was the one who was supposed to be taking care of her daughters. As she glugged the wine, her thoughts spiralled and the more she hypothesised, the more convinced she was that Elias was guilty. She just didn't know what of.

25

SABINE

When Nicky texted to invite her over for a drink on Monday evening, Sabine was tempted to say no. Work was always busy after a break and she was looking forward to an early night. She reread the message.

> Can you come over for a glass of wine this evening?

If the message had started with 'fancy coming over', she probably would have declined. But 'can you' sounded more like Nicky needed the company and she hated the idea of her being lonely, especially after what she'd shared on the last evening in Zante.

She could still hear Nicky's voice as she sobbed down the phone line the day she'd thrown Julian out. She could hardly speak when Sabine arrived at the house half an hour later. 'He's gone,' she'd said, tears cascading down her face. She'd shown Sabine the video Julian's mistress had sent, and even Sabine was shocked at how depraved that man was. She'd known he was a slimeball, but this was next level. She had optimistically thought that Nicky would channel her fury and become a firebrand woman scorned, but instead, she seemed to be weaker than before. 'Now I have to cope on my own,' she'd said, through tears. 'I can't do it. I don't know how.'

Sabine was shocked at quite how convinced Nicky was that she wouldn't cope without that prick. It wasn't as if he ever did anything for the girls, or around the house, as far as she was aware. She'd disliked Julian intensely – ever since he tried to slide his hand up her thigh in the back of a taxi soon after he and Nicky met – and she'd always presumed Nicky would come to her senses one day and split up with the creep. She deeply regretted not telling her friend what her new boyfriend had done, but she'd been so convinced Nicky would soon see him for what he was and dump him, she'd decided it wasn't worth the upset. She'd been so sure it wouldn't last. She'd even practised how to explain why she'd stayed quiet, because looking back, it was a terrible decision.

When Nicky then announced they were engaged, just four months after they met, it felt too late to tell her what a sleaze he was. Instead, Sabine convinced herself he wouldn't be unfaithful now he and Nicky had made a commitment, even if he was still a dick. Nicky seemed so happy, and Sabine couldn't bear to burst her bubble. After Nicky finally showed her the video, through floods of devastated tears, Sabine was even less inclined to share what had happened. She could have saved Nicky from all that hurt more than twenty years before, but she'd chosen not to. The guilt of that weighed heavy on her.

At their engagement party, Sabine had cornered Julian after she'd had a few drinks. 'Just to be clear,' she said over the music pulsing from the PA system, 'I made the mistake of not telling Nicky what you did in that taxi, but if I get even the hint you are behaving like that again, I won't hesitate.'

Julian pulled his top lip over his teeth. 'I'm sorry, I don't know what you're talking about.'

'Don't play the innocent. You know exactly what you did.'

He held up his palms. 'Seriously, I have no idea.'

Sabine wanted to slap his smarmy face. 'When you tried it on with me in that cab.'

He let his head drop to one side and pouted. 'Sounds like wishful thinking to me.'

Nicky came over then, her face glowing with happiness, and Julian wrapped his arms around her waist and pulled her tight against his body. He kissed her deeply, then opened one eye to look at Sabine. With a rising mix of fury and ick, she shook her head and walked away.

Now, Sabine believed she had some making up to do. She arrived at Nicky's at seven-thirty. 'I've brought wine.' She held up a bottle of Picpoul. 'But I can only have one because I'm driving.' The house smelled slightly mildewed. Sabine had put the heating on at her own house when she'd got home from Greece to counter the miserable weather. She put her hand on the radiator in the hall. It was cold. Instinctively, she knew not to mention the cold or the smell. Nicky would see it as criticism. 'What did you have for dinner?'

Nicky turned towards the kitchen where a bottle of wine, already three-quarters finished, sat on the worktop next to a bowl of crisps and a pot of hummus. 'Bits and bobs. No point cooking for just me.'

She was drinking alone. That wasn't a good sign. Sabine put the wine in the fridge, noticing the shelves were all but bare. 'Bits and bobs of what? There's nothing in here. We've been home for two days. Why haven't you done a big shop?'

'Like I said, there's no point when it's just me. The girls are back tomorrow. I'll go to the supermarket before Julian drops them off.' Her words slurred.

Sabine closed the fridge and examined Nicky's face. Despite the light tan from last week, she looked drawn. 'You need to look after yourself, not just other people, you know.'

Nicky poured a glass of wine and handed it to her as Sabine surveyed the kitchen. 'I know what will cheer you up.' She placed her glass on the counter and walked to the far wall. She stroked the cream paintwork. 'A bit of colour.' She stood back. 'Maybe not colour exactly, perhaps a green-ish grey.' She turned, assessing the space. 'Yes, on these two walls.' She moved to the pine cupboards. 'And we could get new doors on these. It wouldn't cost too much to transform this room. I could bring some colour swatches over next week when things at work have calmed down a bit.'

She turned to Nicky hoping to see her face brightening. Instead, her chin was puckered, and her bottom lip trembled.

'You don't have to change the cupboard doors,' Sabine said, suddenly concerned. 'Or anything if you don't want to. Is it too soon? What's wrong?'

Nicky ran her hand through her hair, which was unusually greasy at the roots. 'I can't afford new doors.'

'I get a brilliant discount.'

'I can't afford the water bill, never mind discounted kitchen glow-ups.'

Sabine knew things were tight, but she had no idea basic bills had become an issue. 'I didn't know things were that bad. I'm sorry. I'm not surprised you were a bit...' She stopped. This wasn't the time to be critical.

'A bit what?' A deep V formed between Nicky's eyebrows.

'Well, you were bound to be anxious with all that going on in your head.'

'It wasn't that I was anxious about,' said Nicky. She stood and retrieved her glass then took a big slug of wine.

The atmosphere in the room changed and Sabine didn't know why. 'Okay...'

'I was anxious because I was anticipating what would happen between Lola and Elias, and surprise, surprise, I was right to worry.'

She took another drink and Sabine wondered how many glasses Nicky'd had before she arrived. Her eyes had a glassy quality, and the imprecise way she waved her arm suggested she was more than a little bit tipsy.

'It's a shame things didn't work out, but that's what they do at that age, isn't it? They get obsessed and think they're in love, then they fall out and go chasing the next shiny thing.'

'My daughter is not a shiny thing.' Nicky spoke slowly.

Sabine blinked. She was stone-cold sober and struggling to keep up with Nicky's changing mood. 'No, that's not what I meant. I just meant it's not a big deal, is it? It was a holiday romance, and clearly now it's over.' Nicky swayed. Sabine tried a soothing voice. She could do without this tonight. She'd tried to change Nicky's anxious behaviour on holiday, but nothing she said or did seemed to make a difference, and now this. 'I think you're having a stressful time, and everything feels bigger than it is. Let's not blow it out of proportion.'

Nicky put her drink down heavily, the base clanking against the granite. 'That's all right for you to say, it wasn't your child in tears in the plane.'

'I'm sorry Lola was upset, but... what do you want me to say? Teenage relationships end.'

Nicky moved closer. 'What did he do?'

Sabine's hackles rose. 'Why do you presume Elias did something?' The alcohol on Nicky's breath made her want to turn away. 'How do you even know it was him that ended it? It could have been Lola.' It was typical of Nicky to assume her innocent little girl was the victim. Elias hadn't exactly been full of the joys of spring since they got back. 'It could easily have been Lola that broke it off.'

'Why would she do that? Boys like Elias...'

'Go on.' Sabine set her jaw. She didn't care how upset or drunk Nicky was or what she'd been through with Julian, she didn't have the right to come at her son. 'Boys like Elias what?'

Nicky's neck moved as she swallowed. 'I know what teenage boys are like.'

'And Lola is an angel, is she?' Trying to steady her rising anger, Sabine widened her eyes in a challenge.

'I know my daughter.'

Sabine laughed. 'Do you? Do you really? Do you know her as well as you knew your husband?'

Nicky froze. 'What?'

'Nothing.' Sabine blanched. Maybe she'd gone too far, but Nicky had pushed her to it. She moved Nicky's glass to the side. 'How much have you had to drink?'

'What did you mean?'

The hairs on Sabine's arms stood to attention. 'Look, I don't know what you want from me. You seem to be accusing Elias of doing something to Lola, but neither of them has said anything bad happened. I know you're having a terrible time, and I'm sorry for all the stuff that happened in your marriage, truly, but just because things are rubbish for you at the moment, you can't invent problems that aren't there, and you certainly can't start accusing people of things out of the blue like this.'

'I know something went on. Lola had a bruise on her thigh.'

'What? And that's down to Elias as well, is it? What exactly are you suggesting, Nicky?' Surely she couldn't be saying what she thought she was? A headache throbbed in Sabine's temple.

'She said she fell, but I don't think that's what happened.'

Sabine had heard enough. 'Stop right there. I'm not listening to any more of this crap. If she says she fell, then she fell. Aren't things bad enough without you inventing more shit to worry about?'

'I'm not inventing it. Elias hurt Lola. I know he did.'

'Don't you dare accuse my son.' Sabine pointed in Nicky's face. 'Your head's a mess, I get that, but clinging on to this ridiculous notion like a dog with a bloody bone is stupid. Fanciful. Just because your husband is a shit, it doesn't mean you can tar every man with the same brush.'

'This has nothing to do with Julian. Have you got any idea what it took to tell you the truth about my marriage? I can't believe you're throwing that back at me.' Her face contorted in rage.

'What am I supposed to think when you start making things like this up? He's my son, for God's sake, my only child, and you're making dangerous and damning insinuations about him with absolutely no grounds. You've clearly got an issue with men but it's pretty clear that Elias is not the problem here.' She paused to breathe. 'You need to sober up and get some sleep.' Sabine stood and left the house, slamming the door behind her.

26

NICKY

The alarm went off at 8 a.m., making Nicky's heart leap in her chest. She'd spent most of the night replaying the argument with Sabine, only drifting into a feverish sleep about three hours ago. The throat-closing certainty Elias had hurt Lola was stronger than ever. She was an idiot for having drunk so much again. She hadn't been able to resist buying and opening a bottle each night since she'd come home from holiday. The second glass was the one that dulled the silence in the empty house. She always planned to stop there, but somehow the bottle was always empty before she stumbled up to bed.

Last night she'd told herself she needed Dutch courage to ask Sabine for Elias's version of events, but there was no excuse for getting smashed on a Monday night, especially when all it did was make her brazen and combative. She rolled over and groaned, half-remembering Sabine saying something about Julian, but she couldn't recall exactly what.

She hauled her body to the side of the bed where her phone was charging. There were no notifications. What was she hoping for, a message from Sabine telling her everything was okay? A loving message from Lola? Even Julian had stayed silent. She pushed everyone away. Was it any surprise she was alone?

There was no choice but to do a shop before the girls got back, but the lights and noise of the supermarket made it feel like a battleground. Despite her limited funds, she bought the crisps Betsy liked, and the ridiculously overpriced chocolate Lola was always asking for. She was trying to buy their love with treats – not only pathetic, but dangerous too. Everyone knew you shouldn't use food as a reward or a consolation. Or alcohol. She would do better next week. For now, she needed her children to like her. She threw a packet of paracetamol in the trolley, set her jaw and marched past the wine aisle, keeping her eyes averted.

She was putting the last of the groceries away when a key scraped in the lock. The sound of Betsy's chatter reached her, and it was all she could do not to run into the hall. Instead she walked nonchalantly through to where Julian was rolling the suitcase inside. Betsy flew at her and flung her arms around her. 'I missed you.'

'I missed you too.' Nicky hugged her tightly. Lola was standing behind Julian. Nicky tried to catch her eye, but she stared at the floor. 'You all right, love?'

'Yeah.' Lola nodded. 'I'll take this upstairs.' She kicked off her trainers then rolled the suitcase to the foot of the stairs and began to lift it up step by step. Betsy squeezed past her on the stairs, and soon it was just Nicky and Julian in the hallway of the home they'd shared until a couple of months ago.

'Coffee?' she said. She'd made a plan in her head on the way back from the supermarket, but carrying it out was another thing altogether. She was going to ask him for his keys. He had no right to let himself into this house any more. But she wanted to know if Lola had disclosed anything, so first she had to be convivial.

Julian blinked, looking as shocked as if he'd been offered a kiss with tongues. 'Erm, yeah. Why not?' They went through to the kitchen and Julian sat at the table in the same chair he'd always sat in at breakfast and dinner. He filled up so much space. Nicky's stomach made a fist.

She filled the kettle and spoke over the running water. 'How were the girls this weekend?'

'I told you,' Julian said. 'Lola was a right misery.'

'Yeah, she seemed a bit off when we were on the plane.'

Julian tutted. 'She's a teenage girl. Hormonal and dramatic are her default settings.'

Typical of him to put it down to hormones. Whenever Nicky had pushed back during their marriage, he'd tell her she was being irrational because of her hormones. It could never have been down to her treatment by a man. Rage simmered inside her. Nicky reached into the cupboard for two mugs. She wanted to smash them into her ex-husband's face. 'That's a bit harsh.'

'Is that right?' He stretched his arms then put his hands behind his head and knitted his fingers. It was a familiar movement and now Nicky could see how smug it looked. He was a self-satisfied, middle-aged narcissist, and she hated him with every cell in her body. 'Well, you'd know, wouldn't you? I can hardly get her off her phone.'

'So much for spending quality time with your children.'

His expression changed and her muscles clenched tight. She forced herself to breathe evenly.

He stood, his eyes narrowed. 'You know what, I'll give the coffee a miss. I thought we might be able to have a civilised conversation, but you're clearly not capable of that. Is it any wonder that Lola can't control her moods, when she's got you as an example?' He lifted his palms and moved towards the door.

'Why has Sabine always hated you?' She hadn't planned to say that, but now it had come out, she really wanted to know.

'What are you talking about?' Spit flew from his mouth with the words.

Nicky clenched her fingers at her sides. She wasn't going to back down any more. 'She's never liked you.'

Julian gave an artificial laugh and lifted his gaze to the ceiling. 'She's your best friend.' He made quote marks with his fingers. 'You two have always been weirdly close. She's hardly going to be best pleased with the man who you think cheated on you. She probably thinks she's being loyal.'

She let the 'you think' go, despite all the evidence she'd seen with her own eyes. 'It's not that. She seemed fine with you when we first got together, then both her and Leo seemed to go off you overnight.'

He huffed. 'Maybe I don't fit with their leftie, liberal, arty-farty ideal. Perhaps they could see I wasn't impressed by their trendy North London vibe.' His voice was mocking. How had she ever thought she loved this man?

'Perhaps it's just because you're a dick.' She'd never said anything like that to him before. It was liberating.

Julian laughed. 'Are you drunk?' He peered at her. 'I thought you looked rough when I arrived, but I didn't like to say.' He took a step towards her, and she instinctively stepped back. 'If you've taken up day drinking, I'm not sure I should leave the girls with you. Perhaps I should go and get them.'

He moved to the foot of the stairs and opened his mouth. Panicked, Nicky put out her hand. 'Of course I haven't been drinking.' She hoped he couldn't smell the remnants of last night's binge. 'I'm just tired. I'm sorry.' The apology came out in a rush. She dropped her eyes. She wasn't even slightly sorry, but she couldn't give him any reason to suggest taking the girls away with him. She didn't know if he could, legally, but she knew she didn't have the money to fight any case he brought. She realised she wouldn't put it past him. How had she been married to this odious man for so long? Sabine was right; she didn't really know him. She hadn't even seen him clearly until recently.

He eyed her suspiciously, then shouted, 'Bye, girls.'

Betsy replied. There was no sound from Lola's room. Julian turned to Nicky. 'See? That's the manners you taught her.' He moved to the door and went to open it.

'Can I have your keys, please?' Nicky said. She kept her eyes on the polished floorboards, her heart rate increasing.

When she glanced up, his hand stilled on the catch. After a second, he said, 'Unless you've forgotten, it's my name on the deeds and the mortgage.'

'You don't live here.' She held out her hand, hoping he wouldn't notice it tremor. 'I'd like your keys.'

'My children live here.'

'Then give me a key to your flat,' she said, emboldened. 'My children spend time there too, so by that argument, I should have keys to your place.'

'Oh, for fuck's sake. I don't know what's got into you.' He took his keys from the pocket of his jeans and waved them in front of her. 'I suppose Sabine put you up to this?'

'Nope,' said Nicky. 'This is me not putting up with your shit any more.' She held out her palm.

A smile crept on to his face. 'Do you know what?' He snatched the keys into his fist. 'I think I'll keep these. You never know, I might decide to move back in.'

'You don't get to make that decision.' Sweat prickled in her armpits. All the strength she'd felt a minute ago drained away.

'We'll see.' He shoved his keys back in his pocket and turned to leave.

When he slammed the door behind him, her body thrummed with adrenaline. He couldn't just decide to move back in if she didn't want him to, could he? A sound came from upstairs. She listened. It was Lola crying. She would have to worry about Julian later. Her daughter needed her. She was sick of her and her girls being taken advantage of by men. It ended now. She would find out what had happened to Lola, and she would do something about it.

Nicky knocked on Lola's bedroom door, then went in without waiting for a response. The blinds were down, daylight seeping in at the bottom edge, highlighting Lola's scattered possessions on the windowsill: a pink pen with a feather at the tip, a jug she'd painted at the pottery place in town. The things of childhood. Nicky's eyes took a moment to adjust to the gloom. She could make out Lola, face down on her bed. The crying was quiet now, muffled by the pillow, but Nicky could see her daughter's body shuddering. If she was still this upset days later, then Nicky's instincts were right. Something terrible had happened. She'd waited until she got home to let it all out. That was oddly reassuring. 'All right if I switch on the light?'

Lola shook her head, so Nicky took her hand off the switch. She pushed the door closed behind her and went to sit on the mattress beside her crying child, resting a hand on her back. 'Want a cuddle?' To her surprise, Lola lifted herself to sitting and flung her arms around her neck. The sound of her sobs, so close to Nicky's ear, speared straight into her heart. 'Oh, sweetheart.'

She hugged Lola to her, feeling her narrow ribs expand and contract under her hands. 'Oh, love.'

She made shushing sounds and stroked her head from the crown down the length of her silky hair, saying, 'It's okay. It's all right.' After a minute, Lola's breath grew steadier. 'Want to talk to me about it?' Lola loosened her arms and sat back, crossing her legs. She lifted her pillow and hugged it into her middle, looking to Nicky like the small, sad little girl she'd comforted when she lost her favourite stuffed elephant, or fell over in the garden all those years ago. It didn't feel like years, though. It felt like yesterday.

'I'm scared you'll be angry,' said Lola, glancing up, then back down at the bed.

'I won't be angry. I promise.' She left it a beat. 'Is this about Elias?' Nicky kept her voice quiet and calm. Lola nodded, fresh tears dropping on to the pillow.

'What happened, sweetheart? One minute you were both as happy as Larry, then... You haven't cried like this since you lost Ruffles.'

Lola's lips twitched upwards at the mention of her blue elephant toy. 'I don't know how to...' Lola stopped. 'I can't say the words. It's too...' She covered her face with her hands.

Nicky took a breath. 'I think something happened between you and Elias on the last night of the holiday. Am I right?'

Lola fell on to the bed and shoved her face into the pillow.

'Why don't I ask you questions, and you can nod or shake your head?' Nicky recalled a parenting podcast she'd listened to once that said teenagers find it harder to talk when face to face with their parents. It suggested going for a walk or talking in the car. Face down in a bed in the half-light would have to do. 'Are you upset because Elias broke up with you?'

Lola nodded.

Nicky took in a long breath. 'That's what Betsy wanted you to tell me?'

Lola wiped her nose on the back of her hand. 'That's the bit Betsy knows about.'

Blood thundered in Nicky's ears. 'But that's not the only thing upsetting you?'

'No,' said Lola, her voice muffled but distinguishable. She thumped her fist into the mattress. 'This is so embarrassing.'

'Don't be embarrassed. I want to help you, sweetheart. I hate seeing you so upset.' She kept her voice level, then waited a second. 'Can you tell me what happened?' That wasn't a shaking or nodding question, but the anxiety swilling in her stomach needed her to get to the point.

'We went to the beach after everyone had gone to bed.'

Nicky closed her eyes, then opened them again. It took all her strength to say calmly, 'You and Elias?'

Lola nodded.

'You planned it?'

'See, I knew you'd be angry.'

'I'm not angry, I'm trying to work out why you're so upset.' A lump formed in her airways. 'Did things happen between you and Elias at the beach... sexual things, I mean? Is that what you meant when you said "it's not just that?"'

Lola turned her head slightly. One eye peeked out at Nicky. Nicky set her face to neutral, then tried a gentle smile. 'It's okay, sweetheart. I'm not angry.' She was angry. The outrage from all the times she'd been screwed over by men flared inside her: that stupid boy in sixth form who'd brought her parents' disapproval down on her, Julian and his years of abuse.

Lola sat up and tucked her legs in, resting her sad face on her knees. 'We drank some vodka.'

'Vodka?' Nicky couldn't help her voice rising in pitch. She swallowed to try to quell the fury, but it still burned in her throat.

'I knew you'd be like this.' Lola hid her face behind her knees.

Panic tightened Nicky's chest. She couldn't stop now. With considerable effort, she made her voice soft. 'So, you drank some vodka. What happened then?'

Lola's shoulders rose and she let out a shuddering breath. 'We... we had sex.'

Nicky froze. She knew it. A buzzing started in her ears. Elias had sex with her and dumped her immediately afterwards. He was just like all the other men. He thought women and girls were only there for his gratification. All the things Julian said about little tarts who didn't have any respect for their bodies flashed across her brain. The hypocrite. And Elias was no different. She wanted to sob for Lola, to scream. Instead, she said, 'Okay. Did you use protection?'

'Yeah.' She continued to cry.

'Okay. It's okay, sweetheart.' Nicky's skin burned. It wasn't okay. It was all that was wrong with the world. Why did the men have the power? Why did she and Lola have to suffer because of their inability to be decent and good?

'I'm sorry, Mum.'

'What are you sorry for, love?' She spoke gently as her heart galloped in her chest.

'I feel... ashamed... I didn't want...' She stopped and sobbed into her folded arms.

'You didn't want to what, darling?' Sweat sprang up along Nicky's hairline. 'Please, Lola. Tell me what you mean.'

Lola shook her head.

'Can you tell me why you're upset? What exactly happened with you and Elias?' Even saying his name made her want to smash her hand into the wall. 'Did he—'

'The next morning, he said he thought we should stop seeing each other.' Lola spoke through her sobs.

A bright flame whooshed through Nicky. She gripped her fists so tightly her nails dug into the flesh of her palms. 'He finished with you the morning after he had sex with you?'

'Don't say it like that.'

'Like what?'

'All angry, as if it happened to you. I knew you'd react like this. That's why I didn't want to talk to you.' Lola stood, arms crossed tightly.

'You keep telling me I'm reacting angrily when I'm really not.' She thought she was covering it well. She wasn't screaming or smashing things, despite the violent urge to. She got to her feet, forcing her hands to unfurl. 'I'm just trying to work out exactly what happened. I'm not reacting like anything.'

Lola shook her head. Tears poured down her cheeks. 'I feel bad enough. I don't need—'

Nicky moved to her daughter and gathered her in a hug. White-hot acid swirled in her abdomen. 'I'm so sorry this was your first experience.' Her mind went back to the boy from church who'd cried after they had sex, then confessed their sins. She hated him with every molecule in her body. 'Elias didn't... he didn't hurt you, did he?' She didn't know if she meant physically or emotionally. All she knew was how wounded and humiliated she was after her first sexual encounter.

'I can't talk to you about this.' Lola's sobs wracked through Nicky's body as if they were her own.

'I saw the bruise on your thigh and the graze. Did that... Was that because...?'

Lola's crying grew louder. 'I was drunk.'

'How drunk?' said Nicky. This was getting worse and she could hardly contain the distress pushing at her skull. She bit down on the inside of her cheeks and pulled Lola to face her. 'How drunk were you, Lola?' Lola tried to turn away, but Nicky held on to her shoulders. 'Were you too drunk to consent?'

'Mum, don't.' She pushed Nicky's hands away and fell on to her bed.

'Did you consent to have sex with Elias, Lola? How did you get those bruises?'

'I can't talk about this any more. Please, Mum. Please leave me alone.'

Nicky felt dizzy. This was what men did. They took what they wanted and left destroyed women in their wake. 'But we have to talk. If you were drunk, then you can't have—'

'Leave me alone!' Lola shouted.

'Lola, you don't understand. If he got you drunk and had sex with you, especially if he hurt you, and then dumped you—'

'I knew you'd react like this. This is why I can't talk to you. Get out of my room!' Lola shrieked, and Nicky had no choice but to do as she was told.

28

NICKY

An hour later, Nicky's insides were still molten lava. She was overwhelmed by thoughts of what her daughter had been through. She allowed Betsy to watch TV downstairs with a packet of crisps, then, as if jet propelled by her fierce mother's instinct, she raced back to Lola's room. She didn't knock this time. Her agitation wouldn't allow it. 'Do you think we should go to the police?' she said in a rush. 'We probably should have gone before, because, you know, evidence, but if we go now then you can still make a statement. They'll be able to see the bruise at least.'

The blinds were up now so she could clearly see the horror on Lola's face. 'What? No. What are you talking about?' Her top lip rose in a grimace showing her perfect, even teeth. It was only six months since her braces had come off. If she'd still been wearing braces would Elias have seen she was still a child and left her alone?

Nicky held up her phone. 'I've been trying to work out whether British police have any jurisdiction in Greece, and I'm not sure, but—'

'No.' Lola shook her head. 'This is mad.' Her eyes darted

around the room as if she was looking for a means of escape. 'I'm not going to the police. There's no... I just want to forget it ever happened.'

'Sweetheart—' Nicky wanted to cradle her to her chest and tell her everything would be all right. She would make it all right. She wouldn't let men destroy her. It ended here. She remembered Sabine's refusal to go to the police after Toby raped her and saw the pattern repeating and repeating. Men hurt women, and women carried the scars and the shame again and again and again.

'No, Mum.' Lola was crying, and every sobbing convulsion sent a shiver of pain through Nicky. Lola covered her face with both her hands and bent forwards. 'I wish I'd never told you. I knew you'd act like this. I can't talk to you about anything without you feeling like you have to fix it.'

Nicky took a step forward. 'That's not—'

Lola dropped her hands. Her eyes sparked with anger. Lola was rarely angry. She was a good girl. She was compliant and helpful.

But Nicky knew that it was shame making her defensive, and Lola would know that in time too. She wouldn't allow Lola to make the same mistakes she had, and she wouldn't be passive any more, not when her daughter's physical and emotional wellbeing were at stake.

'You treat me like a little kid who needs to be wrapped up and kept safe, and I'm not.'

Nicky was tempted to tell her that she was, and in her eyes she always would be. 'Trying to stop bad things happening to your children is a mother's job.' It was her only job and she was failing again, just like she had a million times before.

'You take it too far. You want to be in my life, in my business all the time.'

'Your business?' Nicky almost laughed. She was a sixteen-year-old school kid, not the CEO of Apple.

'Yes.' Lola raised herself to her full height, an inch taller than Nicky. 'I need you to let me have a life of my own. I don't need you interfering and having a massive emotional reaction on my behalf. Honestly, Mum, I have to think about how you'll react before I tell you anything, that's why...' She let her hands flop at her sides. 'I want to be able to be upset without you being upset.'

That was preposterous. She was asking her not to be a mother. 'You're only sixteen. Something awful has happened to you and all I want to do is help. How am I the villain here?'

'You can't fix everything. And I don't even want you to.' She turned to the window and gazed out across the garden. 'At least Dad treats me like an adult.'

An acidic laugh escaped Nicky as she thought of all the times Julian had made her intervene with the girls so he didn't have to. He was the one with the strong views on what a teenage girl should and shouldn't be, yet she was always the bad cop. 'Does he?' The bitterness was clear in her voice.

Lola stared out of the window, her arms folded tightly around her. Nicky could feel the space between them growing wider and didn't know how to cross it. For the last hour she'd been gearing herself up for action. She was going to do whatever it took to be a good mother. She would show Julian that she was up to the job, even when things were at their worst. She was ready to take on the world to support her daughter and now that fiery energy had nowhere to go.

'I think I might ask Dad if I can live with him,' Lola said quietly.

The air left Nicky's lungs. 'What?'

'His flat is nearer my sixth form.' Her voice wobbled. She turned, her eyes full of tears. 'It would only be one bus from his.'

'I'd drive you every day.' It was all Nicky could think of to say. In that moment she would crawl the distance on her hands and knees with Lola on her back if it meant she would stay. The truth about what kind of man Lola's father really was flooded her mouth, but she kept her lips tight. It wasn't fair to load that on to a child. And she was still a child.

'It's not... I just think it...'

'You think you'd prefer to live with your dad? Full time?' Her voice wavered. She coughed to try to disguise it. How had a discussion about Elias turned into this? It didn't make any sense. The room took on a dreamlike quality, blurred around the edges. Lola was a willowy silhouette against the window. Her beautiful, precious girl wanted to leave this room behind. She wanted to leave her for that prejudiced, controlling and intentionally cruel man. Her fingers itched to bring out her phone and show her what kind of man he really was. She wanted to rewind time and let her see that she really was hurt by his jibes, that it wasn't okay to talk down to your wife, to belittle her at every opportunity, whilst making out that she couldn't take a joke if she got upset. But in her heart, she knew that Lola couldn't have been oblivious to what went on. Despite everything Nicky had done to smooth things over, she'd caught the furtive glances between the girls, the sweetness in their voices when they addressed their father when he was in one of his moods.

He'd never been abusive towards them. Nicky always told herself she would have left him immediately if he had. But that didn't mean they hadn't been hurt by living in a home like theirs. Yet, still, Lola would prefer to be with him.

Desperation constricted Nicky's lungs. She wanted to make Lola see that her dad would never look after her the way she did. But she couldn't, because her vigilant care was the reason Lola wanted to escape. And she'd been a bad enough parent without bad-mouthing her father.

Lola turned back to the window. 'I don't know. Maybe.' The next words came out quietly. 'Would you be all right if I did?'

Nicky put a hand to the door frame to stop her knees from giving way. 'Of course I'd be all right. I mean, I want you with me, but you'll be off to uni in a couple of years anyway, so I can't hold on to you forever, can I?' The pain of knowing Lola was concerned about how she would cope made her insides liquid. That's how much she had failed as a mother. Her daughter felt protective of her, but despite that she still wanted to walk away. 'You don't have to worry about me. You never have to worry about me.' Lola turned and rushed at her, wrapping her arms around her neck. There was so much love in that embrace and somehow that made it worse. Her daughter loved her, but she still didn't want to live in the same house as her. She would never forgive herself for this. Never.

As she held Lola in her arms, another, equally painful thought came to her. Perhaps this wasn't really about Julian or even Nicky. It definitely wasn't about public transport. Lola had only mentioned moving in with Julian after they'd talked about Elias. Maybe it was the memory of that night she wanted to escape. The experience could have been so traumatic, she couldn't bear to even live with the people who were on that holiday with her.

She held her child even closer, a new sense of purpose swelling inside her. She'd made mistakes, but Elias was the biggest problem here. If she could fix that, then maybe Lola would stay.

29

SABINE

'What the hell are you talking about?' The phone was hot against Sabine's ear. Surely she couldn't have heard Nicky correctly?

'He can deny it all he wants,' said Nicky's voice through the phone's speaker, 'but the fact is, Elias had sex with Lola when she was too drunk to consent. He plied her with vodka, then took advantage of her. She's in pieces here. I'm waiting for her to calm down, then I'll talk to her about next steps.'

'Next steps? What do you mean?'

'Speak to your son about what he's done. I've got to go. My daughter needs me.' The line went dead.

Sabine tasted bile at the back of her mouth. She put the phone down with a shaking hand. Nicky's voice had been cold and calm on the phone. Somehow it would have been better if she'd sounded hysterical, then Sabine would have been tempted to dismiss what she'd said as exaggerated nonsense. But she was clinical in her accusation, and Sabine was left with her dreadful words ringing in her ears.

She thought about calling Leo to ask what he thought she should do, but she'd made light of the brief relationship between

Elias and Lola when they got back from Zante, and it would be a shock to hear this accusation out of the blue. She decided it would be better to discuss it with Elias before mentioning it to his father.

Elias was currently out with friends. She'd been glad when he said he was heading out that evening because he'd been moping around the house since they got back from holiday. It wasn't like him, and she'd wondered if he was more upset about splitting up with Lola than he'd let on. Like Nicky, she'd initially presumed he was the one who'd finished it, but recently she wondered if Lola might have dumped him. She didn't like the idea, which she knew made her a bad person, but what mother didn't think their child was the best, the most worthy of love? She hadn't quizzed him about it. She wasn't like Nicky, all up in her kids' business.

Now, sitting nursing a glass of Malbec and waiting for Elias to get home, it crossed her mind there might have been something else behind his taciturn behaviour. No. She wouldn't allow her mind to go there. She cursed Nicky for even putting the thought in her head. At 11 p.m., she heard the front door click open. She stood, a nervous fluttering in her abdomen. 'Elias.' She crossed the open-plan room.

'Hey. How come you're still up?' He shook off his jacket and hung it in the under-stair cupboard. It must be raining. Droplets of water shimmered in his dark curls.

She had the urge to run her hand through his hair like she used to when they sat watching TV together when he was small. 'I had a call from Nicky.'

He stilled. 'Yeah?' He sat on the bottom step and undid the laces of his trainers.

She waited for him to ask how Nicky was, or something else about the call. That would be a normal response. Why wasn't he speaking? 'Aren't you curious about what she wanted?'

Elias stood and walked towards the kitchen, leaving his shoes at the bottom of the stairs. 'I presumed you two talked all the time.'

'We do.' She paused. 'We did.' Elias took a glass from the cupboard and ran the tap, holding his finger under the water, then letting it tumble into the glass. She hadn't mentioned the argument she and Nicky had yesterday. She'd tried to put it out of her mind, but now Lola had made an accusation, she couldn't pretend none of it was happening. 'But this was about you and Lola.'

Elias's shoulders dropped. 'Oh?'

'Can we sit?' She gestured to the table.

He sat, rolling his glass between his hands, watching the liquid swirl up the sides.

'She's in a bit of a state.'

'Lola?' He looked up with real concern in his brown eyes. That was reassuring. She berated herself. She didn't need reassurance from her son. She knew him. He was a good person.

'Well, yes, but Nicky too. She said...' She steeled herself. 'She said you and Lola had sex.'

Elias closed his eyes, lifting his eyebrows so his lids pulled taut. 'Wow. This is not a conversation I want to be having.'

'Me neither,' said Sabine. 'But I'm afraid we have to... because that's not all she said.'

He opened his eyes and peered at her askance. 'She had details? I knew Lola and Nicky were close, but that's weird, right?'

'She said you were drinking vodka.'

Elias let his head hang back. 'Yes. We had some vodka. It's not a crime, is it?'

'Well, it is, actually. You're both underage.'

Elias huffed. 'Okay. Technically it is, but come on, it's not like we weren't drinking the rest of the week. Sorry, I get it was sneaky to take it from the villa, but it's not that big a deal, is it?'

'Was Lola drunk when you had sex?' Sabine forced herself to say the words.

Her son's brow puckered. 'What?'

She placed her hands on the table and took a deep breath. 'Nicky thinks you got Lola drunk and took advantage of her.'

'You what?' Elias rubbed the back of his neck. Colour rose in his cheeks. 'Is she seriously suggesting that? That's crap. It's bull-shit.' He drew his shoulders back. 'Is that what Lola's said? Did she accuse me of having sex with her without her consent?'

'I don't know exactly what Lola said. I've only spoken to Nicky and that's what she suggested happened.'

'But that's bollocks.'

Sabine put out her hand. 'Before you get angry, run me through your version of events.'

His eyes grew wide. 'My version? You make it sound like I'll make it up.' His voice was high, and Sabine's heart thumped against her ribcage.

'No, that's not what I'm saying.' She reached for his hand and held it tightly. 'Of course I don't believe you've done anything wrong. I just want you to tell me what happened that night.'

'Well, for a start, I didn't take the vodka from the villa, she did,' he said, pulling his hand away and crossing his arms.

'What?'

'Don't look so surprised. I'd ask if I wanted it, wouldn't I? I don't need to lift alcohol.'

The disappointment on his face made her ashamed. 'Sorry.'

'I didn't even know she had it until we got to the beach.'

'But you did plan to sneak out together?' Sabine asked.

'Yeah, we planned that. She thought her mum was watching

her all the time and she just wanted a bit of time to herself – well, with me. For us to be on our own.'

'Is that all you planned? I'm sorry for asking, but I need to get it clear in my head.'

Elias rubbed his neck again. He took a gulp of water. 'This is so embarrassing. I can't believe we're doing this.'

'I know. I'm sorry.' She wasn't enjoying this any more than he was.

He leaned his forearms on the table. 'Before we went, she told me she wanted to lose her virginity.'

Sabine nodded. 'She told you that? It was her idea?'

'Yeah. I didn't push her, for God's sake. I'm not that guy.' He stared at her imploringly.

Sabine wanted to hug him, but there was more to say first. 'I know you're not. It's so weird she's said something different to Nicky. Why would she do that?'

He slapped the worktop, then took in a breath as if trying to calm himself. 'I have no fucking idea. Honestly, I did it all right. I asked for consent all the time. I made sure she was comfortable with every last thing. Jesus, I was so careful... I just can't believe she's said that I... It was her. It was her all the way. I was happy to wait. I promise you, I didn't even suggest it.'

Sabine looked down at the counter. She couldn't face him when she said the next sentence. 'Nicky said Lola had a bruise on her thigh.'

'That wasn't me.' He blinked fast. 'She fell over a couple of times on the way back to the villa. She was knocking it back at the beach. I thought she was nervous, but I didn't realise she wasn't used to drinking. Most girls I know get smashed on spirits every weekend. I don't think Lola does, though. I didn't realise she was that drunk. I swear I didn't take advantage because of that, though. Like I said, I'd already told her I was happy to wait.'

'Wait?' Sabine was confused. 'You planned to carry on seeing her? I thought you finished with her straight afterwards?'

Elias shook his head. 'No. That's not what happened. Jesus, this has all been twisted.' He took a gulp of water. 'I went into her room the next morning and she was acting all weird. She wouldn't look at me. I sensed she was regretting what we did, and I felt shit about that. I got the feeling she was about to dump me, so I tried to make it easy for her. I said something about how things would be different when we got back home, and if she just wanted to leave it as a holiday fling, I'd understand.'

'And what did she say?'

He lifted his palms. 'She said yeah, that was probably for the best. I was gutted, to be honest. I liked her a lot. I was going to ask her to be my girlfriend when we got back. She's different when she's not around her mum, really funny. She was cool. But I wasn't going to beg. When she was all tearful that day, I thought it was because she regretted having sex with me, because she wasn't really into me. That hurt. It was embarrassing, but it was more than that. Honestly, I thought we could be a thing. That's what I wanted.' He pushed his hair off his face. 'I can't believe she's said all that. It's not true.' He gazed at her with pleading eyes. 'That's not me. You've got to believe me.'

Sabine did. Of course she did. He was her son, and he wouldn't lie.

Lola had refused to say anything else to Nicky. She'd barely left her room and Nicky was struggling to keep her emotions and thoughts under control. When Sabine texted, suggesting they meet at a local park the next day, Nicky agreed. She was early and the air conditioning had turned off with the engine and now Nicky was sweltering. It felt like summer at last. The sun beat down relentlessly. She'd struggled to sleep a wink last night, since her thoughts kept returning to that beach, seeing images of Lola, overpowered, crying out for her mother.

She opened the door, but the air wasn't any cooler outside. Sabine's Range Rover pulled into the car park. Nicky's pulse thundered in her ears. It was no surprise her heart rate was up; a lot was riding on this meeting. Since Sabine had chosen a public place for them to discuss what Elias had told her, it was clear she thought so too.

Standing and closing the driver's door, Nicky pulled her linen trousers away from her sticky thighs. Sabine emerged from her car looking as fresh as ever in a blue floaty dress she'd worn at the start of their week away. Nicky had said how much she liked it.

Sabine complained it was dry clean only when she dropped a splodge of tzatziki down the front. She must've had it dry cleaned since she got back. The thought added to Nicky's fury. Of course Sabine could pay someone else to clean her clothes for her. She paid someone to clean her house too, whilst she spent her precious time choosing expensive fabrics and overpriced kitchen cabinets for wealthy clients who could afford to hire her for an extortionate fee.

Up until the last week, she'd always admired Sabine. She thought of her as artistic, entrepreneurial and business savvy; but watching her step from her enormous car, that admiration morphed into seething resentment. Lucky her, with her doting, arty husband, enormous home and gas-guzzling car. Julian was right. Sabine had it all and she'd forgotten how normal people lived. She probably never gave a thought to Nicky having to scrub her own toilet and iron her own clothes. With a privileged upbringing like Elias was being given, was it any surprise her son felt entitled to take what he wanted when he wanted, no matter the cost?

Sabine scanned the car park, her gaze eventually finding Nicky. She didn't smile. She marched in her direction. Nicky forced her feet to move towards her. 'Hi.'

They didn't hug or kiss each other's cheeks like they usually would. Nicky was glad the day demanded sunglasses, and they didn't have to meet each other's eyes; she was finding it hard to hold back tears.

'Hi.' Sabine's voice was curt. 'Let's walk.'

She turned towards the iron gates at the entrance to the park and Nicky stepped in time, trying not to focus on how clean and white Sabine's trainers looked in comparison to hers. She thought of the second-hand designer trainers she'd eventually agreed to buy for Lola for her sixteenth birthday. She could hardly get her head around the price, especially for 'preloved', but Lola had begged and pleaded for them. They were designed by some sports star Nicky had never heard of, and she'd eventually given in, blowing more money than she could afford on second-hand shoes. She would bet the same money again on Elias having similar trainers, but without someone else's foot-sweat already soaked into the insoles.

They passed a woman holding the hands of two small children, a girl and a boy. The girl had corkscrew pigtails like Betsy when she was small. Nicky keened for the feel of small fingers in her palm. Life was easier then, when the girls' hands were safely in hers. 'So, what did Elias say?'

Sabine took in a breath. 'Well, for a start, he says Lola took the vodka from the villa. He didn't even know she had it until they got to the beach.'

Nicky rolled her eyes behind her sunglasses. 'Did he?' They walked on. 'How does that fit with him drinking beer earlier in the week? He clearly likes a drink. Lola rarely drinks alcohol.'

'Is that right?'

Nicky's skin prickled. 'Yes, it is.'

'Or is she just good at hiding it from you?' Sabine ignored Nicky's tut. 'She was drinking whenever you weren't looking last week.'

Nicky started, then remembered Sabine needed to get Elias off the hook. 'You would say that.' A flock of pigeons took off from the path in front of them, making her jump as their wings flapped in a grey cloud before dispersing.

Sabine huffed. 'She would have a beer by the pool then put the bottle next to Elias's lounger so you wouldn't think it was hers. She drank wine when they were cooking. She's sixteen, I didn't think it was a big deal.'

Typically arrogant of Sabine to decide what was right for someone else's daughter. 'Then why hide it from me?'

'Because I knew you would see it as a big deal, like you do with everything else when it comes to the kids.'

The sun burned the straight line of Nicky's parting and sweat gathered under her arms. Inside, she seethed. 'So, you thought you had the right to decide whether my daughter was old enough to drink? What about Betsy. Did you sneak a couple of tequila shots into her Coke?'

Sabine shook her head. 'You have to overreact about everything, don't you? That's why we are where we are.'

'I'm not overreacting.' A man wheeling a bike along the path in the opposite direction slowed and watched them. She lowered her voice. 'And we are where we are because your son got my daughter drunk and had sex with her when she was in no fit state to consent.'

'That's not what happened.' Sabine stopped, deep lines ridging her brow above her glasses. 'It was Lola who suggested they had sex, not Elias.'

'Is that what he told you?' Nicky felt like laughing, the suggestion was so preposterous. She felt like crying too.

'Yes. He said Lola wanted to lose her virginity.'

The heat made her faint, or it could have been the mention of her daughter's virginity in such a public place. She imagined what Julian's reaction would be and shuddered. They passed a bed of purple dahlias, the petals on their enormous heads perfectly symmetrical. 'How do you explain the bruise on her thigh?'

'Jesus, Nicky. You can't truly believe Elias had anything to do with that? Apparently, she fell over a couple of times on the way back to the villa.'

Nicky spun to face Sabine. 'She was so drunk she fell more

than once, but Elias maintains she was sober enough to ask him to have sex with her? Does that sound convincing to you?' Sabine's mouth tightened. Nicky wished she could see her eyes. She needed her friend to understand how implausible Elias's story was. 'I'm sorry, Sabine, but I think you know as well as I do that Elias isn't telling the truth.'

'Don't you dare imply that I shouldn't believe my son.'

A burning sensation in Nicky's chest made her want to roar. 'I can't believe you're being so blind.' She wiped moisture from her top lip. 'Actually, I can. You're his mother, of course you believe him, but that doesn't make what he says true.' She remembered the night at university when Sabine wouldn't report what Toby did to her. 'I bet if, when we were back at uni, that creep Toby's mother had heard what happened to you that night, she'd have blamed you. She would have said you were leading him on, that you only said he didn't have your consent because you were embarrassed or ashamed. She would, wouldn't she?' She was on a roll now, the words coming fast. 'That's why most girls don't report rape, isn't it? No one believes them, or they blame themselves as much as society blames them. And the men get off scot-free, their mothers convinced their little angel boy would never violate a woman like that.'

'Stop right there.' Sabine grabbed Nicky's arm. 'Don't you dare equate Elias with that bastard.'

'He's a bastard now, is he? I thought he was innocent?' Nicky shook her arm from Sabine's grip, triumphant at her point being proved.

'Lola consented. She only changed her story the next day.'

'Your son took what he wanted, then dumped her.' Nicky's temples throbbed. Her skin was on fire.

'That shows how much you know.' Sabine pointed a finger in Nicky's face. 'That's not what happened. Lola finished with him.' She put her hands on her hips, as if she'd won the argument.

Nicky fought for breath. The dry air burned her throat. 'He's lying about that as well?'

Sabine rolled her head back. 'When will you get it? Lola couldn't even look at him in the morning. He saw she was struggling and gave her an out, and she took it.'

His excuse was clever, Nicky had to give him that. 'She couldn't look at him because of what he'd done to her.' Nicky's voice was strained with the effort to make Sabine see the truth.

Sabine threw her arms in the air. 'You've told yourself the story that works for you, haven't you? The one that keeps your girl the innocent victim and Elias the big, bad sexual predator. But that's a load of crap. Can't you see, Lola couldn't look Elias in the eye because she was ashamed of what she'd done? You did that to her. You passed down your prudish, conservative values and when she did what every other girl her age is doing, she felt ashamed. She was probably hungover and self-conscious and didn't know what to do with herself. And that's on you, Nicky.'

'Oh my God, is there nothing you won't say to make your narrative fit? Lola never showed any interest in sex until Elias came along.'

'Not to you,' said Sabine. 'How could she? From the little I know of him, her father's views on women's rights belong in the 1950s, and you just let him get away with that because you were too scared to stand up for yourself or your girls. And you're so buttoned up she probably thinks you'd send her to a nunnery if she even so much as looked at a boy's crotch.'

Nicky shook her head. Sabine might be right about Julian, but she was wrong about everything else. 'You don't know anything about me and Lola. We talk. How do you think I know what Elias did to her?'

'He didn't *do* anything to her, he did something *with* her. But you can't get your head around that, can you? You see sex as something men do to women. Do you know how warped that is?'

Nicky's vision blurred. There was some truth in what Sabine had said. She didn't see sex as a loving act. It never had been for her. It was something to be got through, something men needed and women didn't.

Sabine carried on. 'I think sex is a massive issue for you, and you're seeing what happened through that distorted lens.'

'How fucking convenient for you to think that, rather than facing the truth about what Elias did to Lola.' She pointed a finger. 'And don't think I've forgotten about that girl in Zante. You told me she was lying about what happened last year, but that doesn't sound quite so plausible now, does it? So maybe you should look at your own life before judging mine, and look at your son? Your actual son, I mean. Not the ideal version you've made up in your head.'

'Ha!' Sabine took off her sunglasses and glared at her with ice-cold eyes. 'Pot and kettle! I suggest you take another look at Lola too. And while you're at it, take a look in the fucking mirror.' She turned back in the direction of the gates and marched away.

31

SABINE

Sabine seethed all the way home from her meeting with Nicky. She wished she'd never suggested taking her and the girls to Zante. No good deed goes unpunished, wasn't that the saying? She was certain Lola was lying. Almost certain. Since Nicky had brought up that girl's accusation from last year – Cassia, she remembered now – there was a tiny, niggling question in her mind, and she hated her for making her doubt Elias for even a second.

Inside the house, she shouted up the stairs, 'Elias?'

'Yeah?'

She realised she'd half wanted him to be out so she didn't have to have this conversation. She kicked off her trainers and made her way up to his bedroom. 'Can I come in?'

'Yeah.'

He was propped up against the cushions on his bed. The sun shone through the skylight in the roof, brightening the room which, to Sabine's distaste, Elias had insisted on painting a blue so dark it was almost black. His electric guitar sat next to him on the bed, plugged into the small amp on the floor.

'Writing the next viral sensation?' she said, nodding at the guitar.

'Nah, I'm not feeling it.' He unplugged the lead from the guitar and the amp gave an electric squeal.

'Still down about Lola?'

He shrugged.

'Okay if I sit?'

Elias took the guitar and leaned it against the wall, then sat next to Sabine on the bed. 'What's all this about?' he said, adjusting a cushion against his back.

'I've just been for a walk with Nicky.'

Elias lifted his eyes to the ceiling. 'Right. What am I meant to have done now?'

Her heart started to thump. She couldn't believe she had to have another conversation like this. 'Nothing. I told her what you said.'

'And?'

She sighed. 'She maintains Lola is telling the truth.'

'Well, she isn't.' Elias peered at her, his dark eyes questioning. 'You know that, right?'

Averting her eyes from his, Sabine said, 'Of course.'

Elias slapped his hands on the mattress. 'You don't, do you? You don't believe me.'

'I do, it's just—' Elias went to get up. She grabbed his hand to keep him next to her. 'Hear me out. I do believe you, but there's a couple of things niggling at me.'

'Go on,' he said, his eyes boring into hers.

'Well, it's just that... you aren't always completely honest with me, are you?'

'What do you mean?'

'Like when I asked if you were smoking weed up here.' She

scanned the room for evidence of it now but couldn't see any. 'You swore you weren't, but me and your dad could both smell it.'

Elias's eyebrows lifted. 'You think because I pretended I wasn't smoking a bit of weed, that makes me a sexual predator?'

'No, of course not. It does show you're happy to lie, though.'

He rubbed the back of his neck. 'I'm seventeen. Of course I'm going to lie to my parents sometimes. I thought you'd go mad about the weed, rant on about it being a gateway drug and all that crap. I was trying to save myself the hassle. It wasn't a big lie.'

Sabine believed him. And it wasn't a big deal. She'd tried plenty of substances herself when she was younger, not that she was going to tell him that. But there was still something poking at her. She raised her eyes to the dark wood fan in the centre of the ceiling and steeled herself. 'It's just that, all this made me wonder about what happened last year.'

'What do you mean?'

'In Zante.' She watched his face contort when he realised what she meant, her skin tingling at his obvious shock.

'Are you serious?' He whispered the words, his lips twisted in disbelief.

'For Andreas to still be so angry this year... I just wondered—'

'If I'd assaulted Cassia as well as Lola? If I'm a serial sex offender?'

'No.' Was that what she thought? She feared it might be, and that sent shivers of horror through her. Surely she wasn't capable of believing that about her own flesh and blood, her beautiful boy?

'Oh, my God, Mum. Are you serious?' He put his fingers to his brow. His jaw hung open. 'Andreas is a psycho. Everyone knows that. Cassia is as mental as he is. I can't believe you think I might have done something to her. I told you exactly what happened, word for word.'

'I know, but—' The events of last year twisted in her head. She'd believed him without question. Had she been blinded by her love for him? Had she been wrong?

'But what?' He stood, rubbing his neck in fast movements. 'Demitri was there. He told you what she was like. She wouldn't leave me alone. I said I wasn't interested and when she kept turning up, I told her to fuck off, that I wouldn't touch her if she paid me. That's all.'

'I believe you. It's just that... I don't know, if two girls are saying things about you—'

'No smoke without fire, eh? Is that what you think?' Two angry circles reddened his cheeks.

'That's not what I think.' This was getting out of hand. She wanted it to stop. She stood and reached for him, but he drew away.

'Can you leave, please.' He shoved his hands in the pockets of his jeans, drawing his arms into his sides. He stared intently at the carpet.

'I just want to talk.' Sabine's voice cracked as she dipped her head to try to make him look at her. She'd somehow made her beautiful son think she thought he was a sex attacker. That's because, although she hadn't fully realised it, she had allowed the suggestion to permeate and live in the darkest place in her mind. How could she? He was her boy, her gorgeous, perfect boy. 'Look at me.' He glanced up, then back at the floor. The pain in his eyes was unbearable. 'I believe you, Elias. Of course I do.'

'I would like you to leave.'

She would have preferred him to tell her to fuck off. This calm, polite request felt so distant, so cold. She made her way to the door, then stopped and turned. Elias was facing the bed, his shoulders hunched. He shuddered. She crossed to him and put her hand on his shoulder, but he shook it off. 'I don't want you in here.' There were tears in his voice and Sabine's heart broke for her child. But there was nothing she could do. She left his room, closing the door quietly behind her.

32

SABINE

Fifteen minutes later, Sabine was nursing a cup of iced tea at the kitchen island, listening to the birdsong through the open bi-fold doors. The sound of birds was meant to be soothing, but it would take more than a few blue tits having a chat to lift her mood. An entire aviary couldn't touch it. Every cell in her body felt drained of life. She'd set fire to her relationship with her son, and she didn't have the first idea of what to do now.

She heard Elias's footsteps on the stairs and froze, bracing herself as he crossed the living space and approached the kitchen. He pointed the phone he was holding in his hand towards her. 'I didn't want to do this, but I don't feel like I've got a choice any more.'

'Do what?'

Elias climbed on to the grey leather stool next to her. 'Look at this.'

'What?'

Elias put the phone on the worktop in front of them and pressed play on a video, then crossed his arms, mouth set in a rigid line. Stubble darkened his jawline and Sabine hankered for the boy he had been, so she could say 'Silly Mummy made a mistake. I'm sorry. Will you forgive me?' and he would give her a cuddle and run off to play on his trampoline, forgetting all about the spat they'd had minutes before. But this was far more serious than a spat and she didn't know how to manage this grown-up version of her son. He felt like a stranger for the first time ever.

Sabine turned her eyes to the screen and watched in confusion as a pert bottom clad in Calvin Klein boxer shorts jiggled to a music track she vaguely recognised. She gaped at Elias, waiting for an explanation, but he kept his eyes on the screen. 'Why are you showing me this?'

He didn't reply, just swiped to another video. In this one, a hand ran down a flat stomach, stopping at the top of a pair of lacy pink knickers. Elias scrolled to the next video with a flourish that seemed deliberate. A torso dressed in a blue bikini danced provocatively to a track which seemed to consist entirely of a man repeatedly swearing. Sabine's mouth filled with saliva when she realised she recognised that bikini. 'This is Lola?'

'Yep.' Elias scrolled to the next video.

Heart racing, Sabine pressed stop. She didn't want to see any more. 'Are you sure?'

Elias picked up the phone and started to scroll. 'There's one with the side of her face in if you don't believe me.' He squinted at the screen as images flickered, the first notes of music distorting from the speakers as he moved from one clip to the next.

Sabine put her hand on his forearm. 'I do believe you. It's just that I can't get my head around it.'

'You thought she was the girl she is around her mum, but she's not.' He put the phone down with a clatter and pointed at the screen. 'I'm not saying she's like that all the time either, but she's not the sweet little innocent Nicky thinks she is.' He crossed his arms again, a lawyer having made his case.

'So, she what... makes porn?'

Elias laughed, but stopped abruptly, as if remembering he was furious with her. 'If you think that's porn, you're more sheltered than I thought. Everyone makes content like that. Loads of girls do, anyway. They've all got shadow accounts their parents don't know about.'

Sabine blinked. 'Have you?'

Elias shook his head. 'Nah. I don't need one. It's not as if you've ever stopped me doing whatever I want, is it?' There was something like derision in his voice, like that was a criticism. 'And, like I say, it's more the girls.'

'But, why?'

Elias shrugged. 'Attention, to get likes. For the kicks, I don't know.' He tapped the phone screen. 'I knew about this way before we went on holiday.'

Sabine's head was spinning. 'How?'

'We're connected. Everyone around here our age is. You come up in each other's feeds, and we all follow the same people.'

'On Instagram?'

'Insta, TikTok, Snap, all the platforms.'

'But you and Lola acted like you didn't know each other at the start of the holiday.' None of this made sense. She was struggling to keep up.

'We didn't. We haven't seen each other since we were kids and you used to take us to those soft play places in the holidays when you weren't working.'

In her mind's eye, Sabine saw a tiny Lola sitting quietly, gnawing on a brightly coloured plastic ball in the ball pit whilst Elias launched himself into the middle, shrieking in joy. Nicky had loved those trips to soft play, but Sabine soon started to make excuses for why she couldn't go along. All those screaming toddlers. It was an assault to all five senses, and much as she loved her son and her friend, that was not the way she wanted to spend her downtime. She'd suggested Elias's childminder might want to go along with Nicky, but then Nicky said she wasn't desperate to go back either. Looking back, Sabine could see now it was her company Nicky had wanted, and a brief twinge of guilt squeezed her heart. Elias had loved that place too. She'd been selfish, and it was dawning on her that it probably wasn't the only time.

'I'd seen her feed, though,' Elias continued. 'I knew she wasn't as buttoned up as she seemed, that's for sure.'

Sabine tried to work out how this fitted with what Nicky said about Lola. 'But Nicky checks Lola's phone. She takes it off her at night. She doesn't allow any technology in her room, but that's clearly her bedroom. When is she making these films?'

'She's got a burner.'

Stills from TV crime thrillers raced through Sabine's head. She saw shady thugs shoving envelopes of cash across counters, and dealers handing out illicit phones to their mules. 'Where the hell did she get a burner phone?'

'Don't look so shocked. She's not secretly involved with County Lines. It's her dad's old one, that's all. That's what she told me.'

Julian. She should have known. 'Does he know she's got it?' Nicky could be as vigilant as she liked, but she'd bred with a moron who couldn't see beyond himself and who was now free to act as he liked around the girls. It must be killing her.

'I didn't ask.'

'But you talked about this account?'

'Yeah, she asked which one I liked best. She's nothing like you think she is when she's with people her own age.' There was a softness in his eyes when he spoke.

Sabine tucked her chin into her neck. 'Clearly.'

'And you don't need to get all judgy. She's not making porn, just some sexy videos. She really hadn't been with anyone before that night. She's not like that.'

'I can't believe you're defending her after what she said about you.' Indignation billowed inside her like smoke.

Elias lay his palms flat on the granite. 'Yeah, well, I know I didn't do anything wrong, so I feel like... I keep thinking of messaging her, but you see all that stuff about messages being used as evidence. I don't want it to look like I'm pushing her into saying anything or having a go at her. I don't want to be accused of something I'm not guilty of, either. When even you didn't believe me, I thought I'd better show you this, so you could see Nicky has a warped view of what's really going on with Lola.'

Sabine covered his hand with hers. 'I'm so sorry. I do believe you.'

He took his hand from under hers. 'You didn't, though, did you?'

She drew in a quick breath. She couldn't recover this by lying. 'Nicky got inside my head. I'm so, so sorry.'

'But you know me.' He shook his head. 'I thought you did.'

'I do. It was...' There was no way to justify it. 'I made an awful mistake. I'm so sorry.' He didn't raise his eyes to hers and she wanted to sob and beg his forgiveness, but she was the adult so she should act like one. It would take time to heal the wound, if it could be healed at all. She picked up his phone. 'You know I'm going to have to make Nicky aware of this, don't you?'

Elias groaned.

'I won't have her maligning you, when she doesn't have all the facts.'

He nodded.

'And I really am sorry.'

Elias rolled his lips over his teeth and she knew she was

nowhere near forgiven. She'd betrayed her own son and didn't know how she would ever forgive herself. He stood and sauntered back to his room and Sabine sat alone in the kitchen, her stomach hollow with regret. The room was quiet except for the hum of the freezer, the chirp of birds in the garden and the sound of her phone keys as she started to tap out a text.

33

NICKY

Nicky's phone beeped. She peered at the notification: a text from Sabine. Even the sight of her name made her stomach acid gurgle. Gritting her teeth, she clicked on the message.

> If you want to know who your daughter really is, find her second phone.

Fire raged across Nicky's skin. Sabine was playing tit for tat, was she? Just because she'd been told some home truths about Elias, she had to pretend Lola hid secrets from Nicky too. Well, that was rubbish. Lola didn't have another phone. Why would she? If she did have a second phone, Nicky would know about it because she knew her daughter. They were close. She closed down the screen, went back to her laptop and carried on scrolling the recruitment website for jobs.

Her eyes kept wandering back to the phone. What had led Sabine to think Lola had another device? Elias must've told her that. She clicked on a job advertisement for an admin assistant, but after rereading the top line three times, she shut her laptop and stomped upstairs to Lola's room, swearing under her breath.

She wasn't looking for a phone. She was just going to prove Sabine wrong.

She stopped in the doorway, scanning the room. The pink pen with the feather was still on the windowsill next to the painted jug. The bed was unmade, the pale green quilt thrown back, the pillow dented in the middle where Lola's head had rested. Nicky felt like an intruder. Lola and Betsy were both out with friends and they weren't due back for hours, but her heart still raced when she imagined being caught searching through her daughter's possessions. It wasn't as if they were on good terms at the moment. It occurred to her that might be Sabine's motivation: to sever her bond with her daughter for good. She put her hand on the cold door frame. She shouldn't do this. It wasn't ethical. But Sabine had been specific. She would take a look, but only to prove Sabine wrong.

With a monumental effort, she stepped into the room, wondering where she would hide something if she was a sixteen-year-old. Not that Lola was hiding anything. She was certain of that. She patted the pillow. Nothing hard in there. She picked the pink and green cushions off the floor and pressed them between her palms. Nothing. This was ridiculous. What did she think she was doing?

She didn't stop, though. Next, she opened the drawers under the white desk that doubled as a dressing table. All she found was a mess of makeup, half-used blushers with no lids and lip gloss seeping from the tube on to the bottom of the drawer. That irked Nicky. Outwardly, Lola was so neat and ordered. Nicky had presumed the inside of her drawers would match that. Perhaps she should have examined the inside before, rather than trusting Lola would keep things in order. She was still a child, after all.

She started to screw the wand back into a tube of mascara, then thought better of it. When Julian lived with them, she used to clear up after the girls because he hated mess. But he wasn't there, and if she was working, Lola and Betsy would have to learn to pick up after themselves. She would make Lola do it when she got home. That was a better life lesson. You make a mess, you clear it up. She started to feel guilty about not teaching them that all along instead of taking the route which would most appease Julian. God, parenting was exhausting. Nothing was ever simple. Unless you were Sabine, she thought with a new surge of fury. If you were Sabine, you farmed parenting out along with everything else you deemed beneath your attention.

Turning to the built-in wardrobe, she tugged one of the brass handles to open the door. At least one side looked neat. Lola's dresses and skirts hung in bright rows. The shelves on the other side were in disarray, hoodies and leggings shoved in, unfolded. She huffed. Lola was in trouble when she got back. Nicky always reminded her to put her clothes away carefully since she'd taken the time to wash, dry and iron them for her. She pulled out a T-shirt she remembered ironing earlier in the week. It was criss-crossed with crumpled lines. That was downright disrespectful. Nicky had better things to do with her time than pointlessly iron clothes that were going to be screwed up by an ungrateful child. It occurred to her she didn't, in fact, have anything better to do. It was something she did to fill her empty hours. No one she knew ironed clothes any more and if Lola wanted something pressed, she was old enough to do it herself.

Her fingers prodded around the top shelf, then the second. Nothing was hidden. Of course it wasn't. She'd been sent on a wild goose chase and Sabine was probably laughing into her expensive coffee at the thought of having sent her into this unnecessary spin.

She kneeled to examine the bottom shelf where pairs of joggers were jumbled together. She pulled at one pair, then they all tumbled on to the carpet. Nicky huffed. When she began to fold the grey jersey, her fingers touched something slim and hard in the pocket. She reached inside and pulled out a red tube. Initially, she thought it was a lipstick and was irritated that Lola had left it in the pocket of her joggers. What if it had gone in the wash? It was bigger than an average lipstick, though. Nicky peered at the writing on the side. *Strawberry Ice*. She stared at the black tip, understanding seeping in. It wasn't a lipstick. It was a vape. Lola had a vape in her bedroom.

Heart pounding, she took up another pair of joggers and scrunched them between her fingers. Nothing. Maybe Lola picked the vape up by accident, thinking it was make-up. That theory was shattered when, in the next pair, she found another vape. Green this time. Apple Peach, apparently. She put her hand to her mouth. After finding the first one she could persuade herself that it was a mistake, or that Lola was just holding on to it for a friend. Now there were two, and Nicky had to accept they weren't accidentally left in the pockets. They were hidden. Lola vaped and concealed it from her. She was destroying her young lungs with whatever toxic chemicals made Strawberry Ice and Apple Peach flavours and she was taking in nicotine, a highly addictive substance. She couldn't believe her girl could be so stupid. They'd had endless conversations about the dangers of vaping. How smug Nicky had been when Lola agreed with her that only a fool would inhale flavoured poison.

Nicky believed her when she said she'd never do anything that dumb. She'd lied to her face. What else was she hiding?

Her heart plummeted, and it felt like she was moving in slow motion when she pushed her hand to the back of the shelf. There, in the darkest corner, just like she suddenly knew they would, her fingers touched something flat and cold.

34

NICKY

Leaving the tangle of clothes on Lola's bedroom floor, legs shaking with adrenaline, Nicky took the phone down to the kitchen and set it on the table. She sat heavily and stared at it, her insides twisting with dread. It was an explosive about to detonate. This piece of technology threatened to blow up her relationship with her daughter. And what would Julian have to say about this? He'd use it against her. She could hear him now, sneering at her for not having any idea what her child was up to in her own house.

Sabine's message replayed in her head. If she really wanted to know Lola, she should look for her second phone. Well, here it was. And there was something on there that would show her Lola's true self. Saliva collected in her mouth. She pressed the power button and watched the screen come to life.

It needed a passcode. Nicky wilted. She didn't even want to know what was on this phone. She was already reeling from finding the vapes. She stood and filled the kettle. Maybe a coffee would help her focus. Perhaps she should wait for Lola to get home and confront her with the phone and make her open it in front of her. She imagined Lola's face as she presented her with it and cringed as she anticipated the fallout. There was no way this would end well. Whatever was on there was bad. She could feel it in the pit of her stomach.

Sabine's message meant she knew more about what Lola was up to than her own mother did. That made her pick it up and press in the code she knew from regularly checking Lola's phone. It didn't open. She thought back to the meeting at Lola's secondary school where the deputy head told all the parents, in the sternest of terms, to interrogate their children's phones. That was the word he'd used: interrogate. That's why she insisted on knowing both of their passcodes. But Lola had used different numbers for this one. Clearly, she didn't want her mother to have access and there could be no good reason for that.

A heaviness settled in her chest. Despite Julian being the one who'd insisted on it, she'd genuinely thought she was doing the right thing, making sure both girls knew she would randomly check their devices. She believed she was making sure they weren't targeted by unsavoury characters as well as ensuring their content was always appropriate. She'd thought she was saving them from online bullying and random dick pics. She honestly thought they would thank her for it when they were older. It hadn't crossed her mind either of her children would be sneaky enough to get hold of another, secret phone for conducting nefarious activities. If she was entirely honest with herself, if either of them was likely to, she would have bet her life on it being Betsy, not Lola.

There was a roaring in her head. She realised it was the boiling kettle when it clicked off, leaving the kitchen silent again. At a loss, she tried Lola's birthday, then Betsy's. Both drew a blank. On her own phone she searched up how many times you could try a passcode before the device is disabled. Five times.

She'd already used three. She scanned the room, looking for inspiration, but the tired kitchen units and scratched worktops told her nothing. Her gaze rested on a framed picture sitting on a shelf amongst cookbooks she rarely used. It was of the four of them when Lola was about seven and Betsy was an adorable, chubby-cheeked toddler. They sat between their parents, Julian on one side, thinner than he was now, and Nicky, smiling, on the other.

The photograph was taken in Whitstable when they'd been to the south coast for a day out. It had been a scorcher, and they'd had a lovely day on the pebble beach, Julian swimming with Lola, Nicky paddling with Betsy. She almost smiled when she remembered holding Betsy's hands as the sea washed over her chunky legs, how she lifted her feet in their tiny pink crocs and kicked against the frothy waves. She could taste the fish and chips they'd eaten before getting the train back home, tired, sunburnt and happy. Briefly happy, at least. The memory of Julian running his hand up her top and cupping her breasts as she washed out all their water bottles at the sink came back to her. She pushed the memory away.

She crossed the room and took the picture down to have a closer look, examining Julian's face to see if his malignance was evident in two dimensions. She stared into his inanimate eyes, wondering how she'd tolerated him for so long. She opened a drawer and shoved the picture inside.

The thought of Lola or Betsy noticing it gone almost made her put it back on the shelf, but then a thought came to her. Julian. Lola might have got the phone from him. He upgraded every time his contract allowed, always wanting the newest gadget. He never traded in his old phones. Both the girls had their parents' old devices, but the one on the worktop wasn't a current model. It was very likely it was from before Betsy was first given a phone. She'd only been allowed to have one since she finished primary school a few weeks ago, so it wasn't unlikely a couple of old phones might have been left in drawers over the years.

She picked the device up and tapped in Julian's code, wondering if, even if it was his, he'd changed the numbers in an attempt to keep his secrets. The screen sprang to life. Of course he hadn't. He'd been arrogant enough to believe he could get away with anything, and that she'd be too scared to snoop on his phone. To her shame, he'd been right. Her cheeks burned with fury. She'd been worried about how Julian would react to Lola having another phone, when this one was his all along.

Only a few apps showed on the screen, all of them social media sites Nicky knew of. She swallowed hard, then opened TikTok. The logo came up, then a video of a young girl in leggings and a sweatshirt, dancing to 'Stand By Me'. Above her head, 'how to dance like a forty-year-old' was in bold white type. That wasn't too bad. Quite wholesome, really. Nicky swiped up to the next video. It was an actor she recognised from a crime drama having a dance-off with his teenage son. Nicky started to breathe more freely. This wasn't too bad. She wasn't on TikTok herself but if Lola liked to watch silly clips of people dancing, then there was no harm in that.

She saw a black icon that looked like a head and shoulders with 'Profile' written underneath. She tapped on that. A circle at the top of the page showed a picture of half of a beautiful woman's face. Underneath was a grid of posts. Sweat broke out on Nicky's skin when she began to understand what she was viewing. She clicked on the first video. A bottom clad in Calvin Klein shorts jiggled and bounced. Bile rose in Nicky's throat when she scrolled on. A woman's midriff gyrated in a provocative dance, showing snatches of a blue bikini. Only it wasn't a woman's body. It was a girl's. She knew because she recognised every freckle on that toned stomach. She'd bought that bikini in John Lewis, complaining at the time that it was barely there, just triangles and string. But, aware that Julian was no longer around to judge, she'd let Lola talk her into buying it and now, here she was, parading her perfect teenage body to anyone who cared to watch, to a soundtrack of a man rapping disgusting profanities.

She clicked back to the home page and looked again at the heavily filtered image of half a face. Half of Lola's face. She could see it now. This was her daughter's account. This was what Lola was hiding from her. Nausea gripped her when she realised Sabine was right. Nicky had no idea who her daughter truly was.

35

NICKY

It was difficult to keep her voice from shaking when Nicky called the mother of Betsy's friend to see if Betsy could stay a bit longer than planned, telling her that she was running late.

As anticipated, the mum was hugely sympathetic and offered to keep Betsy overnight. Nicky thanked her and accepted her kind offer.

She put her phone down on the table next to the one she'd found in Lola's room and waited.

At seven o'clock, Lola opened the front door. 'Sorry I'm late,' she called. 'The bus didn't come for ages.'

Nicky knew exactly when Lola would be back because she'd been tracking her on the Life360 app. She knew Lola hadn't left her friend's house for the bus stop until six-thirty, which was the time she was meant to be back. Another lie. How easily they came to her daughter. How naive and blind Nicky had been.

'I'm in the kitchen,' said Nicky. 'Come through, I need to talk to you.'

'I'll be down in a minute,' said Lola.

Feet thumped on the stairs. She listened as Lola's footsteps trod along the landing, into her room, then stopped dead. She imagined Lola staring at the jumble of clothes on the floor, then rushing to the bottom shelf. She pictured her stricken face, the fresh lies formulating in her head as she desperately tried to find excuses for why the vapes and a secret phone were hidden amongst her joggers.

She waited for the sound of Lola retracing her steps. Trying hard to keep her breathing steady, she listened carefully, but there was no movement upstairs. Exhaling a long, shuddering breath, she stood, took the phone in her hand, and went upstairs to Lola's room.

Lola was sitting on her bed, her elbows on her knees, head in hands. She didn't raise her eyes when Nicky sat on the mattress next to her. Nicky placed the phone in between them. 'Please explain why this was hidden in your room.' She steeled herself to be asked what she thought she was doing going through Lola's private things.

Lola shifted her head minutely to glance at the device. 'It's just Dad's old phone.'

Just? She wasn't going to play the victim, at least. That was something. 'And why was it hidden in your wardrobe?'

'I'd forgotten it was there.' Lola's voice was sulky.

'Don't lie to me.'

Lola let her hands drop. 'Okay. It's because you go through my phone and take it off me at ten at night, as if I'm Betsy's age. All my friends are on the group chat after that. I was missing everything and it wasn't fair.'

Nicky's shoulders ached from the tension. She hadn't even scoped out the group chats. What if it wasn't only friends Lola was talking to? What if it was dirty old men pretending to be teenage boys? 'Are you chatting to anyone else? Anyone you don't know?'

Lola's lip curled. 'No. I'm not that clueless.' Her tone was so like Julian's, it stopped Nicky in her tracks. Of course those years of hearing their mother denigrated would have sunk in. Why should they respect her when they had seen her treated like rubbish for all of their lives? She'd allowed it to happen. And she'd also shown them that it was acceptable for a man to treat a woman like shit in a relationship. She was a terrible mother.

But if messaging strangers was clueless, what was parading your body in public for all and sundry to see? Sensible? Measured? Socially acceptable? 'Is that why you vape as well, because everyone else does?'

'Actually, everyone my age does vape,' Lola snapped. 'At least we're not smoking. And it's nothing compared to what loads of people my age are doing.'

'Is that right?' The fact that was probably terrifyingly true made Nicky shiver. She heard her mother's voice telling her she didn't care what everyone else was doing. She'd say Nicky lived in her house, so had to follow her rules. And Nicky had promised herself she'd never turn into her mother, but Sabine said she had anyway. Although, if that was the case, Lola certainly wasn't following any rules she'd laid down.

'Yes. But I'm sorry. I'll stop. I promise.' Lola still sounded more defensive than contrite.

'If I check with Gaby's mum, and Izzy's, will they tell me they're happy with them vaping?'

'You can't do that.' She shook her head as if Nicky was being absurd.

'Why not? If everyone is doing it and all the other parents are okay about it, then what's wrong with talking about it?'

'You don't need to talk about it. It's just how things are. You're stricter than the others. You must know that? Other parents aren't freaked out by their kids growing up.'

That sounded like Sabine speaking too. She imagined the two of them having private conversations whilst they were in Zante, both pointing out what they hated most about Nicky's inadequate parenting. What neither of them knew was that half the rules had been thought up by Julian. It was him who wanted to keep the girls sweet and innocent, constantly telling Nicky that she wasn't parenting them well enough. The irony that it was his negligence that had led to where they were now made the acid burn her stomach lining.

She picked up the phone. It almost slipped from her sweating palm. 'Are all the other parents okay with this too?' She unlocked the phone with Julian's numbers. Lola's face went grey. She clearly hadn't expected Nicky to work out the passcode. She tried to snatch it from Nicky's hand. Nicky lifted it away and tapped on to Lola's TikTok account. She held it in front of Lola's face.

'Turn it off,' said Lola, her mouth contorting with distress.

'Look at it,' said Nicky, staring at her daughter's perfect bottom twerking on the screen.

Lola pushed her arm away. 'Don't, Mum. Turn it off.'

'Why?' said Nicky, scrolling to the next video, then the next. 'If you're happy for the world to see you like this, why not me?' She brought the phone towards her. 'Or your dad. Which one should I send to him? Which is your favourite?' She was being cruel now, she knew, but she wanted to show Lola how much she'd hurt her. She wanted her to be ashamed. If she was ashamed, she might stop.

'Mum, stop it.' Lola was crying now. 'Don't send anything to Dad. Please. Turn it off. Please, Mum.'

The sound of Lola's desperate voice broke through Nicky's furious trance. She closed the app. 'What the hell were you thinking, posting all that sexualised stuff?'

'I don't know.'

'You must know. You're an intelligent girl. You did this by choice. No one held a gun to your head, did they?'

Lola covered her face and cried into her hands.

'Have I ever really known you? Is that who you really are?' That was the question that kept running through her head. She'd lived an inauthentic life herself, pretending that her husband was a decent man, and their marriage was as happy as any other. She'd even told herself that story. How else could she have lived with the shame and guilt of not being good enough, or strong enough to leave? It had taken witnessing his betrayal in that video for Nicky to do what she should have done the first time Julian didn't take no for an answer. Her weakness had led to her daughter suffering. She would never forgive herself for that, or the terrible example she'd set.

Lola sobbed hard. 'No. It's not. You have to believe me.'

'But it's here.' She waved the phone. 'It's out in the world, and you intentionally did that. I don't understand why.'

'I don't know why.'

'Do you need the attention that badly? Is that how you want to be seen? What about the talks we've had about feminism and the male gaze?' Those conversations were always out of Julian's earshot. He would have scoffed and called it 'woke bullshit'. She had tried to introduce it, though, even if she didn't exactly live it. She'd wanted better for her girls. She saw now that it was a role model they needed, not empty words. 'Was that you just telling me what I wanted to hear?'

'No. Please stop.' Lola covered her face.

'What happened to the Lola I know?' The question ricocheted around Nicky's head. Where was her sweet, sensible girl?

'I'm here,' said Lola. 'I'm still here. That's not me. I need you to believe me.'

'How can I when I've seen you reduce yourself to nothing

more than a body, making provocative videos for God knows who to ogle?' Nicky was living proof of what happened when men didn't respect women. She couldn't bear for Lola to suffer in the same way.

'Please forget you've seen those. I won't do it again.' Tears streamed down her face. 'Please, Mum. Please don't see me differently.'

'I can't unsee things, Lola.' She took her daughter's arm. 'Look at me.'

Lola turned her head away.

'Look at me.' She held Lola's chin. 'I need to know why you did this. I need to understand.'

'I don't know.'

She released Lola's chin and dropped the phone on the bed. 'Come on. You're a bright girl. You must know.' All the adrenaline that built up as she'd waited for Lola to come home drained away, leaving her exhausted and terribly, terribly sad.

'It didn't seem like a big deal,' Lola said, rubbing her hand over her wet face to wipe away her tears. 'It's a private account.'

'You have over a thousand followers. How is that private?'

'It's only people I have mutuals with. I don't accept anyone who isn't connected to people I know.'

Nicky wanted to scream. She'd seen dozens of news reports of kids being targeted by dangerous predators because they thought they were a friend of a friend. That was exactly why she monitored her daughters' phones, or thought she did. 'I can't believe you think that's safe. I thought you kids were supposed to be tech savvy. You should know it only takes one of you to allow a random person in to make them appear legitimate.'

'I'll delete the account.'

Nicky sighed. 'How do you know those posts haven't already been shared thousands of times?'

Lola threw herself back on the mattress. 'It's not like I'm naked.'

'That's not the point.'

'What is the point?' She propped herself up on her elbows. Her cheeks had regained their colour and there was fire in her eyes. 'What about women's empowerment? Shouldn't I be allowed to post what I want when I want? It's my body, I can do what I like with it. Isn't that the point of feminism? My body, my choice.'

Nicky almost laughed. 'Are you really going to argue that you parading around in your underwear to a rapper swearing about bitches and hoes is feminism in action?'

'That's so like you.' Lola dropped her head back.

Nicky couldn't believe Lola was turning this back on her. 'You are sixteen years old. What you've posted is completely inappropriate.' Lola had stopped crying and was looking increasingly defiant. Nicky was losing control of the situation. She needed to step up and parent properly. 'And you are grounded for a month.'

Lola stared at her with wide, angry eyes. 'It's the holidays. You can't ground me until I start college.'

'I can,' said Nicky, crossing her arms, 'and I'm taking both phones until I can trust you to use one safely.' She hadn't planned to say that, but now she had she could see it was the only sensible course of action. It's what Julian would tell her to do, she knew that much.

'No,' said Lola. 'Absolutely not.'

'You don't have a choice, Lola.'

Lola stood. 'Well, I'm moving to Dad's.'

'What?' Nicky reeled like she'd been hit with a wrecking ball. 'You don't get to make decisions like that. You are a child.'

'I am not!' Lola screamed. 'This is exactly why I don't want to live with you any more. You act like I'm a little kid and I'm so over pretending to be perfect because you worry about me all the time if I act like a normal teenager. I'm sick of you expecting so much from me. I don't want to act like I'm some kind of angel any more and I can't breathe for you trying to manage my life.'

Nicky sat, frozen. She blinked to clear the image of the girl standing over her. This wasn't Lola. This wasn't her sweet, even-tempered girl. But her vision didn't clear to see the image of Lola she knew and loved. The angry, snarling version with scarlet cheeks was still standing there, staring down at her with hatred in her eyes. 'Lola, I—' She rubbed her hand over her face. She didn't want to tell Lola what an awful man her father was, but she had no choice. 'I don't think your dad is likely to be any less strict than I am. It was him who wanted me to—'

'Don't start blaming everything on Dad.'

'I'm not, I'm just saying he has strong views on how he wants you to behave.' She was floundering. 'I don't think he will agree to you moving in with him, anyway.' Julian had only ever weaponised custody. He had never suggested he wanted to co-parent, unless it was an attempt to make her back down.

'Dad actually said I can move in next week,' she said. 'I've already talked to him about it, so there's nothing you can do to stop me.'

36

NICKY

Lola refused to come out of her room for the whole evening. Nicky had her phones, so she had no idea what she could possibly be doing in there. Maybe she had a third. Maybe she had twenty. What she'd said about moving in with Julian was like a wound in Nicky's side and that evening, replaying the argument over and over in her head, Nicky felt like she was bleeding out. She couldn't talk to Julian about it. Not yet. She hadn't decided what to tell him about the TikTok account. She knew one thing: he would make sure Nicky knew it was all her fault.

Too drained and anxious to eat, she craved a glass of cold white wine. She wanted the crisp taste on her tongue, the haziness at the end of the second glass. The desperation she felt to find solace in the last dregs of a bottle was enough to tell her it was a terrible idea. She couldn't keep drinking the way she was and still take care of her girls. She was missing things. Important things, and she had no choice but to admit that could be down to the fact she'd been softening the edges of the world with alcohol for longer than she cared to admit. It was time to take control of at least that area of her life.

She took the bottle of Pinot Grigio from the fridge door, unscrewed the cap and poured the yellowy liquid into the sink. The fruity, citrus smell made her craving worse, and tears poured down her cheeks as the last of the bottle swirled down the plughole. She shouldn't need a drink this badly. It wasn't right. She threw the bottle into the recycling, where it clinked against all the others. She winced. No more, she told herself. No more.

Her mind couldn't settle on anything, so she gave up and decided to go up to bed. She took a sandwich upstairs for Lola. She pushed open her door. Her heart plummeted when she saw how Lola had occupied herself. Her clothes sat in piles on the floor and drawers were open, the contents ready to be put in the big blue Ikea bags she must've dragged out from the space at the bottom of the airing cupboard. She was packing. She really was planning to leave.

Frightened she would start to sob and beg her child to stay with her, Nicky put the plate with the sandwich on the desk and left, closing the door behind her. She went into her room and forced herself to type a message to Julian, asking him to meet her the following morning.

* * *

She didn't sleep, and when she saw Julian sitting at a table by the window of the café at the time they'd arranged, appearing rested and relaxed, she wanted to smash his head into the glass. The low-level fear that had made her tiptoe around him for decades was gone, replaced by white-hot rage. So much of this was his fault.

'I got you a latte,' he said as she approached, pointing at the tall glass sitting on the table.

'Thank you.' She should throw it in his face, not thank him for it. She hung her bag over the back of the chair and sat.

'You wanted to talk about Lola?' He crossed his legs. She always hated the way he crossed his legs. She scrutinised his face, his thick lips always ready with a self-satisfied smile, hooded eyes, heavy with condescension.

'Yes. She says she wants to live with you.'

He nodded. 'Yeah, that's what she told me.'

'So, what did you say?' She was being more direct than she'd ever been with him and she could see from the way he stiffened that he didn't like it.

'I said okay.' His eyes became dark slits. 'Why wouldn't I?'

Nicky's focus faltered. She hadn't expected this. She didn't expect him to want to cramp his style with live-in offspring, and that suited her just fine. It was understood that the girls would live at the family home with her. 'Because she needs to stay at home. With me.'

Julian held his hands out to the side. 'But why?'

'Don't be ridiculous, Julian. You know full well why. She needs a proper home, not a flat—'

'Yeah, I get that,' said Julian. 'That's why we need to talk about arrangements.'

'What?' Nicky gripped the coffee. The sides of the hot glass burned her fingers, but she needed the pain to stop herself from wailing.

'I'm changing jobs,' Julian said. 'Jumping before I'm pushed, to be honest. There's a round of redundancies on the way and after that there'll be a scramble for any available work.' He gave an exaggerated sigh. 'This move is the only guarantee of future income, but I'll have to take the basic salary and hope I can make up the rest in performance-related bonuses.'

He took a sip of coffee. Nicky knew it would be a cappuccino with one brown sugar. She knew what coffee this man liked and how he liked it. She knew the size of his underpants and what his sweat smelled like, and she hated every single thing. He carried on. 'I can't afford for you to keep the house and rent somewhere as well. And it's only fair that we both have a place with space for the girls, especially now Lola wants to move in full time.'

The floor was unsteady under Nicky's feet. This couldn't be happening. He couldn't be taking her home as well as her daughter. Not after everything else he'd done.

'Of course, you can get a lawyer to look things over,' he said, 'but there's a risk that, because my circumstances are changing so significantly, your monthly allowance will have to come under review too. Lawyers are expensive. If you hire one, then it's only sensible for me to do the same. If you agree to sell the house and split the proceeds, I won't question the rest of the arrangement.'

Was he trying to make it appear like he was doing her a favour? She was already struggling to get by on the money he'd begrudgingly allocated to her and she hadn't had a chance to do any real job hunting. Not that she felt qualified for anything these days after so long out of the workplace.

'I can't sell the house,' she said. 'The girls need stability. They need their home.'

'I agree.' His head dipped to the side. 'And since I'm going to be Lola's main carer, I need a decent place as much as you do.'

Rage bubbled up. 'Carer?' A few heads turned in their direction, but she didn't care. 'How exactly are you going to care for her? Give her another phone so she can parade around in her underwear on the internet for any pervert to see?'

Julian glanced around. 'Keep your voice down. What are you talking about?'

Nicky leaned forwards. 'She used the old phone you gave to

her to make sexy videos and then posted them on the fucking world wide web.'

The colour drained from Julian's face. 'Sexy how?'

'Dancing around provocatively in her underwear.'

He shook his head. 'I can't believe you let her do that.'

Nicky's head throbbed with the effort of not screaming. 'I didn't. It was the phone you gave her. I didn't know anything about it until I found it at the back of her cupboard.'

'I didn't give her a phone.'

'Then why did it open with your passcode?'

He rubbed his hand over his face. 'I mean, I keep my old phones in a drawer.'

Nicky threw up her hands. 'There you go. Have you counted them recently?'

Julian pursed his lips. 'Don't blame me for this. She was under your roof. Whatever she's done, she did it on your watch.' He pointed a finger across the table. 'You can't do a thing right, can you? The sooner she's living with me, the better.'

All the energy drained from her. Parenting was so, so hard and she had got it so wrong. But however bad she was, she knew in her bones that Julian was worse.

He sat back and crossed his arms. 'We need to sell the house. When Lola lives with me, I'll keep a proper eye on her so—'

'You haven't done a day's parenting in your life. You wouldn't know where to start.'

'I'll do a better job than you.'

'Is that right? Where were you when they were growing up?'

'I was working.' His voice was low and deliberate. It was the tone he'd used again and again over the last twenty years to shut her down. Well, she wasn't his wife any more and he didn't get to close down conversations because he didn't like where they were going.

'Ha. That's your excuse for everything. You think I couldn't smell the beer on your breath when you came home from working late? You think I never called the office to check if you were still there at the girls' bath time, or at the weekend?'

Julian averted his gaze. Why hadn't she said all this before? Even when he left, she stayed quiet, her voice stolen by years of him grinding her down. He was a liar, a bully and a bore and she'd had enough of putting up with his self-important bullshit.

'Well, if you've found it all so hard, you should be glad I'm stepping up now.'

'Stepping up? You've just seen an opportunity to get your hands on a better place to live. This isn't about Lola at all, is it? You don't see yourself as the kind of man who lives in a two-bedroom flat and think that, if Lola lives with you, you have the right to buy somewhere bigger.'

The muscles in his jaw twitched and she knew she was right. The thought of her precious girl being used so callously by her own father made her want to wail. She sat straighter. 'Should we even split the girls up?' Her heart rate increased with the risk of what she was saying. 'Maybe Betsy should live with you too? You'd be busy then, wouldn't you? She has gymnastics on Tuesday, art club on Thursday and football at nine on a Saturday morning.' She counted them off on her fingers. 'So you can say goodbye to your weekend lie-ins. And no doubt she'll join the netball club at her new school in September, so there'll be more running around for that.' She dropped her hand and glared at him.

'I'll be working,' he said.

'So will I,' Nicky snarled back. 'The budget you expect me to live on is paltry. I hardly have enough money as it is, and now you want me to move as well. I'll have to work all hours to just get by. So why shouldn't you do half the parenting?' She was on a roll.

'Did you think you can just swoop in and take Lola now she's sixteen and fairly independent? Did you think, she's only got a couple of years until uni, I can do that and get a nice place to live out of it? Well, that's not how parenting works.'

'I know that,' Julian snapped. 'And if you're such an expert, tell me why Lola can't bear to live with you any more.' He stood. 'The wheels are in motion, whether you like it or not. I'll arrange for an estate agent to come around and value the house next week.'

He stood and marched out of the café, leaving Nicky to stare after him, wondering how the hell she'd managed to lose her best friend, her daughter and now her home in less than a week. Something had to change. Though a screaming voice in her head was saying what needed to change was her.

37

NICKY

The house was quiet when Nicky got back home. Betsy wasn't due back for another couple of hours and Lola wasn't downstairs, so Nicky went through to the kitchen to make a cup of tea. Even opening the cupboard to take out a mug suddenly felt poignant. It came with a memory of Lola when she was only four, climbing on to the work surface to try to make Nicky a hot drink when she was heavily pregnant with Betsy. Thankfully Nicky found her before she tried to use the kettle. She could still feel the weight of her in her arms as she lifted her down. She'd been torn between telling her off and smothering her in kisses for her kindness. She'd never told Julian about that. She was already curating her life for minimum conflict, even then. She'd lived her life according to his expectations and demands. There was little left of her. What a waste.

She sat, too exhausted to finish making the drink. She thought about that angelic little girl who always wanted to help. How could she be the same person who lied and vaped and paraded her semi-naked body for all to see? A memory of bringing newborn Betsy home from the hospital floated into her mind. She'd sat where she was now with Betsy still in the car seat at her feet. Lola peered at her baby sister with such wonder in her gaze. She'd stroked her tiny face with one finger and looked up at Nicky with shining eyes. 'Thank you for having a little baby sister for me, Mummy,' she'd said.

The memory brought tears to Nicky's eyes. Between them, she and Julian had destroyed the happy family they'd had the potential to be: him through his controlling and narcissistic behaviour, her through attempting to varnish over the cracks with buckets full of pretence. She had wanted the perfect family, so she play-acted one. She wanted her children to be perfect so much that Lola had pretended in exactly the same way she had. Liars beget liars. It was only natural.

She let her head hang. Her job was to protect Lola when she was small and vulnerable. She had failed. Now she wanted more than anything to get it right, but how? Maybe she had to accept her role in Lola's life had changed along with her girl. Perhaps now her job was to allow her bright and beautiful child to be imperfect, to make mistakes without her interference. How else would she learn to trust her own decision-making? Maybe it was time to allow her little bird to fly and be there for her if she fell. The more she thought about it, the more sense it made.

Lola was a kind and giving girl. She'd demonstrated that over and over again. But she was also a teenager, thrumming with hormones. She was growing up, despite Nicky's desperate need for her to stay the same sweet girl she had always been, and Nicky wasn't helping her. Instead, she was forcing her to sneak around behind her back and pretend to be the child Nicky needed, not who she wanted to be. If Lola hadn't shown her true self to Nicky, it was because Nicky hadn't wanted to see it, and Lola was intuitive enough to know that.

She picked up her phone. She needed to talk to Sabine. Even

before she'd brought the screen to life, she remembered that wasn't an option and the hole inside her grew deeper. She thought about Sabine's last message. She already knew Lola had been showing Nicky a facade. A new thought speared her brain. What if Sabine was right and what Lola had led her to believe about what had happened in Zante wasn't the full story? The thought made her stomach churn. She forced herself to stand and climb the stairs to Lola's room.

Lola was folding a T-shirt when Nicky knocked then pushed the door open. From the purple smudges under her eyes, she looked like she'd hardly slept either. 'Can we talk?'

'I've made my mind up and you can't change it. I'm moving to Dad's.'

'Not about that,' said Nicky, gently. She sat on the bed next to a pile of socks and tapped the empty space next to her. Lola sat. 'I want to talk about Elias.'

Lola dropped her head. 'Do we have to?'

'I think we do. I told Sabine Elias had sex with you when you were too drunk to consent—'

She stopped at the sound of Lola gasping. 'I never said that.' She turned to Nicky, her eyes full of tears.

A chill crept up Nicky's spine. 'You told me he took a bottle of vodka down to the beach.'

'No, I didn't. I said we drank some vodka. I didn't say he took it.' Her voice sounded desperate. 'I know what I said. I was careful.'

Careful. What did that mean? Nicky's brain went back to the conversation with Sabine. 'Did you take the vodka?'

Lola nodded. 'It was in the cupboard. We were going home the next day so I didn't think anyone would miss it. I know I shouldn't have.'

Nicky groaned. She'd been so adamant Elias was the culprit.

It began to dawn on her that she'd been wrong about more than the alcohol. 'And did you get the bruise on your thigh from falling over?'

Eyes wide, Lola nodded again.

'I thought Elias hurt you.'

'He didn't hurt me, Mum. He wouldn't do that.'

That's what Sabine had tried to tell her, but she hadn't listened. Blood rushed to her cheeks. 'And did you initiate sex?'

Lola rubbed her forehead. 'Do we have to do this?'

'Yes. Did you?'

She let out a long breath. 'Yes, but only because I was the only one in my friendship group that hadn't done it yet.'

Nicky let that sink in, along with the understanding of what she'd done to her poor friend's son. She'd had no real idea of what was going on right under her nose and it was more her fault than anyone else's. 'I just need to get this straight. You took the vodka. You drank it voluntarily. You initiated sex and you fell over on the way home, right?'

Lola nodded.

Nicky's mouth was dry. She'd accused Elias of assault, and he had done nothing wrong. She'd thought he was a monster, when really the monstrous behaviour was all hers. 'Why didn't you tell me when I first asked you?'

Lola gave a bitter laugh. 'Are you kidding? Have we ever had an honest conversation about this stuff? Whenever you broach sex, you start every conversation with "I know you wouldn't ever" and end it with "would you?" I'm not an idiot. I know what you want to hear so I give it to you, then we're both happy, or at least living in peace. Honestly, you have no idea of the vibes you give off. It's like you're always on high alert. It's exhausting. There's no way I can tell you the truth about what I'm up to, even though I'm not doing anything everyone else isn't, because you'd freak. It's easier to pretend I'm Mary Poppins, or you are. I don't know.'

Every word was a blow, and Nicky couldn't even argue. That was how they existed: in a bubble of denial. One thing didn't quite add up, though. 'Why did he finish with you the next morning?'

'I've been thinking about that and I'm not sure he actually did.' Lola's eyes filled with tears.

'What do you mean?'

'The next day I had awful hangxiety.'

'Hangxiety?'

'Where a hangover makes you really anxious.' She picked at a cuticle on her thumb that was already bloody and raw. 'I felt like I'd acted like those girls Dad's always going on about, and I was so ashamed. I was sure Elias would think I was a tart for suggesting we did it, and I was so embarrassed, I thought I was going to die.'

Nicky nodded, hating Julian even more with every word. She knew the feeling all too well. She just didn't know her daughter did too. 'Go on.'

'I knew you'd be so disappointed if you found out. You always act like sex is something to be ashamed about, like it's something boys do to girls.'

The echoes of Sabine saying something very similar reverberated in Nicky's mind as the hatred switched to herself. She'd done this to her girl. 'I'm so sorry. I should never have made you feel like that.'

'I was so worried about what you'd say if you knew and feeling really guilty... and anyway, when he came in my room the next morning, I couldn't even look at him. He was dead sweet at first, then I hid under the covers like a stupid baby, and he must've thought I regretted what we did. He said if I wanted to call it a holiday fling, that was okay with him.'

This was what Sabine had told Nicky. So, it was true. Nicky's heart broke for both kids, trying to navigate this nascent relationship at their tender age.

A tear rolled down Lola's cheek. 'But looking back, he sounded so sad when he said it, and it wasn't as if he looked like that was what he wanted. He said it was okay if it was what I wanted. At the time I thought he was dumping me, and I reacted all defensively and said it was, but now I think he was just trying to be kind.'

'Oh, sweetheart.' Nicky put her hand on Lola's leg, grateful when she didn't shift away.

'I really liked him,' said Lola. A tear dropped on to Nicky's hand. 'And I ruined everything.'

'I'm so sorry, lovely,' said Nicky. And she was. She was sorry for Lola, for Elias and for the damage she'd done to her friendship with Sabine. She scanned the room, at the piles of clothes her beloved daughter had gathered as she prepared to leave, at the walls and the ceiling of the house she would soon lose. 'I don't think it was you who ruined things. I think it was me.'

If she carried on like this, Betsy would leave as soon as she was able and Nicky would be left with no family, no friends and no home. Her wall of pretence, her dysfunctional relationship with Julian and her overbearing need to keep Lola safe had turned into a stranglehold that was suffocating both of them. Was it any wonder her precious child struggled free? 'I have ruined so many things, but now I want to try to put things right.'

She wanted that more than anything in the world, but she had no idea how.

38

SABINE

When Sabine opened the door to find Nicky standing outside, heat flared in her chest. She was tempted to shut it in her face. As though reading her thoughts, Nicky raised her hand. 'I know I don't deserve it, but please listen to what I've got to say. I've come to apologise.'

'You could have called.' Sabine stood, legs apart, arms tight across her chest. She didn't want to have to see Nicky's face. Not after what her stupid accusation had done to her relationship with her son.

'I wanted to do it in person. I owe you that. I wanted you to see how truly sorry I am.'

Sabine scowled but opened the door and marched through to the kitchen. Nicky kicked off her shoes and followed her. 'Everything Elias said about what happened in Zante was true,' she said breathlessly, as if she needed to get her words out quickly.

'I know.' Sabine spoke slowly, glaring at her. Nicky's eyes were swollen and red. She looked like shit. Good. She deserved to after what she and Lola had put Elias through. That wasn't what she was most angry about, though. It was that they'd made her doubt her son, and he'd known it. How did you repair something like that?

'I'm so sorry for what I said.'

The words sounded weak to Sabine. Sorry was nowhere near enough to make this better. 'Have you any idea of the damage Lola could have done with her lies?'

Nicky shook her head. 'It wasn't Lola. It was me.'

Sabine clenched her fists. 'What do you mean?' An image of Elias's appalled expression when she'd quizzed him about that night appeared in her mind. If Nicky had invented Lola's version of events for some twisted reason, she wouldn't be able to stop herself from punching her in the face.

'I mean Lola told me what happened and... she was... I guess... very vague about the facts the first time we spoke, because she didn't want me to fly off the handle, but she never actually said Elias did anything wrong. I heard what I... what I feared happened, or at least what fit with my view of Lola and the kind of kid I thought she was.'

'Christ.' Sabine slammed her hand on the granite island. Her palm stung with needles of pain. 'That's even worse. You and your messy head made Elias into a monster to fit your own fucked-up narrative?'

Nicky's face crumpled. 'I know, I'm so sorry.'

Did she honestly think a quick apology and a few crocodile tears would solve this? 'The apple doesn't fall far from the tree, does it?'

Nicky glanced up with a question in her weepy eyes.

'You were made to feel guilty and ashamed by your mum, and now you've passed on the baton. Congratulations, you win the award for terrible parenting.' It was an awful thing to say, but it felt good all the same.

Nicky dropped her gaze. 'I can't argue with that.'

Sabine wanted her to argue. She wanted a screaming match to expel all the pent-up emotions pushing at her throbbing temples. 'And I take it you found the phone? Do you know what kind of girl your little angel is now?' She didn't really mean that. She didn't judge Lola anywhere near as harshly as she knew Nicky would, for the videos, at least. But she wanted Nicky to suffer for making them suffer.

Nicky blushed. 'Yep. You were right. I didn't have a clue who she was.' Tears collected in her eyes. 'I've been such a fool. I'm so sorry.' The tears began to fall, and soon they were followed by heaving sobs. 'I realise now that I've been wilfully blind to so many things. I've made so many mistakes.'

'You're telling me.'

'This is just the latest fuck-up in a long line. I've ruined my own life, as well as other people's. I'm so sorry. There's so much I should have told you.'

Sabine stiffened. 'What else?' If it was anything to do with Elias, Sabine would twist Nicky's arm around her back and march her from the house.

'Julian, what went on in my marriage, it was...' She hiccupped through her words. 'He's... he's not a good man.'

Was that it? 'I know. You told me. He's a coercively controlling prick, and you're well shot of him.' She tutted. 'And if you think you can deflect from what you've done, or play the poor me card, you can think again.'

Nicky shook her head. 'That's not what I'm trying to do. I'm culpable. I'm not trying to get out of it. I just want to be honest now because me pretending is partly what led us here. I want to tell you what Julian is really like, but I don't expect you to forgive me because of it.'

'Go on then.'

'I should have told you years ago. He... he was abusive... physically.'

Goosebumps prickled Sabine's skin. 'You said he wasn't violent. Are you saying he was?' This wasn't what she'd expected to hear.

'Not regularly, not much more than the odd shove, or rough —' Nicky put her hand over her eyes. 'It wasn't that, exactly. It was what he made me do... What he did to me.'

The implication made Sabine's blood chill. 'Are you saying what I think you're saying?'

Nicky nodded. 'I've been reading up on coercive control since... and apparently it's not unusual to use sex as a weapon...' Her words were lost in juddering breaths.

'Come and sit down.' Sabine's fury was starting to shift from Nicky to Julian. She led Nicky to the sofa and sat next to her. She had so many questions. 'Are you trying to tell me he raped you?'

'I didn't see it like that for a long time. At first he painted it as being hurt that I didn't find him attractive enough to want sex all the time. I'd give in and go along with it because he made me feel like I was rejecting him otherwise. He said it was about wanting to feel close to me, to be intimate, you know?'

Sabine nodded, to show she was listening, when really she wanted to scream and swear. 'At first?' She steeled herself for what she was afraid was coming next.

'Then he stopped asking. I'd wake up at night with him on top of me and I'd be pinned down so I couldn't move. Sometimes he'd come up behind me in the kitchen if I was at the sink and push my face down on the draining board and do what he wanted to me. I didn't shout out because the girls would be asleep upstairs and I was terrified I'd wake them and they'd witness...'

'Their father raping their mother?' The horror of those words was only just sinking in.

'He told me it was my duty as a wife. He said it wasn't his fault I was frigid.'

Sabine took Nicky's trembling hand. 'How long was this going on for?'

'It got worse after I had Lola. He accused me of going off sex, but I'd had stitches and I was really sore.'

Sabine winced. 'Years and years, then? God, I'm so sorry. Why didn't you tell me?'

'I didn't tell anyone. I barely admitted it to myself.'

'But...' She stopped. Nicky's chest was rising and falling as she took in gulps of air. This was not the time to challenge her life choices. She was doing enough of that herself. 'I wish I'd known.' It occurred to her then that Nicky's response to Lola having sex made more sense now. If her only experiences were bound up with shame and coercion, then was it any surprise she would be frightened that it would be the same for her daughter? 'I'll come with you to the police if you want to report him.'

'I don't know. I don't have any evidence, and they'd need that, wouldn't they? Otherwise it would just be my word against his, and he'd just say I was bitter because he'd been unfaithful.' Nicky rubbed a hand over her face. 'And what would that kind of accusation do to the girls? He's still their dad. They've got half his DNA.'

Sabine was torn. The rage inside her wanted to demand that Nicky exposed that bastard for who he truly was, but she remembered her reticence about reporting Toby back when they were at university. You couldn't tell another person how to feel about something that happened to them. 'I don't mean to be cruel, but you might find that the girls know more than you think – Lola at least.'

'I can't bear to think about that.' Nicky covered her face. 'I've made so many terrible mistakes and I don't know how to fix any of it. I thought that things would get better when Julian went, but everything I did to try to make the girls safe and happy has backfired. I've realised I was trying to parent them to Julian's expectations, not mine. I don't even know who I am any more. It's like his voice is in my head all the time. It's like I'm some kind of messed-up remote control robot that he can still operate from a distance.' She wiped her fingers under her eyes, smearing mascara across her cheeks. 'And now I have no idea who Lola is either.'

Sabine was desperate to say more about Julian, but understood she shouldn't push. After a moment's quiet she said, 'I'll make some tea.'

She gave some thought to what Nicky said as she made the drinks in silence. She sat opposite Nicky, placing steaming mugs in front of both of them. 'Just because Lola did a few stupid things, it doesn't mean she isn't the same girl she always was.' The relief that Elias's innocence had now been confirmed was allowing the muscles in her shoulders to release. She looked at the broken woman in front of her and found pity where the anger had been.

Nicky sipped her tea. 'I sort of know that – I understand it, at least – but I can't feel it. Does that make sense? I feel bereft, somehow.'

'You're grieving for the girl you thought you had, probably.'

'But she wasn't real, and neither was I. We haven't been truthful with each other, so where does that leave us? I've pretended to myself that we're close, but we hardly know each other.' Fresh tears fell from her eyes, rolling through the black streaks and carrying them down her face.

Sabine thought about who Lola truly was as she watched the steam rise from her drink. 'I'm not sure that's true,' she said. 'She is that girl. She wouldn't have been able to pretend for that long if she didn't have that side to her. But that's not all she is.' Sabine thought about it. 'If you re-frame it, this could be a good thing.'

'I don't understand.'

'You should hear Elias talk about her. He says she's funny and clever. He really liked her, and that boy is choosy.' She wagged her finger. 'And at least now you get to see the whole picture, not just the false front. You get to have a proper relationship with her, as long as you accept her for who she truly is.' She took a sip of her tea. 'And you could try to be yourself with her too.' She put a hand on Nicky's shoulder, surprising herself that she wanted to comfort her, despite wanting to kill her only minutes before. She'd always been her chosen family. That was hard to erase. 'I'd quite like to see the old Nicky back. The one who's only a third stress hormones, not three-quarters.'

Nicky gave a sad smile. 'Yeah, let's not hope for miracles.' She took a drink. 'I'm so sorry for what I've put you and Elias through. I'll understand if you can't ever forgive me.'

Sabine nodded and left it a moment. She wasn't ready to let it go completely, but she felt deep in her gut that she still wanted Nicky in her life. 'I know you're sorry. I just wish it had never happened.'

'I've been an idiot.' Nicky glanced up. 'Understatement of the century.' After a moment she said, 'Lola really liked Elias too. She regrets how she behaved at the end. And I hear what you're saying, but I think I've done too much damage to repair things with her.' More tears collected on her lower lids and dropped on to her cheeks. 'How did you get it so right with Elias?'

It was Sabine's turn to blush. 'I'm not so sure I did.' This was something she'd been thinking about a lot since all this started. Lola might have hidden her true self from Nicky because of her anxiety and expectations, but Elias was an enigma to Sabine too. She was beginning to think she'd taken too much pride in his independence. What kind of mother casually says 'he brought himself up' about their child?

Nicky's head cocked to one side.

'Let's just say there's a conversation to be had. This hideous business has given us all food for thought.'

Nicky nodded. 'I wish I'd talked to Lola more. Even if I discount the damage Julian did, she made me see I went on and on about the things that scared me, like drugs and alcohol... and sex, and she found it easier to agree with me. There was never a proper discussion because I framed things as good or bad, and she didn't want to hurt or upset me. She had to navigate things on her own because I was so black and white.' She rested her forehead on her hand. 'How pathetic am I that my kid wants to be the one to protect me?'

Sabine's pity grew. 'That's because she loves you. And that's the best foundation you could have, especially if you want to change the way you communicate. If you both want things to get better, loving each other is a great place to start.' She thought about her relationship with Elias. There was no doubt they loved each other, but hearing what lengths Lola went to to hide things from Nicky perversely showed how much she cared about what her mother thought of her. Sabine wasn't sure Elias gave her a second thought. They both went about their days without much consideration for the other. She'd been so sure they were a close family, but really, they simply lived alongside each other.

'Lola wants to live with Julian.' Nicky spoke quickly, expelling the words as though they were painful in her throat.

'What?'

'I know. That's how bad a mother I am. She would rather live with a controlling man who's shown hardly any interest in her upbringing than stay with me.'

'How much do you think she knows about how he treated you?'

Nicky shrugged. 'I don't know. The awful thing is, she probably thinks it's normal for men to talk down to women, and to make all the rules. I've given lip service to feminism, but I haven't followed it through with actions, and that's what they learn from, isn't it? And he's her dad, right? I always made sure I didn't show it when I was hurt or... scared.' She let her gaze fall to her hands.

'I want to kill the bastard.' Sabine said it with such force that Nicky jumped, then let a small laugh escape through her nose.

'You and me both.'

'I bet she does know what he's like, deep down. Now this has all come to a head, she probably thinks moving away from you is her ticket to freedom, but it won't last,' she said. 'Once she realises he wants her home even earlier than you did, so he doesn't have to think about where she is, never has her favourite food in, and isn't around to give her lifts everywhere, she'll come home to her own bedroom soon enough. Especially if you and she start to talk to each other more openly.'

Nicky shook her head. 'Her bedroom won't be there. Julian wants to sell the house.'

Sabine sat straighter. 'He can't. You need a place for the girls.'

'He's moving jobs, so he won't earn as much, and if Lola moves in with him, he says he needs somewhere big enough, so we'll have to sell up and share the proceeds.'

Sabine felt indignant on her behalf. 'Has he been made redundant?'

'No. He says he's jumping before he's pushed, though. He'll be on basic wage unless he meets his targets.'

'And then he'll get bonuses, right?'

Nicky shrugged. 'Yes, but he says he won't be earning as much.'

'He says that, does he?' Sabine's outrage was returning. 'And he's never lied about anything before?'

Nicky sat up straight. 'Good point.'

Sabine held her breath, then let it go. There was no point hiding anything from Nicky any more. She'd done it to protect her, just like Lola had tried to protect her, but all it did was keep her in the dark, and Sabine was realising secrets never stayed secrets forever. 'I'm sorry, Nicky, I should have told you years ago, but I knew Julian was a sleaze from the off...'

Dimples appeared on Nicky's chin, and it was clear she was trying not to cry again. 'What do you mean?'

'Do you remember when the four of us stopped going out as a group?'

'Yes. I knew you didn't like him. Julian said it was because he wasn't an "arty-farty North London leftie".'

Sabine gritted her teeth. 'Actually, it was because he groped me in the back of a cab one evening after we'd all been out.'

Nicky stared at her. She didn't speak.

Sabine panicked and started to talk quickly. 'You hadn't been together that long, and I didn't say anything because I was so sure it wouldn't last between you. I saw how attentive he was at the start, how he made you feel like some kind of princess, but I still thought you'd see what I saw before too long. He seemed inauthentic, somehow, but I couldn't say that to you because you were besotted with him. Then you got engaged and it seemed like it was too late. I had to hope it was a one-off.'

'Was it a one-off?'

Sabine shrugged. 'He didn't try it on with me again, but after you showed me that video... I can't say I was surprised. Neither was Leo.'

'So the two of you have been keeping this a secret and laughing at me for how long? The best part of two decades?'

Nicky's face was flushed. She gripped her mug so tightly her knuckles went white.

'God, no. That's not what... I wanted to protect you.'

Nicky stood and marched to the bi-fold doors. 'What is it with everyone trying to fucking protect me? Am I that weak and pathetic that I can't ever be told the truth about what's going on under my nose?'

'It's not that,' said Sabine, rising and standing next to her friend. 'You're an anxious person. You feel strongly about right and wrong. You see the world in absolutes.' She fought to find the right words. 'If I'd told you about what happened in the cab, what would you have done?'

'I don't know. You didn't tell me.'

'You'd have dumped him, or dumped me, and he was the one showering you with love and attention, and your mother loved him. She thought I was a bad influence. You would have picked him, I know you would.'

'You don't know that. And I would have had the choice. I would have at least had the facts. I might not have ended up married to a man who destroyed my confidence, treated me like staff and seemed to think I should be grateful for the opportunity to be shagged by him, whether I wanted to or not.'

If Sabine had had any idea that was happening to her friend, she would have staged an intervention right at the start. But would Nicky have listened to her? She spoke gently. 'Or, he would have lied, and you would have turned against me, and you wouldn't have been in my life any more.'

Nicky turned to her with tears pouring down her cheeks. 'But then you left me anyway.'

The pain on her face made Sabine stiffen. 'What do you mean? I didn't leave you. I've always been there for you.'

'You went to live in the States.' Her voice stuttered through her sobs. 'He systematically separated me from all of my friends, but I insisted on holding on to my relationship with you, even though every time I saw you, I had to put up with his sulking and temper. I needed you more then than I've ever needed anyone, and you left.'

'But I didn't know. I'm sorry. I had no idea it was like that for you.' Tears gathered in Sabine's eyes. 'If I'm honest, I was keeping my distance on purpose.'

Nicky looked up. 'Why? What did I do?'

It was time for the truth. All of it. 'After I had Elias, I had four miscarriages.'

'What?' Nicky blinked wet eyes. 'When? Why didn't you say anything?'

'I got pregnant again when Elias was four months old. It was a mistake and Elias was still so little, so Leo and I decided to terminate the pregnancy. I didn't tell you because you were trying for a baby at the time, so it seemed cruel that I already had a baby and was about to have an abortion.' Sabine thought back to that time. If she could turn back the clock, she would have done things so differently.

'But you said you had miscarriages?'

'When Elias was two, we decided to try again, but each time I got pregnant, I started to bleed before the twelve-week scan, and I lost my babies.'

'Oh, love.' Nicky came over and wrapped her in her arms.

Sabine let the tears come, and once they started, she didn't think they would ever stop. 'I didn't say anything because deep down I thought it was my fault. I felt like I was being punished for ending the first baby's life. Every time the bleeding started, I hated myself a little bit more. In the end we gave up, and I tried to be happy that at least we had Elias.' She smiled through her tears. 'If I'm completely honest, I've always envied you having two.

Betsy is such a joy. I couldn't stop myself from feeling resentful that you got to do it a second time when I couldn't. I was glad to be overseas. It stopped me having to face you when I had all these complicated feelings.'

'Oh, love. I'm so sorry. I can't bear the thought of you going through all of that. It must've been agony.' Nicky went to the kitchen island, tore off a piece of kitchen roll, and rubbed it below her eyes, then passed one to Sabine. 'What a pair we are. I used to think we told each other everything, but it's true that you never do know what goes on behind closed doors.'

'True. I don't want to have any more secrets, though.' Sabine felt lighter for having told Nicky about her darkest time. She should have known no one would judge her as harshly as she judged herself.

'Me neither,' said Nicky. She breathed in sharply. 'So, whilst we're being honest, I was always sad you didn't invite me back to Zante after that first time.'

Sabine spluttered. 'You hid that well.' She was glad when the side of Nicky's mouth rose at her sarcasm. 'When things got serious with Leo, we were talking about asking you and Julian to come the next summer, then the cab thing happened, and...' She showed her palms. 'That man has a lot to answer for.'

Nicky sighed. 'But if I hadn't married him, I wouldn't have Lola or Betsy, so I can't regret that.'

'No, but you can't give up your house, either. The man is a proven liar. What evidence have you got he won't earn as much? His word?'

Nicky nodded.

'And that's worth absolutely sod all. Are you really willing to give up the home your girls grew up in without a fight?'

Nicky's jaw set. 'Do you know what? I'm so over him dictating the rules. You're right. I should fight. I'll see a solicitor before agreeing to anything and find out exactly where I stand.' Her shoulders dropped. 'But if Lola goes to live with him, then I want her to have a nice home, too.'

'If,' said Sabine. She took Nicky's hands in hers. 'That isn't necessarily going to happen. Why don't you go home and talk to her again. Let her know you're really listening and that you want to change things between you.'

Her friend dropped her hands and pulled her into a hug that squeezed the air from her lungs. 'I will. Thank you. And I'm going to ask Julian to come around after work tomorrow to put him straight on a few things.'

'How do you think he'll react?'

'He won't like it, but it's time I stopped worrying about how he feels and put myself and the girls first. And I'm still so sorry for everything. I'd like to say that to Elias too. He must hate me for what I said.'

'He's not in right now. I'll speak to him. You go and talk to Lola.' Sabine gave Nicky one last squeeze before seeing her out of the house. When she saw Elias, it was time to have an honest conversation of her own.

39

SABINE

Sabine messaged Elias, asking him to meet her at a pizza restaurant she knew he liked instead of coming home for dinner. When he arrived, she couldn't help smiling as all the eyes in the restaurant seemed to follow her handsome boy to the table.

He kissed her on both cheeks, then sat. 'What's all this about?' There was a nervous edge to his voice.

'Nothing to worry about. The opposite, in fact.' With perfect timing, the waitress brought her glass of wine and the beer she'd ordered for Elias. She thanked the waitress and took up her glass. 'Nicky came over. Lola told her you did absolutely nothing wrong.' Elias didn't lift his bottle to clink against Sabine's glass. 'Don't leave me hanging,' she said. It was her turn to be nervous.

'I don't feel like celebrating being cleared of a crime I didn't commit and should never have been accused of in the first place.'

Sabine lowered her glass. 'Okay. I hear you. I'm sorry.' She wiped her slippery palms on her skirt. 'I wanted to talk to you about that. About a few things actually.'

Elias raised an eyebrow. He took a swig from the bottle.

'Should I have ordered that beer for you? Let's start there.'

He held the bottle in his hand and examined it. 'What do you mean?'

'Well, Nicky and I were talking about the mistakes we've made as parents, and I wonder now whether your dad and I should have been more...'

'Sober?'

Sabine laughed. 'We're not drunks.' Her stomach flipped. 'You don't think we drink too much, do you?' God, this conversation might be heading in a different direction than she expected.

'No. But it is weird you let me drink whenever I want.' He took another swig. 'I mean, I'm eighteen next year, so it's probably okay now, but when I was fourteen, you didn't bat an eye if I took beers upstairs for me and my mates.'

Sabine bristled, then remembered this was what she wanted: the truth. 'I thought it would give you a healthy attitude towards alcohol, to not see it as this forbidden, tantalising thing. I was being European.'

'Being European.' Elias raised his eyes to the ceiling. 'You were being too cool for school. You always were. You said you didn't want to be like other uptight parents with all their rules. But where did that leave me?'

'What do you mean?' She'd thought being a liberal parent was a good thing, but now she could see that she might have taken it too far.

'What did I have to kick against? You said before you knew I smoked weed in my room, and you used it to suggest I was capable of lying, but that's bollocks. If I'm honest, I was smoking too much. I didn't like myself and I wanted to stop, and lying about it to you was my way of telling you I wanted to be parented. I wanted you to kick up a fuss, to do something to make it hard for me, at least. But you didn't. You just shrugged and went back to work.'

Sabine's stomach contracted. 'I didn't know.'

'You did.'

That felt brutal. Because he was right. She did know he was smoking a lot. But she genuinely hadn't thought for a second that it was a problem. She'd believed her son knew what he was doing, and that he'd make the right decision because he always had. But that shouldn't have been down to him. He was a child and he needed boundaries. They'd let him down. 'I'm sorry.'

Elias sat back in his chair. 'Sometimes I wanted a mum, not another friend. I needed a mum.'

She nodded, her insides curdling. 'I'm sorry. I got it wrong and I'm sorry.'

He leaned forwards, resting his elbows on the table. He lowered his voice. 'And I didn't deserve to be doubted like that. If you knew me, if you really knew me, you'd know I wasn't capable of what you accused me of.'

'I didn't accuse you.' Sabine leaned forwards too. 'I never thought you hurt Lola.'

He shook his head. 'There was doubt in your mind.'

Sabine let her gaze drop, the laminated menu blurring through her tears. 'You're right, I'm sorry.' She raised her eyes to his. 'But that was nothing to do with you, not really. I didn't think you could hurt Lola. But the sad fact is that almost every woman I know has had a bad experience with men who don't know when to stop, myself included. There was something in me that knew me saying my son would never do that was the natural response of every mother. It was my immediate instinct to say of course you wouldn't, could never.'

'But I never would.'

'I know that. I truly do.'

Elias nodded. His dark eyes were filled with sadness and she knew she still had a lot of making up to do.

'I need to say it again. I don't think you are one of those men.'

'That's why what Lola did was so wrong, though,' said Elias. 'She's an intelligent girl. She must know how dangerous it is to accuse someone of something like that because every false accusation adds to more women not being believed when they really have been attacked.'

Sabine couldn't believe she hadn't made it clear earlier. 'Sorry, I should have said, Lola didn't ever say you did anything wrong, apparently. She was upset and Nicky saw the bruises on her legs and put two and two together.'

Elias sat forwards. 'For God's sake.' He shook his head. 'Still though, why didn't Lola put her right? I thought she was better than that.' He turned his bottle in his fingers, the corners of his mouth dipping.

'I'm not sure they ever had a proper conversation about it. Nicky went off on one and Lola was too frightened to stick her head above the parapet. From what I can gather, they have a pretty dysfunctional relationship.'

Elias huffed and crossed his arms. 'Great. That makes it better how?'

'I'm not saying it does,' said Sabine. 'It's a reason, not an excuse. Nicky royally fucked up, and she's very sorry. She wanted to tell you in person, but you weren't in this afternoon.' She paused. 'She told me some things about... well, some things that made how she responded make a bit more sense. I'm not condoning what she did, and she does know how wrong she was, I promise, but what she told me made it a bit harder to stay quite as furious with her as I was. I'm not trying to defend her, I just want you to know that it wasn't just about you and Lola. Nicky's had it tough. Families are messy. They're hard to navigate sometimes, and much as I'd like to pretend, we're not perfect, are we?

I've only heard tonight that you wanted something different from me. Needed something different.'

'Yeah, well,' he said, looking unconvinced. 'I'm not sure I do want you getting in my business now. We've got this far with me – how do you put it? – "bringing myself up".' He raised an eyebrow and Sabine wanted to slink under the table and hide in shame.

'Sorry.' She grimaced. 'What can I do to make it up to you?'

Elias smiled and crossed his arms. 'I think a Lamborghini Countach might just about do it.'

'Nice try.' Sabine laughed.

Elias sat back. 'Worth a go.' He grinned at her across the table and, even though she knew she had work to do, Sabine felt genuinely closer to her son than she had in a very long time.

40

NICKY

Nicky was exhausted when she got home but her thoughts were moving too quickly to do anything other than talk to Lola straight away. She could hear Betsy in her room, chatting away to someone, probably on FaceTime. She mustn't have been into Lola's room since she'd been dropped home because if she'd seen the piles of clothes and heard about Lola's plans, Nicky was sure she'd have been met in the hall by her youngest daughter's tear-streaked face.

She wiped the mascara streaks from under her eyes then tiptoed upstairs and tapped on Lola's door. 'Can I come in?' She pushed the door and found Lola lying on her bed reading a book. 'It's a long time since I saw you reading.'

'Yeah, well, I haven't got my phone, have I?'

Nicky had forgotten she'd confiscated both phones. 'Oh, right.' She paused. 'I'll get your phone for you in a sec.' Lola's face brightened. 'But can we have a talk first?'

Lola groaned. 'If it's about that other phone or that TikTok account, you don't have to worry. I'm embarrassed about the whole thing. As soon as I get my phone back, I'm deleting the account and I'm not going to do anything like that again. I don't want anyone to see me like that.'

'But you did,' said Nicky gently. 'And I'd like to understand why.'

Lola puffed out her cheeks. 'Honestly, I just did it because my friends were doing it. Then, when I started to get likes and loads of comments, it got kind of addictive. I suppose it made me feel older.'

'There's plenty of time to feel older, believe me.'

Lola raised her eyes to the ceiling. 'I knew that's what you'd say. I know you and Dad are just trying to get me to enjoy being a kid while I can, but no sixteen-year-old wants to be told being an adult's not all that. The way I see it, you get to make all the choices. No one can tell you when to get in, what to wear. They can't ground you or take your phone away.'

They can, thought Nicky, if you let them. She put a spike in that thought. It wasn't her fault Julian had covertly taken over her life. She'd been kind and trusting and he had taken advantage of that. It was time to evict that man from her head and to be entirely her own person again. She said, 'I hear you. I'll try not to say that kind of thing again.'

Lola frowned. 'Who are you and what have you done with my mother?'

Nicky laughed, the tension in her shoulders dropping a notch. 'I want to understand more about what's going on in your head.'

'I'm not so sure you do,' said Lola. She turned her face to the window. The way the light caught her features reminded Nicky of how she looked on the plane and her heart ached for her beautiful girl, trying to work out who she was and what she wanted, especially with parents who made it so hard. 'You want me to be a good, compliant child,' Lola said, 'and I'm not sure I am those things. Not all the time, anyway.'

Nicky went to the bed and put her arm around Lola's shoulders. 'And I shouldn't have expected that from you all the time. I shouldn't have let my anxieties and expectations impose ridiculous standards on you. It wasn't fair. I should have had the sense to let you be you and given you space to make bad decisions and learn from them, instead of trying to stop you making any mistakes at all.'

Lola smiled. 'I've made some mistakes, don't worry about that. It's just you didn't know about them before.' She winked.

Nicky realised she liked this funny, irreverent side to her daughter. This version of her belonged out in the world, not cocooned here, just so Nicky knew she was safe. And what did safe really mean? Nicky was an adult and she hadn't felt safe in her own home much of the time. If Lola was restricted and forced to stay close to her, then her spirit might be quashed. That wasn't best for her, and what was best for her should be best for those who loved her most.

'Anything else I should know about?' Nicky braced herself.

'Other than my terrible choice of underwear in those videos?'

'It's the fashion choices you regret?' Nicky tucked her chin into her neck.

Lola scrunched up her face. 'Obviously. What else?' She nudged Nicky with her elbow. 'Seriously, I'm taking them down as soon as I get my phone back.' She dropped her gaze. 'Did you tell Dad about them?'

'I did, sorry.'

Lola shrugged. 'You do the crime, you do the time.'

Nicky had expected her to cry, or throw a strop, but clearly her daughter was more mature than she'd given her credit for. She scanned the room, only now noticing the piles of clothes had disappeared. 'Where's all your stuff?'

'I put it away,' said Lola. 'I had time to think, because I didn't have my phone.' She raised an eyebrow at Nicky, who was trying to stop the hopeful joy from exploding out of her. 'I thought about what it would be like living at Dad's and realised it would be different, but it might not be better.' She glanced at Nicky's face, then down at her hands. 'He's not very... dad-ish, is he? And I feel bad about saying this...' Lola picked at her nails. 'But I don't miss him now he's not here. Not really.'

Nicky swallowed. She needed to tread carefully. 'Why do you think that is?'

Lola kept her eyes on her fingers. 'He's always cross and he blames everyone else, even when we haven't done anything wrong. I feel horrible saying it, but he isn't very nice to people a lot of the time and he can be kind of a bully.' She took Nicky's hand. 'I don't like it when he's mean to you.'

'I don't like it either,' said Nicky. She thought carefully about what to say next. 'I hope you don't think that it's normal for couples to behave the way me and your dad did towards each other.' Tempting as it was to lay all the blame at Julian's door, she wanted Lola to know that she wished she'd stood up to him from the start. 'Marriages should be equal. They should be full of love and respect. One of my biggest regrets is not modelling a healthy relationship for you and Betsy. I made mistakes, but I'll do everything I can to make sure you don't make the same ones. You deserve to be loved beyond measure, my darling girl.' Her voice broke with emotion, because it was true. Lola and Betsy were extraordinary. They'd become the incredible young people they were despite their family's dysfunction, which made them all the more special in Nicky's eyes.

'So do you,' said Lola. 'I wish Dad appreciated how kind you are. It's mad that he doesn't seem to know how much you do for all of us.'

It was all Nicky could do not to cry with relief. Lola's words gave her hope that the damage she and Julian had caused her was not too deep to repair. 'I'm glad you think I'm kind. That means a lot to me, especially after all the times I've messed up recently.'

'You're the kindest person I know. It can be a pain when you worry about us, but I know you're only anxious because you care about us so much, and I'd miss you loads if I didn't live with you.' Then Lola nodded her head in the direction of Betsy's room, as Nicky's heart swooped with elation. 'And I'd miss that idiot.' She pinched her lips. 'But don't you dare tell her that.'

Nicky mimed zipping her lips, finding it hard to keep the enormous smile at bay.

'And it'll be okay here with just the three of us, especially if you're going to be less of a nutter...' Lola continued.

'Steady,' said Nicky. She nodded, then. 'I am going to be less of a nutter. And if I forget and start acting... nuttery again, I want us to have an adult conversation about it, okay?'

'An adult conversation, you say?'

'We can try, at least?' She put her arm around her beautiful girl and swallowed hard as she melted into her.

'I'd like that. I love you, Mum.'

The words went straight to her core. What more could she wish for than this? 'I love you too,' said Nicky. 'Every last bit of you.' And she meant it with all her heart.

41

NICKY

Nicky showed Julian through to the sitting room, rather than into the kitchen like she usually would. She wanted him to know he was a guest in her home, and hoped he didn't register the tremble in her hands, or her wavering voice. She told herself that she was not going to be intimidated by this man ever again. She just needed her body to reach the same page.

He sat on the armchair and crossed his legs, a smug look on his face. 'The girls not in?' he said.

'No. They're both at friends' houses.' She hadn't wanted them at home in case Julian decided to kick off when he realised she was going to stand up for herself, and for them. They didn't need to hear him shouting, especially when she'd decided to give as good as she got for a change.

'Farmed them out for other people to look after. How very on brand.' He gave an obsequious smile. 'Get on with it, then. I need to be quick, I have somewhere I need to be.'

Nicky sat on the sofa and tried to appear relaxed, despite her heart thundering against her ribs. 'You might want to reschedule whatever you're doing next, because we have a lot to talk about.'

'No can do,' he said, crossing his legs in the opposite direction. 'I don't see why you insisted I came around. We just need to pencil in a time for the house valuation. Shouldn't take long.' He gave a leering smile that made her stomach turn. 'Unless you just wanted to see me. Can't keep away, eh?'

'No,' said Nicky with a shudder. 'We have important things to discuss. Why don't you make any calls you need to now?'

Julian's mouth set in a serious line. 'No need, the estate agent can do Tuesday morning or Wednesday afternoon next week.'

'No can do,' said Nicky in the same tone he'd used.

Julian frowned. He blew out his lips. 'You're not going to be difficult about this, are you? I told you the score. It's not like there's a choice.'

Nicky stared him in the eye. 'I do actually have choices.'

His mouth went slack. 'Don't start playing silly games, Nicky.' She recognised the tone. It was meant to put her in her place. But she had a new place now, and she wasn't about to be dislodged by this self-important dick.

'I'm not having the house valued until my solicitor has seen your new contract.'

He drew back his chin 'Your what?'

'You don't expect me to take your word for it that you'll be earning less, do you?' She spoke slowly and clearly, hoping to give off an air of calm determination.

'So, you'd rather pay a fortune to a solicitor?' He huffed out a laugh. 'Two can play at that game.'

'Good,' said Nicky, 'because these things should be fair, shouldn't they?'

'What's fair about me paying for you to live the life of Riley, even after we're divorced? I was the one who worked all the hours. Every penny that went into this house was mine.'

'Is that right?' said Nicky. 'And why was it that I stopped work?'

'You didn't want to work after you had the girls.' He said it as if it was fact.

'Which girls?'

His nose crinkled. 'Our girls, obviously.'

'Our girls. The ones you wanted. Am I right?'

'What are you getting at?'

'Did you ever consider giving up work to take care of them?'

'Oh, for God's sake.' His bottom lip stuck out like a petulant child's.

'Because we earned about the same when I had Lola, didn't we? I told you I wanted to go back to work after I had Betsy, but you were adamant it wouldn't be worth it after we'd paid for childcare. It wasn't just that, though, was it? You'd got used to me doing every last thing in the house. You liked not having to do the shopping, or the cleaning or the cooking. You didn't want to have to think about dentists, or haircuts or school nativities. If I went back to work, then you'd have had to pull your weight.' She leaned towards him, narrowing her eyes. 'And you liked being in control of the finances as well, didn't you?'

A flush crawled up his neck. 'Now you're being ridiculous. I'm not staying here to listen to you rewrite the past. When the solicitor finds out Lola is coming to live with me, you'll have to sell the house, whether you like it or not.' He started to stand.

'She's not coming to live with you.' It felt glorious to be able to say that with confidence.

'What? Yes, she is. She asked me the last time she stayed.'

'Have you spoken to her since she last left your place? In fact, have you called either of the girls?'

The redness reached his cheeks. He was getting angry. Nicky knew the signs well. 'No. But they haven't called me either.'

What a baby he was. Her heart pounded, but she shouldn't be afraid of this oversized man-child. He was a bully, but she was ready to stand her ground. 'Well, I have spoken to Lola. We talked things through, and she wants to stay at home with me and Betsy.' What Lola had said about him quivered on the tip of her tongue, but she wouldn't share that with him. It wouldn't be fair on Lola, and she was her priority.

He fell back into his seat. 'She'll change her mind. She's sick to death of being smothered by you.'

'I doubt that. If she does, we can talk about the house then, but until then, let's get moving with the divorce as things currently stand. Email me the details of your solicitor later today. Right now, I'd like to go through some ground rules that Lola and I have agreed.'

He shook his head and laughed. 'You're serious, aren't you?'

'Deadly. Let's start with her phone. She can have it with her in her room as long as she gets to college on time. We won't check it or befriend her on any social media.'

'Are you off your head? She sixteen. She still a—'

'She's a young woman and she needs to know we trust her.'

'You've changed your tune.'

'Yes, I have. I want to have an honest and trusting relationship with both girls going forwards.'

'What, so they can run loose? You want them to turn into the kind of girls you see in town on a Friday night, staggering around drunk, dressed like common tarts?' said Julian.

She gave him a cold stare, allowing a pause long enough for him to know what she was thinking. He set his jaw, looking more furious than ever. 'I also want you to stop saying disrespectful things about women, especially in front of our girls. You're a pathetic throwback, and the girls are too intelligent not to notice that you believe you are better than half the population, despite there being absolutely no grounds. In fact, you're a disgrace to your sex.' She lifted her phone and waved it. 'All the evidence is in here. Added to which, you're a bigot and a bully and when they come of age, I would be surprised if they choose to spend any time with you at all.'

He leaned forwards, his mouth an angry snarl. 'I bet you're feeding them that shit, aren't you? That's why Lola's changed her mind. You're poisoning my girls against me.'

'Unlike you, my only concern is for my daughters, so, no. I haven't said a single bad thing to them about you, or shown them this horrible video. They're bright enough to work it out for themselves over time.'

He rose from his seat and towered over her. 'Don't you fucking dare slander me.'

Her pulse thundered in her ears and it took every ounce of strength she had to look him in the eye and keep her voice level. 'Slander is false by definition, so no, I won't slander you. I will tell the truth.'

'The truth? Who's going to believe a pathetic cow like you over me?' The atmosphere changed. The hairs on Nicky's arms stood on end as his face neared hers. 'You need reminding who's boss in this house, don't you?'

She tried to stand, but he pushed her shoulder so hard she fell back into the sofa. 'Don't touch me.'

He put his hands on her chest and forced her down on to the cushion. 'Don't you dare tell me what to do. It's time you stopped thinking you have a say in what goes on in my family.'

He moved fast, slamming his forearm across her throat, constricting her airways. She fought for breath, tried to push his arm away, but he lay on top of her, shoving a knee between her legs to part them. It all happened so quickly. She couldn't move. She tried to scream but it came out as a croak. There was no one there to hear anyway. She was powerless, just as she had always been. He leaned further forward as his other hand reached to pull at the waistband of her trousers. She struggled, but his arm across her throat got heavier. She was dizzy and breathless and all the power left her.

He lifted his hips and she heard the buzz of a zip. Tears rolled down her cheeks. There was nothing she could do to stop him. She couldn't breathe and she had to let him do what he wanted, or he might end up killing her and then she wouldn't ever be able to protect her girls.

She let her body go limp. As she did, a loud crack sounded at the window. There was another crack, then a smash, and then screaming. 'Get off her, you fucking bastard.'

Julian leapt up and turned towards the splintered glass. Nicky dragged up her trousers and ran from the room. Sabine was on the step when Nicky threw the door wide. She fell into her arms and sobbed. Julian ran past, snarling obscenities at Sabine, but Nicky couldn't hear anything beyond the beating of her friend's heart next to her ear.

* * *

An hour later, Nicky held Sabine's hand tightly as a policewoman sat across from them in Nicky's kitchen. The banging and drilling sound of a glazier replacing the window in the sitting room added to the buzzing in Nicky's ears. A second policewoman came in, turning off the crackle of the radio attached to her vest. 'Your husband has been apprehended, Nicky,' she said softly. 'He's been taken into custody to be questioned.'

Nicky nodded mutely. She turned to Sabine, whose hand was still bleeding through the kitchen roll she'd wrapped it in. She'd cut it smashing the window with a stone after she saw Julian attacking Nicky through the glass. She told the officers that she didn't know why she came around when she knew Nicky and Julian were due to meet, or why she had the urge to peer into the front room, rather than ringing the bell as she normally would. 'It was intuition,' she said. 'I just had this weird sense that Nicky was in danger.' When she turned to Nicky, her gentle gaze told her that extra sense was love. 'It's over,' Sabine said. 'He can't hurt you any more.'

'Thank you,' said Nicky. The words were inadequate to express the depth of her gratitude, but she said them again anyway. 'Thank you.'

They moved together and held each other as they cried for everything they had gone through at the hands of men, of all the secrets, lies and misunderstandings, and with relief that despite it all, they still had each other. Thank God for this woman, thought Nicky with each shuddering breath. Thank God.

42

NICKY

The day after the attack, Nicky told the girls that their father had been arrested. She didn't give them details, and they didn't ask, but the bruises on her neck were plain to see. When she finished speaking, the three of them clung to each other and cried themselves dry. Unless he had the decency to plead guilty, there would be a trial, and then it would all come out, but she would deal with that when it happened. Until then, she would seek expert advice on how to answer any questions the girls had in the future truthfully, whilst causing as little harm to her precious children as possible. The time for covering things up was well and truly over.

By the end of the summer, the resilience they'd shown left Nicky swollen with admiration for them. They were far stronger than she had ever given them credit for. Despite the restraining order which stopped him from coming near her or their home, Julian was allowed supervised visits with Lola and Betsy. No one was surprised when he chose not to take advantage of the visits. Nicky was glad her brilliant girls hadn't been forced to choose whether to spend time with him or not.

Now, it was the end of the summer holidays and life for the

three of them was settling into a new routine. Lola had done well in her GCSEs and Betsy was nervously excited about starting the secondary school Lola had just left ready to go to sixth form college. Everything was changing, but Nicky was coping with it with the help of a therapist called Helen, who she saw on Zoom every week. As well as helping her deal with her trauma and her anxiety, Helen was helping Nicky expunge Julian's voice in her mind and replace it with her own, encouraging her to be kind and gentle with herself, telling her that's what she deserved. She also reiterated what Nicky had learned – that she had to allow Lola to make decisions, and if they led to mistakes, then they were hers to own and to learn from. Helen even told her to strengthen her own boundaries and talk openly about her needs. That was new, and so far, it was working.

'Come on, you two,' she shouted up the stairs. 'I want to get there early enough to get a parking space.' She threw the stuffed picnic bag into the boot and squinted up at the glorious blue sky. It was a beautiful day to be heading to the coast.

Betsy chattered all the way there about her plans for the school year, quizzing Lola from the back seat about the best clubs to join, while Lola told her which teachers were tyrants, and which she could have a laugh with.

When Nicky pulled into the car park next to the sea wall, her guts twisted with nerves. This could be a great idea, or a terrible one, and she had no idea which way it would go. 'Right then,' she said, but stopped when Sabine's Range Rover pulled up in the next parking bay.

'Mum,' said Lola as Sabine waved from the driver's seat. 'What's going on?' Dark curls were just visible beyond Sabine's head.

'Yay, Sabine and Elias,' said Betsy. She stopped abruptly then and stuck her head through the front seats. 'Lola, are you friends with Elias now?'

'You arranged this?' Lola's face flushed red. 'I can't believe you've done this to me.'

Nicky pressed her elbows into her sides. She hadn't anticipated Lola's reaction being quite so visceral. 'Hear me out,' she said. 'I probably should have told you before, but I didn't think you'd come if I did.'

'Really? You think?' She scowled. 'Are you trying to set us up again? Is that what this is?' She put her hand to her forehead. 'God, this is so embarrassing.'

'This isn't only about you,' said Nicky. She had done her very best to listen to Lola over the last few weeks, but Helen reminded her that listening goes both ways in a healthy relationship, and she wanted to be heard too. 'I have apologised to Elias for how wrong I was.' The memory of Elias's stony face as she made her heartfelt apology soon after she told Sabine the truth still made her cringe. He'd been a little less cold the next time she saw him, so she hoped they were on the right trajectory, at least. 'And Sabine is my best friend. What happened... What I did nearly broke our friendship, but after everything that's happened, we decided to have a fresh start and move on, and we would both appreciate it if you could try to do the same.'

Lola kept her head twisted away from the window. 'Did Elias know I was coming?'

Nicky glanced back at Elias, who was taking a bag from the boot. His mouth was a tight line. 'No, he's as surprised as you are.'

'Great.'

'We thought that, if you talked, you might be able to become friends.' She put her hand on Lola's knee and touched Betsy's hand where it gripped the back of her seat. 'I wish you'd all grown up together, like the children of friends usually do, but circumstances meant that didn't happen.' She paused, trying not to let her regret about staying with Julian despite his abuse rise to the surface. 'But now there's nothing stopping us all from hanging out, maybe going on holiday together again, if we can all get on.'

'Yay, Zante!' said Betsy.

'Can you try? For me? If it doesn't work out today, I won't ask again. I promise.'

Lola let out a long breath through her nose. 'We're here now,' she said. 'I haven't really got a choice, have I?'

'Great. Thank you.' Nicky squeezed her leg and opened the car door.

Fifteen minutes later, Nicky and Sabine were walking along the shingle beach ahead of the kids. 'How are the girls doing?' asked Sabine.

'They're amazing,' said Nicky. 'And their friends have all rallied. I thought they'd find it really hard, everyone knowing their dad did something terrible to their mum, but it's like their friends and their parents have formed this protective barrier around them. It's been incredible to see.' She flung an arm around Sabine's shoulder. 'Where would we be without our friends?'

'Where indeed?' Sabine snaked her arm around Nicky's waist and they walked in step.

'How's it going with Elias?' Nicky said. 'Has he forgiven you yet?'

Sabine tipped her hand from side to side. 'We're getting there. I'm trying to spend a bit more time with him. If we make new memories, I'm hoping the old ones might lose their potency.'

'I know you're probably sick of hearing it, but I really am still so very sorry for accusing him like that.' Nicky still wanted to sink into the earth and disappear every time she recalled the way she'd treated Elias.

'Yeah, well, you've always been an idiot. Why change the habit of a lifetime? And I think you've had enough punishment, don't you?' Sabine's tone was light. That was a comfort.

'I'm desperate to turn around and see how they're getting on, but I daren't,' said Nicky, a few paces further on.

'Me neither,' said Sabine, grimacing. 'I've only heard Betsy's voice so far.' She pointed at a coffee shack further along. 'Caffeine fix?'

'Perfect.' From the silence behind them, this wasn't going the way she'd hoped. They took orders from the kids and joined the queue. 'I didn't tell you,' Nicky said, 'I've signed up for a course that starts in September. It's a refresher to make sure I'm up to date with all the new graphic design software before I start applying for jobs.'

Sabine grinned. 'Look at you, getting back on the horse. You were always a brilliant designer. They'll be snatching your hand off when you put yourself back out there.'

Nicky warmed at the praise. 'If I can't get a job, I can always do freelance.'

They waited in contented silence for their turn to be served. A peal of laughter made them both turn. Lola's head was thrown back in delight and Elias was roaring, hands on his knees, as Betsy bounced from foot to foot, giggling. Lola stepped forwards, her eyes bright, her smile mischievous, and said something to the two of them that the women couldn't hear, but it must've been hilarious because Elias's eyes widened, and he let out another guffaw. Betsy wiped tears from her eyes as she danced around the pair, clearly in her element.

Sabine whispered in Nicky's ear, 'I think they're going to be okay.'

Nicky's heart swelled with love for all of them. 'I think you're right,' she said. 'And I think I am too.' As she looked from face to gorgeous face, she believed that might, at last, be true.

* * *

MORE FROM LISA TIMONEY

The next powerful family drama from Lisa Timoney is available to order now here:
https://mybook.to/TimoneyNewBackAd

ACKNOWLEDGEMENTS

My first thanks go to my brilliant editor, Isobel Akenhead, for her enthusiasm, insight and much-appreciated collaborative approach. Being published by Boldwood Books is nothing short of a joy. Their commitment to supporting their authors and building a sustainable career for us is refreshing and incredibly welcome.

Thank you to copyeditor, Jennifer Davies, and proofreader, Helen Woodhouse, for all their hard work and their generous comments about the book.

I owe a huge debt of gratitude to my fantastic agent, Laura Williams, who's opened up so many opportunities for me, and is an all round superstar.

To my lovely early readers, Suzy Oldfield, Nichola Ibe, Sam Salisbury, and Hannah Maynard-Slade, thank you for your time and your honesty. I don't know what I'd do without you.

My thanks also go to the fabulous online reading community, especially bloggers Nicola Winter @nothing.beats.a.good.book and Emily Portman @aquintillionwords. Their support has blown me away. The following Facebook book groups are wonderful, and also instrumental in helping new readers find my books: The Bookload, Fiction Addicts Book Club, The Fiction Cafe Book Club and The Good Housekeeping Book Room. Huge thanks to their brilliant administration teams (especially Kate Rutherford, Teresa Nikolic and Trina Dixon) who give their time for free to spread the bookish-love. If you are looking for a place to share your love of books, I recommend these groups whole-heartedly.

The writing community is the most positive and supportive bunch of people you could hope to find. Both online and IRL, I've found my tribe, my strength and inspiration in the friends I have made since I began my writing life. There are too many to name individually, and I would hate to leave someone out, but if I've met you through writing, I'm talking about you.

Finally, my thanks go to my family. I am incredibly fortunate to live with people who make me laugh every day, ensure my feet are always firmly on the ground, and fill my life with love... and endless new material for family dramas.

If you enjoyed *The Lies Our Children Tell*, I would be very grateful if you could leave a brief review wherever you buy your books. Even a few words can make an author's day, and help new readers discover our books. Thank you!

ABOUT THE AUTHOR

Lisa Timoney is the author of emotional family dramas filled with devastating secrets and explosive revelations. Originally from Yorkshire, Lisa started her career teaching English and Drama. She now lives in London with her husband and two teenage daughters.

Download your exclusive bonus content from Lisa Timoney here:

Visit Lisa's website: www.lisatimoneywrites.com

Follow Lisa on social media here:

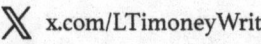 x.com/LTimoneyWrites
instagram.com/lisatimoneywrites
facebook.com/LisaTimoneyAuthor
bookbub.com/authors/lisa-timoney
tiktok.com/@lisatimoneywrites

ALSO BY LISA TIMONEY

The Daughter She Gave Away

The Lies Our Children Tell

BECOME A MEMBER OF

THE
SHELF
CARE
CLUB

The home of Boldwood's
book club reads.

Find uplifting reads,
sunny escapes, cosy romances,
family dramas and more!

Sign up to the newsletter
https://bit.ly/theshelfcareclub

Boldwood

Boldwood Books is an award-winning fiction publishing company seeking out the best stories from around the world.

Find out more at www.boldwoodbooks.com

Join our reader community for brilliant books, competitions and offers!

Follow us
@BoldwoodBooks
@TheBoldBookClub

Sign up to our weekly
deals newsletter

https://bit.ly/BoldwoodBNewsletter